Death of an Angel

Sister Carol Anne O'Marie

Death of an Angel

WHEELER
PUBLISHING, INC.
ROCKLAND, MA

★ AN AMERICAN COMPANY ★

Copyright © 1997 by Sister Carol Anne O'Marie

Published in Large Print by arrangement with
St. Martin's Press
in the United States and Canada.

Wheeler Large Print Book Series.

Set in 16 pt. Plantin.

Library of Congress Cataloging-in-Publication Data

O'Marie, Carol Anne.
    Death of an angel / Sister Carol Anne O'Marie.
      p. (large print) cm.(Wheeler large print book series)
    ISBN 1-56895-442-5 (softcover)
    1. Large type books. 2. Mary Helen, Sister (Fictitious Character)—
Fiction. 3. Women detectives—California—San Francisco—Fiction
4. Nuns—California—San Francisco—Fiction. 5. San Francisco (Calif.)—
Fiction. I. Title. II. Series
[PS3565.M347D44 1997]
813'.54—dc21   97-9213
                                                    CIP

In memory of
Sister Magdalen Coughlin, CSJ
(1930–1994)

Her life was much too short
for those of us who loved her.

Death of an Angel

Monday, November 2
Feast of all Souls

By four o'clock in the afternoon, the storm was at full tilt. Sheets of rain hit hard and stiff against the windowpanes, and the wind moaned around the tower of Mount St. Francis College like a lost soul in search of peace.

A sudden cold draft made Sister Mary Helen shiver. Although that nervous little weatherman on the television had been predicting a storm all week long, this morning she had deliberately left her umbrella in the convent. No wonder! When she left her room, the sky was blue and nearly cloudless. Besides, that poor little fellow was so seldom right.

With thunder rolling in the distance, Mary Helen raced down the deserted corridor toward the Hanna Memorial Library. She checked her wristwatch. Nearly four-thirty! Father Adams, the college chaplain, was celebrating the Mass of the Poor Souls, more euphemistically called the Faithful Departed, at four-forty in the college chapel. She didn't want to be late. So many of her old friends were among those dear faithful departed.

In fact, at her age, which she almost never thought about and even less frequently told, she was beginning to have more old friends who were departed than she had old friends who remained.

As she swung open the beveled glass door, the library lights dimmed, flickered, but remained on steadfastly. The scattering of students studying at the narrow wooden tables tittered with relief.

A peevish "shush" came from behind the circulation desk. Angelica Bowers was on duty.

Poor Angelica, Mary Helen thought instinctively, then chided herself. There was nothing at all poor about Angelica Bowers. She was an educated woman—a Mount graduate, actually—and competent at what she did. A little officious on occasion, but always willing and able.

And fat! The word popped up from nowhere, and Mary Helen felt ashamed. You have little room to talk, she thought, pulling her suit jacket firmly over the five extra pounds that had been following her around since summer vacation.

She crossed the long room quickly. "Is Sister Eileen here somewhere?" Mary Helen whispered, hoping that her friend was ready. Eileen had the knack of getting totally involved in something about five minutes before she was due to quit.

Angelica Bowers studied Mary Helen, her blue eyes peering anxiously out of mounds of damp flesh. She gave her usual tentative smile. "I just saw her," she said. "Let me get her for you."

Grabbing the edge of the circulation desk with both dimpled hands, Angelica twisted and pushed herself off the high stool. Breathing heavily, she just stood for a moment, splayfooted. Once she had recovered both her breath and her balance, she lumbered toward the back room in search of Sister Eileen. Her nylons made a soft scraping sound with every step.

Poor Angelica, Mary Helen thought again in spite of herself.

"We'll just make it, old dear." Eileen circled around Angelica, who was having difficulty positioning herself back up on the check-out stool.

"Good night, dear," Eileen whispered above the drumming of the rain on the tiled roof. "Have a nice evening."

Mary Helen glanced over. Was it her imagination or did Angelica Bowers look as if she were about to cry?

"Why don't you say something to that woman about her weight?" Mary Helen asked, as they turned into the hall leading to the chapel.

Eileen rolled her gray eyes. "Why don't you?"

"Because I'm not her boss, that's why. I have no excuse."

"And what excuse do I have? She does her job."

"So much weight must be bad for her health."

"Maybe for mine, too, if I mentioned it," Eileen quipped.

"It's really not funny. How much do you think she weighs? Two hundred and fifty pounds?"

"Closer to three-fifty, I'd guess."

"Do you think it's glandular?"

"Not after I saw what she eats."

They were walking so briskly that Mary Helen was beginning to pant. "Why would a young woman...What is she? About thirty-four or thirty-five?" she asked.

"At least that, I'd say."

"Still comparatively young. Why would she let herself go like that?"

"Why indeed?" Eileen agreed, pulling open the heavy bronze chapel door.

The comforting scent of incense and beeswax greeted them. The sacristy lights were ablaze, and Father Adams had just kissed the altar stone.

"We made it." Eileen slipped into the back pew. Mary Helen followed, breathing hard.

Making a quick resolution to go back on her own diet and to get more exercise, Mary Helen put Angelica Bowers on the back burner, at least for the moment. Resolutely, she turned her mind to those who no longer had bothersome, imperfect bodies to worry about. "Eternal rest grant unto them, O Lord," she prayed with the entire congregation, "And let perpetual light shine upon them."

A streak of lightning tore past the stained-glass windows. Rumbling thunder blotted out the final "Amen."

Holding tightly to the safety rail, Angelica Bowers exited the Number 31 Balboa bus one slow step at a time. Once on the street, she opened her umbrella, hoping to keep at least her head dry. An unexpected rush of wind turned the umbrella inside out, and pelting rain stung her face. It ran off her thin brown hair and down her neck in cold rivulets which found their way inside her coat collar. Her teeth chattered.

Through watery eyes, Angelica peered down 42nd Avenue at the peaked-roof house five down from the corner. Despite the early dusk and the sheet of rain, the light from the dormer window shone like a warning. Mama was home. But then, Mama was *always* home.

Angelica stood frozen while the other commuters hurried around her, some even nudging her in their eagerness to get to their houses.

4

Somehow the cold, hard rain and the persistent wind seemed preferable to what awaited her.

She started down the darkening block reluctantly, clutching a white paper bakery bag, trying to shield it from the wet. Maybe one of those tree branches swaying wildly overhead will fly off and kill me, she fantasized. Or an electric wire blown from the pole will touch me, and...But nothing like that ever happens to people who want it to, she thought sadly.

With two fingers, Angelica undid the latch, then kicked open the metal gate that shut her house off from the rest of the block. In fact, hers was the only house on the long street that had a fence and a gate to protect their small front yard. Mama had had them installed after the dogs came. Somehow, the cyclone fence made Angelica feel even more isolated from her neighbors.

Grabbing onto the banister with one hand and holding the bakery bag and the useless umbrella in the other, Angelica mounted the slick wooden steps to her front door. More from habit than from anything else, she wiped her soaked feet on the doormat, and it squished under the pressure.

As soon as she put her key in the double lock, the high, nervous barks started upstairs. By the time she turned it, listening for the click, the familiar sound of heavy square bodies pounded across the hardwood floor. One after another, Salt and Pepper, Mama's poodles, thudded, then thudded again, against the door as if trying desperately to keep her out.

"Good watchdogs," Mama had said, insisting, almost ten years ago now, on buying one black and one white Royal Standard poodle instead of the small toy poodles that Angelica would have preferred.

"What about a collie?" Angelica had asked hopefully, when she realized that Mama wanted a watchdog. When she was young, Angelica had loved to watch *Lassie* reruns on television. Wouldn't it be wonderful to have a friend like Lassie?

"Collies are great watchdogs, Mama," Angelica said eagerly.

"Poodles don't shed," her mother retorted. The matter was settled.

Angelica bit back any argument. "Honor thy father and thy mother." She had learned in school that it was one of God's commandments. But God needn't have worried about her mother. Mama did not tolerate disrespect or disobedience or even any back talk. Angelica understood that at a very early age. So instead she hated the dogs almost as much as she hated her mother. Someday, she knew, she must rid herself of them all.

Without a word, Angelica gave the front door a quick push, hoping to surprise the animals, maybe even hit them with the sharp edge of the door just to let them feel her loathing.

But like a pair of mind readers, the poodles jumped clear, then sat erect, one black, one white, a pair of salt and pepper shakers with rounded topknots and black noses held high. In their intelligent oval eyes, Angelica read only contempt.

"What took you so long?" Mama's high whine floated down from the upstairs bedroom. "It's

6

getting dark, and I was beginning to worry. Anything can happen to a girl outside alone. You never know what kind of monsters are out in the streets at night."

And you never know what kinds of monsters are in the houses waiting, Angelica thought. She hung up her coat and watched a small puddle form beneath it on the hardwood floor.

"Answer me!" her mother shouted.

"I'll be up in a minute," Angelica called up the staircase.

"Why are you late?" Mama shouted as if she hadn't heard.

Angelica's stomach knotted with rage. "The bus was just crowded—that's all."

Hearing her mother grunt, she walked toward the kitchen. The poodles trotted after her, their sharp black toenails clicking on the linoleum. She buried the damp bakery bag filled with éclairs and chocolate-chip cookies deep in the pantry, but not before she broke off one corner of a cookie to nibble.

When Mama finally fell asleep tonight, she'd have a big glass of cold milk and those two luscious chocolate éclairs, both oozing with fresh whipped cream. Her mouth watered.

The poodles looked from Angelica to the cupboard. Then, losing interest, they loped up the stairs, their docked tails held high.

Popping the piece of cookie into her mouth, Angelica followed. She'd be able to swallow it all by the time she pulled herself up the staircase, thankful with every step that it wasn't narrower or steeper.

Suddenly the house was stifling. Or was it just her imagination? For too many years to remember, every time she had mounted these steps, she had experienced that same stifling sensation.

"You look like a drowned rat," Mama said when Angelica finally stepped into the dim bedroom.

Mama was the perfect picture of a bedridden invalid, although Angelica sometimes wondered about her mother's illness. She daydreamed about Mama hopping out of bed as soon as she left for work in the morning, roaming the house, those calloused feet bare, snooping, prying, judging, condemning, the dogs behind her sniffing, yapping.

Angelica felt the perspiration break out on her forehead. She reached for a tissue in the half-empty box next to the bed where her mother was perched on a bank of soft pillows. Angelica mopped her face. Tonight Mama's gray hair fell limply over her shoulders and made her thin, pointed face appear even more rodentlike than usual.

The two poodles rested their long muzzles against the white top sheet, and their wide feathery ears spread out. With one bony hand, Mama stroked each coarse, curly head in turn.

"My good girls," she cooed to a background of wind and rain battering the bedroom windows. "My babies." She made kissing noises toward the lethargic animals.

"My angel," she cooed in the same tone, her needle-sharp eyes fastening on her daughter, "are those nuns working you too hard? Making you do overtime? Or maybe you stopped somewhere?" To anyone who didn't know Mama, it sounded as if she was teasing, but

Angelica knew the signs. She felt the familiar tightness in her chest.

"For heaven's sake, Mama, I'm thirty years old," she began. But, as usual, her protestation sounded feeble, even to herself. Actually, she was thirty-six, but Mama didn't like to hear that. "Surely I'm perfectly able to take care—"

"But you're still my little girl," Mama cut her off smiling coldly and wagging one bony finger. "The Sugar Bowl Bakery, maybe? Did you get off the 31 at the Sugar Bowl, pick up some goodies, and then get back on?"

Angelica said nothing, suddenly afraid to speak for fear her mother would smell the chocolate on her breath. She watched Mama's index finger wave back and forth, back and forth, until its long fingernail seemed to pin her like an insect to a mat.

The nail needed to be cut. She stared silently at her mother, then quickly rid her mind of what else she could do with small, sharp manicure scissors.

"Now don't be pouting," Mama's voice was teasing, the way Angelica remembered it when she was a tiny child, when she loved Mama and wanted Mama to love her back. She felt a momentary twinge of guilt, wishing she still felt that way.

"I'm only worried about you because you've never been the same since the accident. You've never been strong. The coma took its toll on you. On us all," Mama added dramatically.

THE ACCIDENT. Mama always made it sound as if she was saying it in capital letters. Angelica had heard about the accident thousands of times. Mama never tired of reliving

9

the event, which had taken place over thirty years ago.

Angelica blocked out the words between Mama's beginning—the big rig losing control on the narrow, foggy approach to Golden Gate Bridge—and her conclusion—Papa dying weeks later in the hospital and Mama, struggling back from the edge of death, living to care for the child who needed her.

Once upon a time, the recital had frightened her. What would have become of her? But now she knew that there were things far more painful than being an orphan.

Mama ended as she always did. "You know, Angel, you're not strong. You've never been the same since the accident."

"I didn't go to the Sugar Bowl," Angelica lied. She felt the deep crevices in her elbows and behind her knees and in her groin fill with moisture. Mama hated a liar. "It's warm in here." Angelica squirmed and wondered if she dared open the bedroom window, but the rain was still teeming, and the trees in the backyards swayed wildly in the wind.

"A guilty conscience turning up the heat, perhaps?" Mama's voice was still teasing, but her eyes had grown frosty, almost as if she knew about the hidden bakery bag.

Angelica glared at the poodles. Had they told? Did they share a secret language with her mother? One that only the three of them understood?

The dogs stared back with wide, black-rimmed innocent eyes.

Angelica groped for the damp tissue she had buried in her cleavage. She blotted her upper lip. "I'd better start our dinner," she said, swiping at her forehead and along the back of her neck.

Finished with torturing her, Mama pushed the remote control and the television set snapped on. "What are we having?" she asked, stroking Salt's head absently.

"Spaghetti and meatballs," Angelica hadn't really given the main course much thought. For her, dessert was the only concern. Spaghetti would do. It was easy and filling, and there was always plenty left over for a midnight snack.

"Don't forget to wash your hands before you start dinner," Mama reminded her. "You never know who's been touching what on those buses."

Angelica felt her face burn with the same swirling rage she felt every night when Mama reminded her to wash her hands. She glared at her mother's sharp profile, longing to tell her that one of these days she'd put her dirty hands around Mama's reedy neck and...The words teetered on the tip of her tongue, aching to be said, to be shouted. But Mama had lost interest in everything except the television game-show host and the noisy, twirling wheel of prizes.

Cramped in the downstairs bathroom, Angelica let the warm water run over the palms of her hands. She studied each one of her fingers, thick and meaty, like ten small pork links at Cala's Meat Market.

A thin strip of turquoise and silver, a long-ago Christmas gift from her Uncle Frank, banded the third finger of her right hand. Flesh bulged on either side of the ring. When she used soap, she could turn it; but no matter how hard

11

she tugged, it would not slide up or down. She could not remember the last time she'd been able to take off that ring.

Angelica stared at her wet left hand. She'd probably never have an engagement ring of her own to put on that ring finger, but one of these days, when Mama was gone, Angelica would take Mama's ring and wear it as her own, even if she had to enlarge it to make it fit. In fact, she would wear both Mama's engagement ring and her wedding band, although the diamonds in both were puny and the settings bland. Angelica didn't care. All the people on the Number 31 Balboa bus would think that she was a happily married woman going home to a loving husband.

Her stomach cramped, and she felt a sudden hollow. She was hungry.

"Don't you know there's a water shortage?" her mother called over the noise of the upstairs television set. "What in the world are you doing in that bathroom?"

Angelica's chest tightened. "Nothing," she called back.

"For heaven's sake, do something!" Mama snapped peevishly. "I'm nearly starved. And don't forget to feed the dogs."

"When have I ever forgotten to feed them?" Angelica grumbled under her breath. She watched Salt and Pepper descend the stairs with slow deliberate steps, like royalty. Pompon tails held high, they moved toward the door and waited with noble aloofness for her to let them out before dinner.

She opened it just wide enough for the dogs to pass. The wind wailing through the crack made Salt recoil. With a surge of pleasure, Angelica gave the poodle a quick shove out into the cold, then kicked Pepper for good measure and hurried toward the kitchen.

The sharp ring of the hall phone stopped her short. She checked the grandfather clock in the corner. Six-thirty. Monday night. Uncle Frank.

She picked up the receiver on the fourth ring. "Hello."

"Hello, Angel!" Uncle Frank's reedy voice rang through the line. She waited for his usual question. "How's my favorite niece this week?"

With a practiced giggle, Angelica gave her usual answer. "I'm your only niece, and I'm fine."

"And how is the old battle-ax? Still alive and enjoying ill health?" Uncle Frank cackled at his own joke.

"She's fine, too." Angelica heard her mother shifting in her bed.

"I am not fine!" Mama's whine echoed down the staircase. "And who is that anyway?"

Angelica didn't know why Mama bothered to ask. Frank, her mother's only living sibling, called every Monday night at six-thirty sharp, as predictable as death.

And why? Angelica wondered. Mama never wants to talk to him and nothing ever changes. One Monday is much like the next. But someday it will change. Everything will change. Angelica felt moisture forming on her upper lip. Some Monday I'll pick up the phone at six-thirty and when Uncle Frank asks, "How's the old battle-ax?" I'll answer, "Dead!" Then *I'll* be the one to laugh.

"Tell him I'm too sick to talk," Mama called down, coughing for emphasis.

"Too sick to talk, huh?" Frank knew the answer. "But not too sick to eat or to issue orders, I'll bet. Honest to the good God, that woman's her own worst enemy."

He said that almost every week. Once Angelica had asked him what he meant.

Uncle Frank had hesitated. "She's just plain jealous," he had said finally, his breath coming out in a rush. "Always has been. Ever since we were kids. Your Papa used to tell me that sometimes, even after they were married, her jealousy was like a coal that came hissing hot from hell!"

Angelica was startled. She'd never heard her Papa say anything like that, especially about Mama. It was almost as if he was afraid of her, too.

"Listen, Angelica honey, why don't you get away for a few days?" Frank began. This, too, was a familiar conversation. Her uncle introduced it every time a school holiday was coming up. What was it now? Angelica thought for a minute. Thanksgiving, of course.

"How can I leave Mama alone at Thanksgiving time?" It was the same question she always asked, inserting the appropriate holiday season. "Besides, she's sick. She needs me."

"Sick!" Uncle Frank snorted. "That old bag is going to live forever. And, God's truth, she's gotten more than her mileage out of that accident. You need to get out and enjoy yourself, be with people your own age. You're still young and...and..." Frank faltered. "You're still attractive, with that angel face of yours."

Angelica ran her hand across her doughy face.

"If it's money, Angelica, I'll give it to you," Frank said.

Money was always a problem for Angelica. Mama handled all their bills and expenses. Every payday, on her way home from the college, Angelica simply deposited her paycheck at the Bank of America branch on the corner of 38th and Balboa. Every payday Mrs. Hart, the teller with the unnaturally coal black hair, cashed the check Angelica had given her and put the money in a bank envelope for her to take home. Mama took out enough for food and household supplies and gave Angelica a weekly allowance. "A generous allowance," Mama called it.

Sometimes Angelica wondered about the money, but she never asked. Mama said it showed poor breeding to talk about money, especially with relatives. One of these days, she'd work up enough courage to ask Uncle Frank.

Ferocious barking started up outside, drowning out whatever else her uncle was saying. A young voice shouted obscenities. The poodles lunged against the gate with resounding metallic thuds.

"What's going on?" Mama screeched from upstairs. "Hang up. He's only talking nonsense anyway. And do something about that racket."

"I'll think about it, Uncle Frank," Angelica promised and hung up quickly.

Angelica opened the front door cautiously. Wet, cold air wrapped itself around her legs. She shivered as the poodles, tired of barking, pushed past her. She could tell by their bared fangs that they were angry with her. Would they tell Mama that she'd kicked them? Angelica's stomach roiled. The two rough bodies flanked her and then, with deliberate aim, shook themselves, spraying Angelica's skirt and legs with

15

muddy drops. Satisfied, the pair trotted toward the kitchen to await their dinner.

"Hey, lady!" a boy's voice called out. Angelica recognized it as the same voice that had been shouting minutes ago. She turned on the porch light and squinted. A small redhead, balancing a bicycle that seemed much too large for him, stood outside the front gate. His body, covered by a slicker, hunched against the rain. He must be the new paperboy.

"Here's your *Examiner*." The youngster held out the plastic-wrapped paper. "Shall I try to lob it onto your porch, or do you want to come out and get it? 'Cause I'm not coming inside your yard for nothing. Them dogs could eat you alive. Don't you ever feed 'em?"

"Try to throw it," Angelica called, stepping back to avoid the rain splashing on the porch.

"Angelica! Stop talking to whoever it is you're talking to and get into the kitchen! You need to towel off these wet dogs and feed them. And what about my dinner?" Mama's voice rang out into the darkness, strong and demanding.

"Who's that?" the paperboy asked.

"My mother," Angelica whispered nervously and began closing the door.

The boy flung one leg over his bike. "How come you still have to do what she says when you're so old?" His freckled nose wrinkled with curiosity.

Her angry tears nearly blurred the youngster as he vanished into the rain. His question hung on the cold air. From the distance, the deep, dismal bawling of a foghorn seemed to echo it. "How come? How come?" it asked. Very quietly, Angelica Bowers closed the heavy front door.

Long after Mass was over and dinner eaten, Sister Mary Helen still couldn't get Angelica Bowers off her mind. She wasn't sure why. Even now, settled in an easy chair in the large community room, where most of the Sisters eventually gathered, Angelica's girth gnawed at Mary Helen like a moth working its way through an old woolen habit.

In one corner of the room, the television anchorman was joking with his cohost before signing off. Why can't they just report the news and be done with it? she thought crossly. What do we care if they enjoy each other's company? But she didn't say anything because a small circle of Sisters were glued to every word as if they were included in the banter.

Young Sister Anne sat cross-legged beside the coffee table, playing solitaire. Behind her on the couch, Sister Therese, who insisted on pronouncing her name "trays," was practicing great restraint by not telling her to move the red jack onto the black queen.

The steady rain gurgled in the gutter just outside the window. Sister Mary Helen stared unseeing at the television set, scarcely aware that some bank was protesting, "We always have you in mind." A show host spun the colored wheel. As usual, old Sister Donata guessed the correct answer.

The wheel spun again. In its blur, Mary Helen saw only the blue of Angelica's anxious eyes peering out from her round, chunky face. The woman seemed always on the verge of tears. And why not? She must be miserably uncomfortable.

Why was she so overweight? She seemed to be an educated, intelligent woman with a decent job.

The television audience "oowed" as a contestant won an elegant and overpriced "gift."

"Who'd want it?" Sister Donata asked no one in particular. Mary Helen nodded absently. Maybe Eileen has more of an insight into Angelica's situation, she thought.

Sister Eileen had spent most of her religious life at Mount St. Francis College. Mary Helen subtracted automatically. Was it possible that they had been nuns for fifty-four years? Or was it fifty-six? Not that it mattered. If there were any insights to be had on anybody, Eileen would have them. I'll ask her as soon as she comes in, Mary Helen decided.

Bored with the show host's jokes, she picked up the *Chronicle*. She skimmed through the hard news, including the report of another grisly rape of a senior citizen in the Sea Cliff district. She read Herb Caen's column and chuckled at *Cathy*, whose dieting problems she understood fully. On her way to the obituaries, she passed headlines declaring "Abuse in Nursing Home," "BART Dispute Unsettled," "Priest Implicated in Scandal"—back-page news these days—and yet another Emporium "40 percent off" sale.

"Dog Eats Dead Owner" caught her eye and made her shudder. Right next to it, as if God-sent, was a large advertisement proclaiming a little prematurely, "Happy Holidays! Our gift of a slim body and good health to you!"

A svelte young woman, sitting amid a breath-takingly beautiful rock formation, gazed into space. A contented smile played on her per-fectly formed lips. "Weight Loss. Incredible Value. Uncanny Results," the ad promised. "Spend one to four weeks at the American In-stitute of Fitness."

A perfect spot for Angelica! What more could anyone want? Mary Helen checked the address. Ivins, Utah. Where in the world was Ivins, Utah?

Fortunately, the community room had an atlas on its bookshelves. Mary Helen blew the dust off it and was so intent on poring over the detailed map of Utah that she didn't hear Sister Eileen settle into the chair next to her.

"Are you planning a trip?" Eileen's question startled her.

"Don't sneak up like that," Mary Helen said when her heartbeat returned to normal.

"Sneak up!" Eileen's bushy gray eyebrows shot up in annoyance. "I swear, old dear, that it's about time you had your ears checked."

Mary Helen, who was often accused of selective deafness, chose not to hear that remark. Ears checked, indeed! She heard as well now as she ever did. If people would only stop mumbling and sneaking around.

"There was a day," Eileen muttered, "when you could hear the grass growing in Ireland."

"I was waiting for you," Mary Helen said, having reached her fill of the "hearing" topic. "Look at this!" She thrust the newspaper ad-vertisement in front of Eileen and watched her read it carefully.

"I was just trying to locate the place," Mary Helen explained. "It should be down here in this corner by Snow Canyon. The atlas lists its population as seventy-seven. Most of the town must work at the fitness institute."

"Why the sudden interest in fitness?" Eileen looked up from the paper. "Do you want to go there, or have I missed something?"

"Of course, *I* don't want to go there." Mary Helen frowned, suddenly realizing that she'd forgotten to tell Eileen of her quickly forming plan. She pointed to a dot on the map. "What I want us to do is to talk Angelica Bowers into taking some vacation time and going there."

"Angelica Bowers! Are you still stewing about Angelica Bowers?"

"She looked so miserable today. I guess I've never really noticed her before. Or if I did, she didn't strike me as being so unhappy."

Eileen's soft face folded sympathetically. "Poor girl! They say she has never been the same after the accident, you know."

Mary Helen perked up. "What accident?"

"It was in all the newspapers and on television when it happened." Eileen stared incredulously at her friend. "Oh, but that was before you came to the Mount, wasn't it?"

Mary Helen nodded impatiently, wishing Eileen would get on with the story.

"It happened so long ago, I can't remember exactly when, but it was one of those awful pile-ups on the approach to the Golden Gate. The fog was dense and wet, and a truck took the curve too fast. At least a dozen people were hurt. Three died. Angelica's father was one of them—not at the scene, but a few days later. Anyway, Angelica herself, who was only about four or five at the time, was in a coma for weeks."

Eileen folded the *Chronicle* and set it back on the edge of the coffee table. It was about time for Sister Therese to swoop down on the Jumble puzzle.

"Somehow, Angelica grew up thinking she was doomed," Eileen said pensively.

"Doomed?" Mary Helen studied her friend.

Eileen nodded. "As if things could never quite return to normal. I first noticed it when she was a student here. She came to class, all right, but never had the stamina to participate in college activities, even social ones.

"When I asked her why, she'd simply say, 'The accident.' When she graduated, I urged her to go on for a master's degree. By then, she was what you'd call sturdy. Nowhere near fat. But she demurred. Her reason? 'The accident.'

"About that same time, her mother who was also in the crash began suffering bouts of back pain, which, I understand from Angelica, became increasingly worse. Now, for all practical purposes, she's an invalid."

"How old is the mother?" Mary Helen wondered aloud.

"In her mid-seventies, I'd guess."

Mary Helen did some quick subtracting. "Angelica must have come late in the marriage," she said.

"Or maybe her parents married late." Eileen shrugged. "Anyway, instead of looking for a job with a future, Angelica took the first clerical opening here at the college library. And she has turned down every opportunity offered her to go on for more education, which, of course, would lead to a promotion.

"As the years passed, her weight increased,

almost imperceptibly. And with each year, she became more withdrawn....Maybe you're right about this...this..." Eileen looked for the paper, but it was gone. "This institute.

"She does have vacation time coming, and didn't the ad say, 'Incredible Value'? Maybe it's not too expensive."

"Do you think finances are a problem?" Mary Helen asked. It seemed to her as if Angelica had enough troubles already.

"I don't really know," Eileen admitted, "but she doesn't make much money here. If her mother is bedridden, what with doctor's bills and real-estate taxes and upkeep...Unless there's something we don't know about, she can't have it too easy."

She brightened. "Maybe her health insurance will cover it."

"Whoa!" Mary Helen said before Eileen gathered a full head of steam. "First, we have to get her to go! And going is only the first step," she added realistically. "As you wisely remarked..."

Eileen frowned, undoubtedly trying to remember what she'd said.

Mary Helen continued. "It's taken her years to put on that much weight. Even if she stayed the entire four weeks, pounds don't come off that quickly. She'll need to join some kind of behavior-modification program or an exercise class when she comes back."

Canned laughter from the television set filled the flat silence while both old nuns considered the problem.

"The fitness institute would be a good jump-start into a program," Eileen offered hopefully.

"You know, we have an old saying back home."

Mary Helen groaned. Eileen seemed able to dredge up an old saying to fit every occasion; and if it didn't, she tailored it.

"Mighty things grow from small beginnings," Eileen proclaimed, lifting her small nose.

"In this case, don't we want mighty things to dwindle?" Mary Helen couldn't resist.

Ignoring her, Eileen rushed on, "At least this will be a beginning. I'll photocopy the ad on the library copy machine first thing tomorrow morning. Then, after she's been told about it, I'll give it to her."

"After?" Mary Helen pushed her bifocals up the bridge of her nose. "Who then shall bell the cat? You seem like the logical one to me."

Eileen frowned. "Me? I work with her and, before I semiretired, I was her boss for years. She might take it better coming from you."

"What reason would I have for even broaching the subject?"

It didn't take Eileen long. "You're the Alumnae Director. Angelica is an alum. There it is!"

"Not so fast," Mary Helen said.

Cocking her head, Eileen smiled triumphantly. "Besides, this whole thing was your idea."

They came to a decision quickly and certainly, using the method they often used in a deadlock. Mary Helen never could figure out quite how Eileen always knew to choose paper when she balled her fist into a rock.

At first, Kate Murphy did not recognize the sound. It was faint, yet persistent, like the warning gong of a buoy way out in the bay. But its ring, ring, ringing kept coming closer and closer until one bell finally penetrated her sleep. The telephone!

Why wasn't Jack answering it? It was a husband's job. After all, the phone was on his side of the bed. Eyes still shut, she felt for the spot where her husband usually lay. Empty!

Her heart jolted. Where was he? "Jack," she whispered as loudly as she dared. She didn't want to wake the baby. She must stop the ringing. "Jack?" she said a little louder. There was no answer.

Fighting down the panic that began to grip her, Kate struggled to untangle herself from the covers. She reached across the empty space in the bed and snatched up the receiver. Dread slid down her back like a raindrop outside the windowpane.

"Hello." She recognized the voice of her partner, Dennis Gallagher, immediately. A homicide! That's what this call is about, she thought, deliberately taking a deep breath.

After all these years in Homicide, she should be used to late-night calls. Yet there was always something terrifying about the cold, relentless ring of the night phone.

Kate glanced over at the clock. Three-thirty in the morning! "What have we, Denny?" she asked, trying to sound wide awake.

Gallagher hesitated. "Jack." His words were fuzzy.

Outside the window, a bird twittered in the darkness. "Jack?" Kate asked. She was Homicide. Jack was Sex Crimes. Why would he want Jack? "He's here somewhere." Her scalp prickled. "He must be downstairs getting something to eat."

"No, Kate." Gallagher's usually booming voice was a husky whisper. "Hell, there's no right way to say this." He cleared his throat. "Jack's at St. Mary's Medical Center. He's in surgery. Doctor thinks he'll pull through okay. I'm on my way over to get you right now." He stopped. "Bill Jordon didn't make it."

"Didn't make it!" The hollow words echoed in Kate's ear. Inspector Bill Jordon was Jack's partner. Like Jack, he was married and had a child, a sweet little three-year-old named Julie. He didn't make what?

Fully awake now, Kate remembered that Jack had told her this morning that he'd be late. Something about working a stakeout with Bill. The partners had a suspect they were pretty sure was the rapist who had broken into several homes in Sea Cliff. He specialized in preying on elderly women, particularly women who lived alone.

"Too close for comfort, hon," Jack had joked when he kissed her good-bye this morning.

"Wait just one minute, pal." Kate wasn't going to let him get away with that! "Didn't you say, 'elderly women'? It's not a problem."

Jack had pointed to the few gray hairs that were beginning to mingle with the red ones at her temples. "Check it out, hon. We better get the sicko quick-o!"

Kate had slammed the door after him.

When her husband wasn't home by ten, Kate had gone to bed. Since he'd changed from Vice to the Sex Crimes Detail, she didn't worry about his safety quite so much. Not that any police work wasn't dangerous, but rapists, molesters, and perverts usually didn't kill their victims.

She knew she'd wake up when he came in. She always did. But tonight she hadn't because Jack had not come home. Bill Jordon never would. Hot tears stung her eyes.

"You okay, Katie-girl?" Gallagher asked softly.

What the hell do you think? Kate wanted to shout, but didn't. Denny was just delivering the bad news. Wasn't it the Greeks who killed the messenger when they didn't like the message? Suddenly she knew how they felt. She willed her whole body to remain calm. This was not Denny's fault. This was nobody's fault, except the sicko's.

"Kate?" Gallagher sounded worried. "Are you there?"

Kate nodded, then realized that her partner couldn't see her. "Yes," she said, her throat tight.

"I'll be there in ten minutes, tops."

"The baby," Kate's mind was swimming. What would she do with little John?

"The missus is on her way to your house now. She'll stay there in case the little guy wakes up. He'll need to see somebody familiar."

Dear old Denny! He's figured out everything, Kate thought, scrambling into a sweat suit. How long had he been with Jack tonight, she wondered. She didn't think to ask. Or if her husband was shot, stabbed or what? The only thing that she knew—the only thing that was really important—was that he was alive.

"Thank God, thank God," she repeated over and over as, automatically, she put John's ducky bowl and mug on the high-chair tray for his breakfast. In a few hours, he'd be waking up and calling for them. Kate swept away a straggling tear. No time for that!

She opened the front door before Mrs. G. rang the bell. "Perfect timing," she whispered, brushing the older woman's cheek with a kiss. "Thanks."

Then Kate was down the front stairs and at the curb before Denny's car stopped completely.

"Where's your umbrella?" he asked, leaning over to unlock her door.

Kate, numb, hadn't even felt the chill drizzle of rain. Yet she was aware of Denny's small kindnesses. Her partner had the car oven warm, a rare treat. A Styrofoam cup of coffee and a twisted glazed doughnut, her favorite kind, were in a cardboard box waiting for her.

"Drink up," he said pulling the unmarked police car away from the curb. Rain drummed on the roof. To the rhythmic swish of the windshield wipers, Gallagher told Kate as much as he'd learned from Jack before her husband lost consciousness.

Apparently, the two officers had waited outside the "perp"'s house, followed him to Sea Cliff, watched him pry open an unlocked window and enter the house, then followed him. The terrified sobs of the elderly woman had led them to an upstairs bedroom.

Shivering despite the heat, Kate listened. Tires hissed in the rain. Had they moved the hospital? She cursed every stop light, every cautious driver. Didn't they know she had to get to Jack?

Gallagher switched on the defroster and glanced over at her. His face took on a dark red glow from the taillights ahead of them. "When Jack and Bill burst in, the perp must have opened fire."

Kate hugged her arms around her body and

27

leaned back in the seat. She felt sick. "Jack was shot?"

"In the shoulder, with one of those goddamn Saturday night specials! Who the hell expects a rapist to carry a gun? A knife, sure. But a Smith and Wesson thirty-eight? For a few bucks, this guy can now shoot six people without reloading."

Kate winced. Denny sounded more annoyed at the man's lack of protocol than at the act itself. Her saner self knew this wasn't true. But somehow her saner self wasn't home right now.

"Neighbors heard the racket," Gallagher told her. "They called 911. The black-and-whites got there in seconds. I picked up the call. The woman was still holding her own when I got there. Jack was trying his best to take care of Bill and to give her mouth-to-mouth. You never saw so much bl—" He stopped, but it was too late.

The car seemed to be closing in on Kate. Despite the rain, she cracked open the window.

"The woman died on the way to the hospital," Gallagher sniffled.

"Did they get the perp?" Kate asked woodenly.

Gallagher shook his head. "We will." He set his jaw.

"Damn right," Kate said, the empty feeling growing in her stomach.

"If we only knew who the hell he was," Gallagher mumbled.

Before the car came to a stop, Kate was out the door and through the emergency-room entrance. The Sister on duty looked up expectantly. "Can I help...?"

"Inspector Jack Bassetti," Kate demanded before the nun had the chance to finish the question. "I'm Inspector Kate Murphy."

The nun hesitated. "I'm afraid he's not up to questions right now, Inspector."

Kate struggled for control. *How could the Sister possibly know I use my maiden name on the job?* Near bursting, she said "I'm also his wife."

Jack Bassetti lay in a small, curtain-shrouded alcove in the recovery room. At first glance, he looked as if he were just sleeping. Kate might have tried to awaken him, too, except for the intravenous tubes, the beeping machines, and the enormous white bandage covering most of his upper body.

Although it was unbearably hot in the alcove, Kate's teeth were chattering now. A nurse slipped in through the curtain silently. Smiling tentatively at Kate, she checked one of the tubes. Her white uniform blended with the white of the curtain. In fact, *everything in the space is white,* Kate thought, her throat closing. The curtains, the sheets, the hospital gown, the nurse's uniform, Jack's face on the pillows. That white face without a smile, without a wisecrack, without the teasing eyes. The zigzag line on the machine and the slight rise and fall of the sheet covering his chest were the only indication that he was alive.

And everything was so quiet! The deadly silence that hung over the cubicle exaggerated the beep of the monitor until it was strident.

In the distance, Kate heard the squeak of crepe-soled shoes on polished floors, the swish

29

of curtain hooks being whisked along rods, and the deep, hiccupping sound of a woman's weeping. Was that Bill Jordon's wife, or the victim's daughter or sister? Would that soon be herself?

The curtain walls of the cubicle were moving closer. Before she tiptoed out, the nurse pushed a wooden chair toward the end of the bed. Kate sank into it. Folding her arms on the white thermal blanket covered with a white top sheet, Kate buried her face and sobbed.

She had no idea how long she stayed like that. Her throat ached and her face felt hot and... soggy. The top sheet was damp.

Sniffling, she felt something jiggle. Was Jack moving his foot? She sat up. He was smiling crookedly at her. His lips moved. He was trying to speak.

"Darling!" Kate kissed him all over his stubbly face. She raked her fingers through his curly dark hair, loving every familiar feature. His lips moved again, and she brought her ear close to his mouth. She felt the thread of his breath on her cheek.

"What is it?" she whispered. "What can I do?"

"...Drenching my foot..." His words were halting, but laughter fluttered across his hazel eyes. "...Give...pneumonia, too?"

Relief flowed over Kate and bubbled up into fresh tears. Jack was alive, all right. Surrounded by all those awful machines and that sterile white, only her Jack would make a joke. How lucky she was to have found him, although she'd rather choke than admit it.

"Nobody likes a smart-ass, pal," she whispered just to let him know that she was all right, too. "And remember, you are at my mercy!"

Jack grinned again, rolling his eyes. His lips moved. Kate bent down close to hear. She hoped he wasn't going to ask about Bill. There would be time for that when he was stronger.

"Whatever you do, not my mother!" he said.

His mother! Until this moment, she had not given Loretta Bassetti a thought. Someone would have to call to tell her the news before she found out from the newspaper or the television.

Kate heard crepe soles behind her. The nurse was back. "Time for pain medication," she said in a cheerful whisper.

"Is he in pain?" Kate asked, then wished she hadn't.

The nurse stared at her in disbelief. "He's been shot, honey," she said flatly. "Of course he's in pain."

Kate grabbed the end of the bed. The nurse gave her a wary look. "Why don't you let him sleep?" she said more kindly. "I think the doctor's out by the desk. He might want to talk to you."

Two hours later, with Jack moved into the intensive care unit and the doctor's assurance that her husband was doing as well as could be expected and needed rest now more than anything else, Kate could think of no more excuses not to call her mother-in-law. Dennis Gallagher, after telephoning his wife and assuring Kate that the baby was "doing great," had gone to the Hall of Justice.

Kate found the correct change for the pay phone in her purse. The clock on the hospital wall told her it was well after six. Mama Bassetti was an early riser with uncanny intuition. It would be just like her to sense something, call the house, and get Mrs. G. If that happened, Kate would never hear the end of it.

With a sense of dread, she dropped the coins into the slots and dialed the number. Loretta Bassetti answered on the first ring with "What's wrong?"

At once, Kate's temper fizzed. "What makes you think something is wrong?" she asked.

"It's six o'clock in the morning, Kate. Who calls at this hour of the morning to tell you something's good? Unless it's a new baby. And you're not even pregnant, are you? Neither is my Gina. And if my Angie had a baby, that's not good news, either, since she is not married to that bozo she runs around with. Besides, she tells me they don't live together. As if I was born yesterday!"

Having dismissed Jack's two sisters, Kate was afraid that her mother-in-law was about to start on the long list of his first cousins. Suddenly she felt as if her knees were melting.

"There is some bad news," she interrupted, "but let me start by saying that the doctor says he's doing well."

"The doctor? He?" Mrs. Bassetti's voice rose a notch. "The baby?"

"No, no, Loretta. The baby's fine."

"Thank God."

"Loretta, it's Jack."

Her mother-in-law sucked in her breath. "Jackie?"

"We're at St. Mary's Medical Center now," Kate began as gently as she could. "He was shot

32

last night. He's resting, and the doctor's sure he's out of danger."

"The doctor said that?"

Kate was positive he would have if she had pressed him. "Yes, Loretta." She crossed her fingers.

Kate heard the crackling of the phone lines. "Loretta?" She listened. "Loretta, are you all right?"

Nothing but silence filled the space between them. It was the first time in Kate's memory that her mother-in-law was completely speechless.

Sister Mary Helen wasn't sure what woke her. Suddenly she was wide awake. Her heart was pounding and her fists were clenched. She stared up at the pitch-black ceiling, conscious of the uneasiness that wrapped her like a winding sheet. She tried to shrug it off, but the inexplicable foreboding was almost tangible.

Was it the new whodunit she'd tried to finish before she went to sleep? She felt for the plastic prayer-book cover which she always used to camouflage her mystery novels. She found it on her chest where it must have landed when she dropped off.

She considered that the book might be the culprit, but only for a moment. The story was yet another of the lawyer mysteries that were so popular. If she read many more of them, she might be able to pass the bar examination without any anxiety at all, but she'd hardly wake up scared.

Outside the trees creaked under the force of

the wind and a branch scraped against her window. The drainpipe swallowed great gurgling gulps of rain.

Was it that piece on the ten o'clock news about the rapist who was terrorizing elderly women in Sea Cliff? Mary Helen held her breath and listened. Inside the convent, everything was nighttime still.

She glanced over at her alarm clock. An alumna had given her that clock as a gift, and Mary Helen was glad. With the large luminous numbers, she no longer had to fumble on the nightstand for her glasses to see the time. Three-thirty, it read. Two and one-half hours before the alarm would ring. She'd be dead in the morning if she didn't get back to sleep. And she had a big task in the morning. She needed all her strength and more than her usual share of tact and prudence to tackle the monumental problem of Angelica Bowers. Perhaps "monumental" was a poor word to choose. She needed to be more discreet than that.

Although Mary Helen never admitted it to Eileen, she was elated when she lost their game of Paper, Scissors, Rock. It delighted her to think of having some part in encouraging Angelica to become a new person—thin, happy, attractive. And the young woman *would be* attractive, too. She had a very pretty face. An angel face, really. Mary Helen could not drop the ball on this one.

She set her book on the nightstand, shut her eyes, and tried to relax, deliberately releasing the tightness in her legs and arms. The rain had quieted to a gentle patter. Mary Helen turned on her side.

Today had been the Feast of All Souls, she remembered drowsily. *There could well be a poor soul out there in all that wet darkness who is dying at this very moment. Maybe that was what awakened me; a person in need of my prayers for the courage and the strength to die,* she thought.

"The Angel of Death....You can almost hear the beating of his wings." From somewhere deep inside, the words popped into her mind. She felt under her pillow for her rosary and slowly began to finger the beads.

"Holy Mary, Mother of God." She fell back sleepily on the old familiar words. "Pray for us sinners, now and at the hour of our death. Amen."

Tuesday, November 3
Feast of St. Martin de Porres, Religious

As soon after the morning Mass and breakfast as possible, Sister Mary Helen hurried toward the Hanna Memorial Library. She wanted to catch Angelica Bowers when the doors opened, before any of the students or most of the other staff arrived.

Since she had awakened this morning, she had been trying to decide on the most tactful way to broach the subject of the fitness center. As usual, she decided that the direct approach was the best approach. She'd ask Angelica for a moment of her time. They'd sit down at a quiet library table. She'd tell the young woman of her concern and, finally, show her the advertisement.

Mary Helen was so eager to meet Angelica that she didn't even stop by her own office. She knew that her secretary, Shirley, was perfectly capable of taking care of alumnae business until she arrived.

At the moment, Shirley was probably more capable than she since the college alums were currently working on their annual Christmas Tree Extravaganza, which was scheduled for early December.

Mary Helen readily admitted that Shirley was far more knowledgeable about glittery Christmas-tree decorations, festive and clever table settings, and dance bands than she was. And that seemed to be what most of the meetings centered on these days. Actually, Mary Helen was called upon during this particular affair only when the committee contacted the perennial "big donors." When someone was needed to ask them to sponsor tables, donate trips for raffles, and secure the endless live-auction items, Mary Helen was that someone.

"What's the big rush?" Eileen had asked when Mary Helen stood to leave the dining room halfway through her second cup of coffee. Mary Helen had explained, hoping Eileen picked up her urgency and would get the advertisement copied immediately.

"I already did it," Eileen offered before Mary Helen had the chance to ask. Mind reading is both a good and a bad by-product of a long and close friendship, Mary Helen thought, examining the piece of paper.

The American Institute of Fitness looked even more inviting on white paper than it had on newsprint. Who could resist a chance to look like the trim young lady gazing at the distant mountains?

Throwing back her shoulders and taking a deep breath, Mary Helen tried the beveled glass door leading to the library. She was relieved to find it pulled open.

Although a few of the bullet-shaped overhead lights were on, a sure sign of life, the reading room was completely deserted. From the far end, Archbishop Edward Joseph Hanna, third archbishop of San Francisco, stared down from his portrait positively daring anyone to dog-ear one of his precious books.

The only sounds were a coffeepot perking and the low rattle of cellophane. Both were coming from an office behind the circulation desk. Obviously, the "No smoking, eating, or drinking" sign on the wall did not apply to back offices.

"Yoo-hoo!" Mary Helen called out, hoping it was Angelica.

"We are not open yet!" A frowning Mrs. Kenny peered around the corner. When the senior librarian saw Sister Mary Helen, she tried unsuccessfully to adjust her face. "Are you looking for Sister Eileen?" she asked.

"No," Mary Helen answered politely. "I'd like a word with Miss Bowers."

"She's never here this early," Mrs. Kenny said and returned to her rattling.

Trying not to appear curious, Mary Helen glanced into the room. "When does she usually arrive?" she asked, watching the woman unwrap a box of Danish pastries.

"These were going stale at my house," Mrs. Kenny explained, setting the Dutch apple roll next to the raspberry jelly. "Here they'll be gone by the morning coffee break."

She stepped back to admire her arrangement. "They looked so delicious and were such a bargain at Costco that I couldn't resist. But when I got them home!" She made a face.

Sister Mary Helen clucked understandingly. The convent shelves were full of the follies of Costco shoppers.

"Miss Bowers?" Mary Helen asked again, trying not to sound impatient. "Do you know what time she usually arrives?"

Mrs. Kenny checked the round faced clock on the office wall. "Minutes—no, seconds before we open to the students."

The aroma of fresh coffee filled the room, an especially delicious smell on such a wet morning.

"Angelica is always just under the wire, poor thing," Mrs. Kenny added.

"Why 'poor thing'?" Mary Helen wondered aloud.

The librarian flushed. "I hope I didn't sound patronizing, but have you ever noticed how she walks up the college steps, Sister?"

"As a matter of fact, I haven't" Mary Helen admitted.

"It would break your heart." Mrs. Kenny offered a pastry to Mary Helen, who declined. It would never do to have Danish on your breath when you're talking about a diet.

"I think she actually gets off the Number 31 Balboa across the street at Turk and Chabot, in plenty of time. She's all right on the crosswalk. It's flat. But those steps." Mrs. Kenny rolled her eyes. "There must be at least two hundred of them."

Seventy-eight, to be exact, Mary Helen thought, if you start at Turk Street and walk straight up. She had counted them more than once herself.

"The students don't give the steps a thought," Mrs. Kenny was warming to her subject, "but for those of us who are older, it's a climb. It's really painful to watch poor Angelica. She clutches the banister, climbs a few steps, stops for breath, pretends to admire the azaleas or the rosemary growing on the landings." Mrs. Kenny's eyes cut to Mary Helen to make sure she was still listening—which she was, but just barely.

"Azaleas are lovely, of course," she continued, "in full bloom, but how much pleasure can one derive from looking at the same rosemary bushes every morning?"

"Not much," Mary Helen agreed, picturing the prickly shrubs which grew in a concrete planter like a girdle across the landing.

"So you see, she's not fooling anyone, and it must be embarrassing."

In the distance, Mary Helen heard the library door swinging open and shut. The rest of the staff was arriving. Surely, soon the aroma of freshly brewed coffee would draw them into the office. She wanted to speak to Angelica privately. To do this now, she'd need to watch for her arrival and catch her before she came in.

Again refusing Mrs. Kenny's offer of a Danish, Mary Helen excused herself and moved to the bank of windows to the left of the archbishop's picture. From that vantage point, she had an excellent view of the top of the stairway and the concrete square in front of the main entrance. The rain had stopped, but small puddles were everywhere.

Armed with her copy of the American Institute of Fitness ad, Mary Helen scanned the swelling crowd. Students, professors, and college staff flowed across the square like water to an open drain. She'd have to forget about sitting at a quiet library table to talk. Maybe she'd snag Angelica and find a vacant classroom. The woman would never fit into one of the plastic-and-chrome students' desks. They'd have to stand.

At last Mary Helen spotted her prey at the edge of the square, letting the quicker traffic, which, of course, was all of it, pass her. Angelica's round face was flushed. Damp hair clung to her forehead.

Waddling more than walking, she stood out like a plump wet pigeon amid a brood of finches. Watching her made Mary Helen more determined than ever to help Angelica Bowers do something about her weight.

Leaving the library, the old nun planted herself in the hallway. The noise of feet shuffling on polished hardwood floors and laughter filled the cathedral ceilings of the passage. She watched a horde of dripping umbrellas and raincoats file by. She was beginning to wonder if she'd chosen the right spot when Miss Bowers appeared. Head down, she seemed to be concentrating on every step she took.

"Angelica," Mary Helen reached out and touched the woman's forearm.

Startled, Angelica turned toward her. "Yes, Sister?" Her flat blue eyes blinked with uncertainty.

Like a rabbit's, Mary Helen thought. "May I see you for a moment?"

Fear flickered across Angelica's face. "What did I do?" she asked in a childish voice.

"Nothing. You didn't do anything wrong. There is just something I'd like to talk to you about." Mary Helen ushered Angelica into the first vacant classroom she found. She shut the door gently behind them.

Angelica's apprehensive eyes shifted everywhere except to Mary Helen's face. Avoiding the rows of desks and pretending to admire the view, which *was* admirable, Mary Helen jockeyed Angelica toward the long, narrow windows. Before them, the magnificent spires of St. Ignatius Church were silhouetted against wooded hills. Water-filled clouds with black edges touched the treetops. Miniature workmen on a scaffolding were fixing the dome. Mary Helen wondered absently if it had developed a leak in all this rain.

"I hope you don't think I'm overstepping my bounds," Mary Helen began. Then, clearly over her bounds, she continued as quickly and tactfully as possible to tell the young woman of her concern. She mentioned her discovery of the advertisement and suggested that Angelica not wait for a school holiday, but that she take some vacation time. She was going to go into a follow-up program, but enough seemed enough. Finally, she ended by hinting that if Angelica spoke with her doctor, health insurance might cover the expense.

The entire time that Mary Helen was speaking, Angelica Bowers stood motionless and, what was even more disconcerting, expressionless.

Sister Mary Helen's voice sounded exceptionally loud, even to herself, as her words bounced off the walls of the deserted classroom. She studied Angelica's lumpy face. It never moved into a smile or a frown. Nor did she utter one word, although her thin lips parted once. Mary Helen stopped abruptly, hoping the woman would say something. She didn't.

Sister Mary Helen didn't have a clue to Angelica's reaction. "What do you think?" she asked in desperation.

Angelica studied her face for a long, cold moment, then lowered her eyes and shrugged.

Sister Mary Helen shoved the newspaper copy toward Angelica, who gripped it in one dimpled hand. A ray of light caught the silver in her ring. Mary Helen tried not to notice how the band dug into the thick flesh of the finger, almost covering the turquoise stone.

"Maybe you'd want to take this ad home, read it, and think about it on your own time?" Mary Helen's words curled into a question. "Then let me know if there's anything at all I can do to help. You know, Angelica, you're still young. And you have a very beautiful face," she added weakly. From sheer frustration, Mary Helen heard herself repeating the advantages of the fitness program, as if Angelica couldn't read. She stopped herself just short of getting preachy.

Mary Helen watched Angelica's eyes focus on the paper. She studied it silently, with great care. Outside the classroom, the noise of assembling students grew even louder. Mary

Helen checked her wristwatch. She didn't want to make Angelica late. Worse yet, she didn't want anyone to walk in on them. Angelica seemed uncomfortable enough.

A tight, disagreeable grin played on the corners of Angelica's thin lips. Was she pleased with something, or was she annoyed? Mary Helen wondered. From her expression, it was difficult to tell.

Without warning, Angelica Bowers looked Mary Helen full in the face. Her pale blue rabbit eyes sparked with a strange fire that made Mary Helen uneasy.

"Thank you, Sister," she said. "I will take this home and think about it. A lot," she added with that same odd smile.

Mary Helen patted her hand. "Good," she said sincerely.

Still standing by the windows, Mary Helen watched Angelica maneuver slowly around the desks and out the classroom door. She knew she should feel delighted. She had accomplished what she'd set out to do: make Miss Bowers think about improving her life. Once the woman really studied the advertisement, Mary Helen was certain she would decide to go to Utah, which, as Eileen contended, might jump-start her into a real change. Mary Helen should feel satisfied. Why, then, was she filled instead with such apprehension?

Sister Mary Helen would have worried about it more, except that as soon as she stepped inside her own office, one of the harried alums approached her with an ingratiating smile. "Sister, will you—" she began, words dripping with syrup.

43

Mary Helen knew that it was time for her contribution. She was tempted to finish the sentence with "round up the usual suspects?" Except in this case, "usual victims" was probably more accurate.

She refrained, however, since alumnae committee members, a mere month away from an extravaganza, notoriously had little-to-no sense of humor.

Running her finger down the list of "big donors," Mary Helen decided to begin with Gemma Burke. Not only was Gemma extremely generous, she was always interesting.

Mary Helen listened to the relentless ring of the Burkes' bell. "Eleven, twelve, thirteen," she counted. Gemma must have gone out and forgotten to turn on her answering machine, she thought, replacing the receiver. And I hope to heaven that she doesn't catch her death in all this rain.

Tillie Greenwood hugged her faded pink chenille bathrobe tight around her middle and cracked open the front door. Without looking to see whether the neighbors were out on their porches, she reached for her morning *Chronicle*.

Fortunately, the new paperboy had a good throwing arm. The bundle landed close enough to the door that only her right arm and a bit of her shoulder got wet.

She was just settling down in her breakfast nook next to the heater outlet with a cup of coffee when she heard a noise on her basement steps.

Grasping her robe in a stranglehold at her

neck, she tiptoed across the kitchen floor to the basement door and listened. The steps creaked. Could it be Elvis? Only her son had a key to the downstairs room. Surely, Elvis would have rung the front doorbell. Unless he'd come in very late last night. She listened again.

"Elvis," she whispered, her voice all breathy. "Is that you, sweetheart?"

"Yes, Mommy," a rasping voice answered.

Mrs. Greenwood felt a surge of love. "Mommy!" She just loved it when her grown son called her "Mommy."

Smiling, she threw open the basement door and her arms. "Elvis," she cried, hugging him around his chest. Actually, that was as far up as Tillie Greenwood could reach these days. Her son had grown into what her own mother always called "a tall drink of water."

"What are you doing here?" A quick glance at his thin, pale face and the raccoon circles around his eyes told her something was wrong.

She smiled stiffly, trying not to let her face show her concern. Elvis hated it when she clucked over him. "Like a regular hen," her mother used to say.

"Help yourself to a cup of coffee," Tillie said, giving her son a final squeeze. "Let me fix you a good breakfast. You look like a man who could use some bacon and eggs to warm you up."

Tillie's hand went up to her coppery hair, still wound tight in pink sausage curlers. She must be a sight. She opened the refrigerator door. "Why don't you uncover Mr. Cheeps and change his water while I fix things up?" she suggested cheerfully.

45

Tillie knew how much Elvis liked the little canary. Even in her son's darkest moods, Mr. Cheeps's trills always cheered him up.

"Then tell me, sweetheart, what brings you here so early in the morning? Or did you get in last night after I'd gone to sleep?"

Elvis's velvety brown eyes shifted from his mother's face to the *Chronicle* still snug in its plastic rain wrapper. He sank into a chair.

"Move closer to the heater, sweetheart," Tillie called from the kitchen, which was quickly filling with the delicious aroma of frying bacon. "It's so wet and cold out. You must have been frozen solid in that basement room. Did you spend the night down there?"

"Then you haven't heard," Elvis said hoarsely.

Tillie peered over her glasses at her son slouched on the wooden chair. She wished he'd sit up straight. Slouching like that could give a growing boy scoliosis, she'd read in the Sunday *Parade*. Of course, at twenty-eight, he'd probably done all the growing he was going to do.

"Mommy, answer me. Have you heard?" Elvis' voice rose as he balled his fists.

"Heard what, sweetheart?" She poured the excess bacon grease from the pan. "Do you want one egg or two?"

At first, Tillie Greenwood had thought that she must be dreaming. What Elvis was telling her couldn't be real! Her ears were playing tricks. Just like her eyes, which filled and made everything in the room swim.

Smelling the skillet burning, Tillie pulled it off the stove and sank into an empty chair.

Despite the heat, she shivered. What was he saying about another woman in Sea Cliff being raped and murdered?

Elvis buried his face in his arms. Tillie heard his muffled sobbing. Reaching over, she caressed his hair—that coarse, curly black hair. So pretty. He'd been such a pretty baby.

"What is it you said you're afraid of, sweetheart?" Tillie asked, positive that she had misunderstood.

Elvis looked up, his face wet. "That the police will think I'm the rapist, Mommy." He choked and grabbed her outstretched hand. "And I'm not!"

"Of course you're not, sweetheart," Tillie said when she recovered her breath. "Do you mean the one who's been on the news?" She felt his muscles tense as she ran her fingers gently up and down his tattooed arm.

Elvis nodded.

"Why in the world would anyone think that?" she asked in a whisper.

"You know why." His words were muffled.

Tillie felt a surge of anger. Was that old charge back again to haunt them? Elvis had been a high-spirited youngster, barely out of high school when that old woman had accused him of...of...She couldn't even think about it without feeling a little sick.

There had been no real proof that the woman hadn't egged him on, at least none that Tillie believed. After all, the hussy had been old enough to be Elvis's mother. Tillie knew that her son would never have done such a thing on his own. When things like that happen, it's the woman's fault. She asks for it. That was what Tillie had been taught, and that was what she still believed.

Unfortunately, the jury had thought differently. Just because the woman had a lot of money, her Elvis had been sent to jail. Thank God, her own mother hadn't lived to see it!

But Elvis proved to be a model prisoner, just as Tillie knew he would. He'd learned his lesson, too. He'd never let another woman put him in that position. He'd told her so, and she believed him.

"Do you believe me, Mommy?" Elvis's beautiful velvet eyes were filling again.

"Shsh." Tillie leaned over and kissed him on his nose. "Of course I believe you, sweetheart," she whispered, just as she had hundreds of times when he was a child and she'd come home from work to find that her own mother had punished him for something he hadn't done.

Poor Mother, Tillie thought, staring at the raindrops racing one another down the breakfast-room windowpane. She'd warned Tillie that she was too young to marry and that Elvis's father was a ne'er-do-well, but Tillie hadn't listened. Mother had been good to take them in when Elvis's father disappeared without so much as a note! Even after all these years, Tillie ached with the hurt.

She'd been forced to go to work as a waitress. It was the only job she could find—actually, the only one she knew how to do. What would they have done if Mother hadn't offered? Who would have cared for her baby?

Mother wanted what was best for Elvis. Tillie knew that. It was just that Mother was a little old-fashioned in her demands. Tillie's heart

48

would break to see her son's small bottom red from a spanking. When Mother wasn't looking, Tillie would slip him a peppermint and kiss his nose and rock him and tell him over and over that he was a good boy and that he mustn't be mad at Mother.

"I have an alibi, Mommy." Elvis's voice snapped her back into the present.

"An alibi!" Thank God, Tillie thought, but the expression on Elvis's face was not reassuring. "Isn't that good?" she asked tentatively.

"Yeah, but you're going to be mad at me."

"I'm not going to be mad, sweetheart. Why would I be mad because you have an alibi?"

Elvis snatched his hand away and studied his fingernails. Which, Tillie noticed, were dirty. After all the fuss her mother had made about clean fingernails.

"Because I was spending the night with a woman."

Tillie felt her face flush. She hoped that Elvis didn't notice. After all, he was a boy with a boy's normal desires. Why should she feel embarrassed? She should feel flattered that her son confided in her.

"That seems like a perfectly wonderful alibi to me," Tillie said cheerily.

"Except that she's a married woman and her husband doesn't know about us. I have to talk her into telling the police."

Tillie's stomach pitched. A married woman! A married woman should have better sense than to seduce a boy. Poor Elvis! What could she do to help? Her mind whirled. "Would you like me to call her? Talk to her? Explain?"

The storm in Elvis's eyes cut her off.

"Then what, sweetheart? What can Mommy do?"

"Just don't tell the police I'm here if those effing pigs come by, and I know they will."

Tillie flinched. She hated it when her son used that kind of language. Her own mother would have washed out his mouth with soap.

Elvis must have sensed her discomfort. He stopped and grabbed both her hands. "I'm sorry, Mommy. It's just that I'm so upset. I love this woman, and I don't want to make things hard for her. I don't know what to do, where to go."

"Go nowhere at all, sweetheart," she said softly, looking at him over her glasses. Wasn't that just like her Elvis? Always so sensitive to others. "You stay right here until you can talk your lady friend into going to the police. Mommy will not say a word—not one single word—to anybody until you do."

"Sister, did you leave a message on Gemma Burke's answering machine?" Shirley asked, checking off names on a large donor list.

"She didn't have it on," Mary Helen answered without looking up. Rifling through the mounds of papers scattered across her desk, she wished that she were one of those people whose desks are piled high, yet who can locate what they want in an instant. Not that she'd actually ever met one, but the tales of their extraordinary talent were legend.

"What do you suppose I did with Gladys Soda's phone number?" she asked.

Reaching over, her secretary pulled a small pink piece of paper from one of the stacks.

Mary Helen sighed and closed her eyes. "Right where I left it," she said.

She had been at this "calling benefactors" business for over an hour. As much as she enjoyed talking with them all, her mouth, her mind and her muscles needed a break. In fact, she'd just hung up from Eileen in the library, and the two of them were meeting in the Sisters' dining room in ten minutes for a cup of coffee. Mary Helen secretly hoped that a few of Ramon's homemade scones would be left from breakfast. There was something about asking people for money that left her starving.

"That's odd," Shirley remarked.

"What's odd?" Mary Helen asked without even opening her eyes.

"That Gemma's machine wasn't on. She's always in so much demand, and she's so efficient. It doesn't seem like something that she'd forget to do."

"Maybe she gets tired of answering calls," Mary Helen said, knowing full well that she herself did. To her way of thinking, the telephone had become a tyrant of sorts leaving you at the mercy of whomever or whatever ferreted out your phone number.

"Maybe she was in the shower or something," Shirley remarked, obviously unable to accept the fact that Gemma might not turn on her machine.

"Maybe," Mary Helen conceded. Putting Gladys Soda's number next to the phone, she stood up and reached for her Aran sweater.

"Are you leaving?" Shirley asked anxiously.

"Just for a twenty-minute coffee break. Why

51

don't you take one, too? It does wonders for both body and soul."

"And leave them?" Shirley whispered gesturing toward the conference room where intense, but muffled, voices of alums rose and fell, but never stopped.

Mary Helen frowned. "What's going on?"

"Intercepting monologues for the most part."

"Any success?"

"The committee decided on a color scheme. Red and green. Which I know you're going to say seems obvious for Christmas, but nothing is simple. Anyway, I want to have your part done by the time we get to it on the agenda."

Mary Helen sat back down and picked up the receiver, which was still warm. "Do you want me to call Gemma before I go?"

Shirley scribbled down the number and pushed it toward Mary Helen. With a satisfied smile, she watched the old nun punch the buttons.

"Hello," a man answered on the first ring. "Who's calling?"

Mary Helen was taken aback. The gruff voice was familiar, although she couldn't quite place it.

"Have I reached Gemma Burke's home?" she asked.

"Who is this calling, ma'am?" the voice demanded.

"Who is this answering, sir?" Two could play at this game.

"Don't get cute, lady! This is Inspector Dennis Gallagher, San Francisco Police Department," he growled. "Now, who the hell is this?"

"My, my, Inspector Gallagher! This is a nice surprise! I thought I recognized the voice, but I couldn't place it. And no wonder. You are the last person in the world I expected to hear. I never meant to call you." How had she managed to dial Homicide? Had Shirley written down the wrong phone number? That wasn't like Shirley at all. She really did need that coffee break!

"I was trying to contact Gemma Burke," Mary Helen explained. Then added, just in case he hadn't recognized her voice, "This is Sister Mary Helen."

There was an uncomfortably long silence on the line. She must have caught the inspector at a very bad moment.

"I'm sorry if I've disturbed you," she said. "Wrong numbers are a nuisance."

"Sister Mary Helen?" Gallagher asked incredulously. "*The* Sister Mary Helen from Mount St. Francis College?"

"Yes, Inspector." What in heaven's name was wrong with him? It wasn't as if she was interfering with one of his cases or anything. It was simply a wrong number. "I was calling Gemma Burke and somehow rang you by mistake, so I'll just hang up now and let us both get back to work," she said pleasantly.

"Hold on a minute, Sister." Gallagher cleared his throat. "Is anybody with you?"

"Yes, Inspector. Shirley, my secretary, is here. Why do you ask?"

"I'm afraid I have some bad news. Was this Gemma Burke a good friend of yours?"

"Why, yes. I've known her for years. She's a

good friend to me and wonderfully generous to the college. Why do you ask?" Mary Helen repeated, her stomach suddenly hollow.

The room felt airless. As Gallagher spoke, Mary Helen's mind refused to believe what her ears were hearing.

"What is it, Sister?" Shirley asked when Mary Helen replaced the receiver. "Your face is as white as your notepad. Are you all right?"

Mary Helen shook her head.

"What is it? Is it Gemma?"

"Yes," she said flatly. "Last night Gemma Burke was raped and murdered." She heard Shirley gasp.

It had begun to rain again and the wind tossed a fresh volley of drops against the dining room windows. Mary Helen, staring straight ahead, watched the glass panes blur.

Her mind moved in and out of focus like a broken lens. This kind of thing didn't happen to women like Gemma Burke. Yet it had. Gemma was the sort of woman one meets at luncheons and theater matinees, or talks to in the grocery line, or sits next to in church. Gemma was sensible and capable. In fact, all the victims of the man the media was calling "The Sea Cliff Rapist" were sensible, capable women who locked their front doors at night and didn't take unnecessary chances. Like Gemma, they, too, had been "raped and murdered." Even as Mary Helen repeated the two words so fraught with evil, she felt the heat of her own shock and disbelief slowly curdling into rage.

Across from her at the table, Sister Eileen's gray eyes shimmered with tears. She refilled their coffee cups for the fifth time. Ramon's breakfast scones sat on the plate untouched. "I feel so sad and so helpless," Eileen said.

How must Gemma have felt? Mary Helen wondered, her psyche still unwilling to fully comprehend the terror of waking to find an intruder hovering over your bed. Had Gemma asked, in that "perfect hostess" tone of hers, "What is it that you want?"

And when she realized the stranger's intent, had she tried to reason with him, to cajole him? Or had she recoiled in horror?

"To think the blackguard got away!" Eileen shivered and fished in her pocket for a tissue.

"He'll do it again, you know," Mary Helen said, dangerously calm. "Unless we stop him."

"I expect that the entire San Francisco Police Department is trying to stop him." Mary Helen heard a hint of a brogue creeping into her friend's speech, a further sign of Eileen's distress. "What can we possibly do that they aren't doing already?"

"I'll come up with something," Mary Helen said ominously and watched Eileen stiffen. "But first, I think I'll call Kate Murphy." She scraped back her chair. She must do something—anything—to release some of her mounting fury. If Inspector Gallagher was involved in this investigation, surely his partner Kate Murphy was, too. As much as Kate protested, Mary Helen knew that the young officer valued her help, especially when their joint efforts were successful, as they had been on several occasions. Gallagher, on the other hand, was a very different kettle of fish. Mary Helen would be wise to contact Kate before he did.

"Maybe I can make some telephone calls for her or track down some leads," Mary Helen muttered, knowing full well that even Kate would never allow that officially.

"You're sounding a little too much like one of those murder mysteries you read," Eileen remarked gently. "Not that you shouldn't call her. In fact, it might be helpful for Kate to know that she has our prayers, at least, behind her. Use the phone in my office. It's closer."

Gathering up their soiled cups, Mary Helen started toward the dishwasher with Eileen close on her heels. "I'm sure there's something I can do," Mary Helen muttered more to herself than to anyone.

"Something *we* can do," Eileen corrected.

Stopping, Mary Helen studied her friend's face. Eileen's large eyes reflected her own sense of outrage. Her lips were thin and set. "I thought that you were the one who was suggesting that we pray," Mary Helen needled affectionately.

"Of course we will pray! We always pray. I am not denying the power of prayer." Eileen lifted her short nose and sniffed. "But prayer without good works is dead."

"Isn't that 'faith'?" Mary Helen couldn't resist.

"Whichever! Faith. Prayer. Same church, different pew! Besides, we've an old saying back home..."

Mary Helen braced herself. "About helping the police catch rapist-murderers?" she asked, hoping she didn't sound facetious.

If she did, Eileen seemed not to notice. "Your feet will bring you where your heart is," she said, shooting Mary Helen a knowing glance.

"And our hearts are surely into bringing dear Gemma's killer to justice."

Following Eileen down the crowded hallway, Mary Helen remembered once again why she cherished her old friend. They would do something! That was a fact, although at the moment, she hadn't a clue what two old nuns could possibly do to help Kate Murphy catch a brutal and heinous killer. It just seemed the right thing for them to try.

Gripping the hospital bed railing until her hands ached, Kate Murphy stared down at her husband, willing him to move, to open his eyes, to speak.

Jack had not been conscious all morning, except for the few brief moments in the recovery room. If anything, he looked worse than he had an hour ago. Had he slipped into a coma without anybody telling her?

Kate's stomach knotted as she tried to control the panic that was invading her throat. She'd ask the nurse when her ten minutes in the intensive care unit were up.

She didn't dare look across the high bed at her mother-in-law for fear that her eyes would reveal her anxiety. Except for the occasional tear that slipped down her pudgy cheeks, Loretta Bassetti was holding up extraordinarily well.

Kate had expected hysteria. Somehow, this bloodless calm was worse. Loretta ran her fingers through her son's thick, curly hair. "Jackie," she whispered time and again. *"Carino,"* she cooed softly in Italian, but Jack did not respond.

"Maybe if you brought in the baby," Mama

Bassetti whispered. "Maybe if he hears his baby's voice."

Kate bit back her anger. Even if such a thing were allowed, she would not bring little John in here. She would not allow him to see his father like this! All hooked up to tubes and machines and looking as white and waxy as death.

"I don't think that's a good idea," Kate said coldly, then regretted the hurt in her mother-in-law's eyes.

Once outside the unit, the two women sat in the waiting room on padded blue vinyl chairs made uncomfortable by the thousands of restless fannies which had sat for hours, anxious to see a loved one. Kate wriggled to avoid a spring.

Staring out the window at the bruised sky, Loretta fingered her rosary beads. Kate twisted and untwisted a lock of her red hair until the spot in her scalp was sore. The two had been together for over six hours. For much of the morning, detectives asking questions, visiting police officers, nurses and doctors on rounds provided a distraction. During those long, silent moments when they were alone, each woman tried to mask her own dread with brave words.

"Next time we go in, he'll be awake," Loretta said again.

Kate nodded and surreptitiously searched for a free duty nurse. She must know. Was Jack as bad as she thought he was? And, if so, how could she keep the news from Loretta?

"I think I'll go outside for a cigarette," Kate said.

"You gave up smoking years ago," Loretta remarked blandly.

"I know I did, but I think I'll take it up again." Kate rose from the couch. "This waiting is driving me crazy."

"So go smoke! Good! Then I'll have two of you sick. It's better you should be crazy. Sit down!"

"I can't sit," Kate protested, sounding too much like a spoiled child. "I've got to do something, get some fresh air!"

Loretta closed her eyes. Her lips moved, finishing a "Hail Mary" silently. "So do something," she said finally. "Get some fresh air, but don't think for one minute that you are fooling me."

"What does that mean?" Kate felt a surge of temper.

"That means, go talk to the nurse. Find out if Jackie is better or worse, but don't give me that baloney about going out for a cigarette or even for fresh air."

Kate almost gave herself away with a grin. "What makes you think it's baloney?" she asked.

"I'm a mother," Loretta's brown eyes sparked. "It's our job to know baloney when we hear it. Especially when our kids are trying to feed it to us. With all the practice my kids gave me, I'm an expert on baloney!"

Kate shifted uneasily wondering whether or not to keep up the pretense of getting some fresh air or just to give in and save as much face as possible. She was relieved to see Sister Mary Helen and Sister Eileen step off the elevator before she had to decide. Relieved, but not surprised!

Dennis Gallagher had dropped by several hours earlier to warn her. Loretta was in the cafeteria getting them both a cup of coffee, and he had caught Kate alone in the waiting room.

"Avoid 'Double Trouble,'" Gallagher had boomed. Kate had no problem figuring out whom he meant.

"What are the odds?" he had stormed. "In a city of 800,000 people and a metropolis of over six million, what are the odds, I ask you, of that nun calling the scene of a homicide almost before the body is cold?"

Kate had shrugged.

"Slim to none!" Gallagher answered his own question. "That is what they are! Slim to none! With that kind of luck, she should be a gambler, not a nun!"

A duty nurse stared at them through a small glass window and raised her eyebrows.

"Maybe she's both," Kate had whispered, hoping that Gallagher would notice and lower his voice.

"Yeah, right! Well, I don't need to be a gambler to know that she'll call you at work next, and whoever answers the phone will tell her you're here. So keep your eye on that elevator door." He yanked at his tie as if it were a noose. We don't have enough problems already? With some wacko raping respectable and well-connected old ladies, then bumping them off in their beds. No, now we have to have two more wackos."

Kate tugged on Gallagher's arm. "They are not wackos,"she whispered, "and keep your voice down before we're thrown out of here. They are two extremely savvy older women who have been very helpful to us. Even you have to admit that."

Gallagher ran his palm over his shiny pate. "How the hell do we know that on any one of those cases we wouldn't have done just as well without them—maybe better?" he grumbled. "God knows, they never gave us the chance to find out."

This time the duty nurse stuck her head out the door. She was frowning and had her finger to her lips like a fifth-grade class monitor.

"So, what's your point?" Kate asked quietly.

"My point, in case you may have missed it, is that when the two nuns stop by—and, mark my words, they will—have nothing to do with them. Period! Thank them—not too warmly, mind you, in case they misunderstand—for their interest in the case.

"Although God knows why they can't get interested in something else. They've got a thriving college, hundreds of students, acres of grounds, dozens of other nuns, and every Catholic cause in the greater Bay Area to get interested in and they pick us!" He stopped for breath.

"And after you thank them, you tell them"— Gallagher jabbed the air with his finger—"as firmly as possible to stay the hell out of our way."

"Don't I have enough trouble already? Now you want me to insult nuns?" Kate asked wearily.

"Not insult them, Kate," Gallagher undid the top button of his shirt. "God, it's clammy in this place. Just make it very damned clear that they are not to get involved. I repeat, *not!*"

"And you know how much weight that will carry if they've made up their minds to help

61

us." The rain was still falling and Kate listened to it tap-dance against the window. She wished the sun would come out. Things always seemed better in the sunshine.

"Well, you damn well better make it have some weight, Katie-girl," Gallagher had suddenly lowered his voice. "As far as I can tell, this Sea Cliff rapist guy is a sleezebag who gets his kicks from terrorizing respectable old gals. If these two get in his way, what's to say he won't consider attacking two old nuns his pièce de résistance?"

Kate stared at him in amazement.

His face flushed. "Mrs. G.'s taking a French class on Wednesday nights, but you get my meaning, nonetheless."

Kate did get his meaning and it sent a cold shiver up her spine. Therefore she was prepared when she spotted the Sisters stepping off the elevator.

"Hello, Kate. Hello, Loretta." Mary Helen greeted the two pale, exhausted-looking women with a warm hug. Sister Eileen was quick to follow and to add noisy kisses.

"How is Jack doing?" Mary Helen asked, settling herself on a lumpy chair.

Kate seemed distracted. "I was about to ask the nurse," she said.

"Why don't you go ahead?" Mary Helen encouraged her, although she knew that the nurse would leave any real answering to the doctor.

Within seconds, Kate was back.

Loretta Bassetti studied her daughter-in-law anxiously. "What did the nurse say?"

"Only that he seems to be holding his own, whatever that means."

Mary Helen squeezed Kate's hand. It was cold. "And how are you doing?" she asked.

"Fine," Kate answered too quickly. "I don't know what I'll do if anything happens to him," she whispered, her blue eyes brimming with tears.

The rest of the color faded from Loretta Bassetti's face leaving only two red spots high on her cheekbones. "What did the nurse *really* say, Kate?" she asked hoarsely.

"Just what I told you." Kate's cheeks were blazing, too. "That Jack is holding his own."

The two women stared at one another like two gunfighters, Mary Helen thought, neither wanting to blink.

"Have either of you had anything solid to eat?" Eileen asked. "Let me go to the cafeteria and get you a sandwich or some thick soup," she offered brightly. "I think they have a delicious potato-leek here. Everything seems worse when you're hungry."

Loretta Bassetti, who held the same opinion, offered to accompany Sister Eileen, and the two left with orders.

Mary Helen was glad. She needed a few minutes alone with Kate Murphy.

"I'm sorry about your friend," Kate began before Mary Helen could say a word. Obviously, the old nun thought, Inspector Gallagher had beat her here.

"Thank you." That hollow feeling around Mary Helen's heart returned. "I can't believe Gemma is actually gone. And I can't believe that the same scoundrel wounded Jack." She paused until she was sure she could speak without her voice cracking. "He'll do it again unless we stop him."

Kate nodded miserably. Then her eyes steadied on Mary Helen. "Denny absolutely wants you and Sister Eileen to stay out of this case. He is adamant about it."

Mary Helen fought down the feeling of hurt. "Of course," she said quietly, "but I do think that we have proven helpful, on occasion."

"That is not his point, Sister."

Mary Helen sat up stiffly. "What is then?"

Kate studied her thumbnails. "His point is"— her voice sounded as if it slid off the edge of a knife—"that this low-life is without compunction, without compassion and possibly without a conscience. He is driven. He is unimaginably evil."

Mary Helen's mouth went dry.

"Obviously, he thinks nothing of raping and murdering helpless old women, of shooting police officers, and he might even consider it a feather in his cap to hurt Sister Eileen and you!"

"I see," Mary Helen said. For the moment, she did.

Although the television in Mama's bedroom was still on, Angelica knew from the ragged snoring rising above the noisy canned laughter that Mama was asleep. The dogs must be napping, too, at the foot of the bed.

Like a captive whose guards have dozed off, Angelica tiptoed down the darkened hallway into the kitchen. She didn't turn on the light. The click of the switch might awaken one of them. Enough of an eerie yellow glow filtered in from the streetlights for her to make her way around.

Silently, she slid the bakery bag from the pantry and set it on the kitchen table. Careful not to let the door squeak, she opened the refrigerator and removed the milk. Then she poured herself a large, cold glass and set the carton on the table beside the bakery bag.

Finally, she eased herself onto a wooden kitchen chair. The rim of its seat cut into her thighs. Angelica wished she could sink into the big overstuffed couch in the living room, but she was afraid. In the dark, she might knock into something and wake Mama or one of the poodles. Better to stay put and enjoy, she thought, pulling one of the last two chocolate éclairs from the bag.

The yellow streetlight gave her hand and her milk and even her éclair a jaundiced look. She closed her eyes and bit into the thin shell.

Rich white whipped cream filled her mouth and she felt a dab of it ooze out onto her chin. Velvety chocolate clung to her front teeth. Its sweetness made them sting. Angelica took a long drink of icy milk. With one thick finger, she lifted the cream from her chin. Then, opening her eyes, she licked her yellow finger clean.

Overhead, bedsprings creaked. Angelica sat as frozen as a lizard on a garden fence. Dampness gathered behind her knees and she felt a drop of sweat slide down her back.

One more creak, then silence. Mama or one of the dogs must have turned. Straining, she heard her mother's steady wheeze. She was still safe.

Licking the last traces of cream and chocolate from the fluted paper boats that had held the eclairs, Angelica crumpled the bag carefully. She wondered where to hide it. Mama would never come downstairs. She scarcely was able to get to the upstairs bathroom by herself. Sometimes she didn't make it all the way there, Angelica thought with disgust, suspecting, as she often did, that Mama did it on purpose.

Mama would never find the bag in the trash can under the sink. But what about the dogs? They might rummage through.

She shoved the bag deep into the bowels of the garbage can outside the back door. Like a guilty child, she thought, and rage filled her like boiling water until her face burned.

Angelica crept into the living room. Easing herself down onto the soft couch, she stared out at the rain-soaked street. Deserted. Yet somewhere out there was a rapist. She'd overheard the nuns talking about him when they called the police today.

They hadn't noticed her sitting in the shadows not far from the phone, which wasn't unusual. Most people seemed not to notice her sitting there.

Not that she minded. In the shadows, she overheard lots of secrets and knew loads of private things that no one thought she knew.

Angelica smiled to herself. Wouldn't prim, proper, patronizing Mrs. Kenny die if she knew that Angelica had overheard her talking baby talk and setting up meetings with someone who clearly was not Mr. Kenny?

Angelica stifled a laugh. Mrs. Kenny sounded like an idiot talking baby talk. She wished she could share the joke with someone, but she had no one.

Maybe that was better. When she did talk to people, they either averted their eyes in embarrassment or gave her that pathetic, pitying, cow-eyed look that made her want to slap them.

Like that nun today! The old busybody in her fancy Irish sweater thought that she'd fooled Angelica with her talk of diet centers and getting a fresh start and improving her life.

The only thing that would improve Angelica's life was to have no Mama, no poodles; to have a house all to herself where she could turn on every light in the place if she wanted to and eat and eat and eat until she felt satisfied.

That same old nun was so distressed that a rapist killed her friend. Why, she wondered, staring out at the deserted street, didn't the rapist come in here and—

"What are you doing down there in the dark?"

Angelica jumped. Mama! Had she heard Angelica's thoughts?

"I asked you—what you are doing?" Mama demanded peevishly.

Clearing her throat, hoping the whipped cream didn't make her sound thick, Angelica called, "Do you need something, Mama?"

"Only a little company," Mama whined.

Laboring up the steps, Angelica felt the familiar tightness in her chest. Her damp palms clutched the banister.

"There you are," Mama turned her small dark eyes on Angelica.

"I thought you were asleep." Angelica wiped the perspiration from her upper lip.

"What were you doing while you thought I

was sleeping? Eating chocolate éclairs?" Mama's voice was teasing, almost mocking.

Angelica whirled around, looking for the dogs. They were still at the foot of the bed. They couldn't have told.

"Or were you down there daydreaming about a vacation?"

Angelica blinked. Where had that come from?

Mama's bony fist slammed down on the white top sheet. "That no-good brother of mine has been filling your head again, hasn't he?" Mama demanded.

Uncle Frank's Monday-night call! That was what Mama was talking about. Angelica let out her breath and dulled her mind to endure Mama's usual tirade.

"How many times must I explain to you?" Mama began, her voice soft. "Here, my angel, sit down," she said, motioning Angelica to a bedside chair.

Angelica watched Mama's small eyes. The voice was soft, but those eyes remained brittle.

"Sit down," Mama repeated. "Listen to Mama."

Angelica sat obediently. The chair creaked and her hips hung over the seat.

Mama coughed, the spasm racking her whole body. Her *TV Guide* slipped off the bed onto the floor. "I'd love my little angel to go on a vacation," she began in a saccharine voice. "Nothing would give me more happiness. But, Angelica, you know yourself, you've never been the same since the accident."

Angelica felt Mama's dry, bony hand brush her cheek and the tightness moved up from her chest and across her forehead. A steady stream of perspiration ran down the crevice between her breasts.

"Your pretty angel face," Mama cooed.

Angelica's face burned with rage.

"Don't blush. It's true," Mama said.

If you only knew what was true, Angelica seethed. If you only knew that every time you say "pretty angel face," I want to reach into that tight little mouth of yours and pull out your thin, sharp gray tongue!

"How could you travel alone?" Mama was still talking. "You'd be too frightened. God knows, every time anyone looks at you cross-eyed..."

Angelica didn't listen to the end of the sentence. She didn't need to. She knew it well. "God knows, every time anyone looks at you cross-eyed, you bawl like a baby."

Mama began using that sentence when Angelica was a small child. She used it every time she had shaken Angelica or cuffed her for being sassy or spanked her with a wooden coat hanger; every time she locked Angelica sobbing in her bedroom closet with the promise of no dessert. Mama had used that sentence frequently to explain Angelica's red-rimmed eyes to Papa at the supper table.

Papa never said a word. Angelica was glad. Sometimes, though, he'd look at her and wink. Feeling sick, Angelica would wait, hoping, praying that Mama hadn't noticed. If she did, Angelica knew that Mama would make up some reason to punish her. "Your Papa's spoiled angel face," Mama would jeer, yanking her from her chair and sending the weeping child to her room with a resounding slap.

"I'd go with you if I could." Mama coughed. "But how can I?" She patted Angelica's hand. "No, my angel." Her voice was strong now. "You'd best get rid of those high-and-mighty ideas." Mama's thin lips cracked into a smile.

"I wouldn't be frightened," Angelica said.

Mama's eyes narrowed. "You've never been strong after the accident. I've told you that!"

Loathing filled Angelica's whole body like wet, hot lava oozing moist and sticky from her pores. Why didn't she have the courage to pick up one of the soft down pillows under Mama's head and hold it over her face until those narrow, cruel lips became rigid and silent forever.

How would she explain it? What would she tell Uncle Frank and the police? The thought of being locked forever in a small, cold room with no dessert was more than Angelica could stand. As much as she hated Mama, she hated the thought of jail more. Why hadn't that rapist broken in here?

Angelica rose abruptly, toppling over the bedside chair with a thud. Both dogs started. Salt growled her protest while Pepper only bared her teeth.

"Where are you going in such a hurry?" Mama demanded.

"Downstairs." Without righting the chair, Angelica moved out of the bedroom and into the hall. Grabbing the banister, she began to descend the steps one at a time.

"Why don't you stay here and keep me company?" Mama called pathetically from her bed. "Why do you have to go downstairs?"

"Because I feel like it!" The words shot out.

Angelica's hand flew up to her mouth as though she could grab the words, pull them back. But it was too late. Electric silence filled the air. Her anger drained; a wave of fear replaced it. Her temples throbbed.

"Come here!" Mama strained the words through her teeth.

Angelica hesitated, clutching the banister to still her trembling. She heard the heavy sound of the dogs jumping down from the bed. They flanked her quickly, waiting for her to move, taunting her with their dark oval eyes.

"Do you hear me?" Mama's voice was still strained.

Angelica followed the poodles fearfully, as, tails held high, they led her back like a prisoner to the dock. Drops of perspiration broke out on her forehead. Blotting it with a crinkled tissue, Angelica moved to the end of the bed. She gripped the bedpost and stared down at her mother.

Sitting regally now, on either side of Mama's bed, Salt and Pepper stared at Angelica, black noses held high, and waited.

Shrouded in a white top sheet Mama lay very still, her hand clutching the handle of her thick cane.

"You watch your tone of voice, young lady," Mama spat out, "and pick up that chair and my *TV Guide*." She pointed with her cane.

Angelica moved forward obediently, and bent to pick it up. The sharp blow of the cane cut across her thighs.

"Don't you ever forget who supports you! I'm all you have! Without me, you'd be out on the street, without a roof over your head." Mama hit her again.

Angelica felt the poodles staring at her with contempt as more blows fell across her back and thighs and buttocks. Tears stung her eyes.

"What would you do if anything happened to me?" Mama screeched, still clutching her cane. "Think of that!"

Angelica turned numbly toward her mother and studied the cane, longing to snatch it up and press the thick stick against her mother's neck until all the life left those piercing eyes. Angelica felt the wetness under her arms and around her waist. It rolled down her, soothing her stinging body.

"Now go downstairs!" Mama snapped. "Who wants an ungrateful spoiled daughter?" She patted the head of each dog in turn. "We don't need her, do we, my babies?" Mama crooned. Salt yipped in agreement as Angelica left the bedroom.

Although her eyes burned and her head felt thick, Angelica could not fall asleep. Careful to make as little noise as possible, she pulled herself up, lumbered out of bed, and tiptoed into the bathroom.

Opening the medicine chest she fingered her way past Mama's pain pills, vitamins, sleeping pills, and hormones until she uncovered the aspirin. She shook a couple into the palm of her hand and ran a half-glass of water.

Catching her reflection in the mirror, she was surprised, as always, to see those pigeon gray wings sprouting from her temples. She moved closer and examined her face.

Even with the puffy cheeks and the wattles under her chin, she did have a pretty face: an angel face framed now with angel wings. "But I'm more than just a pretty face," Angelica said to her reflection, the way she'd heard the pretty girls say on Mama's soap operas, and she even sounded silly to herself.

When she climbed back into bed, a single car passed on the street outside. The beams from its headlights prowled across her ceiling, forming eerie shapes like dancing ghosts. She shuddered and closed her eyes. Still she could not sleep. She turned restlessly, her legs tangling in the sheets.

Finally Angelica switched on the bed lamp. She needed something to read. Reading always made her sleepy. Frustrated that she'd finished her romance novel and forgotten to check out another one from the library, she searched her room for something, anything to read. In desperation, she reached for the copy of the newspaper advertisement that the nun had given her this morning.

She examined the girl in the ad thoughtfully. She looked even trimmer and happier than she had before. Now she looked as if she knew a secret—a secret that Angelica was not privy to.

Angelica wondered idly what a girl like that was thinking about while she gazed at those rugged mountains. She was certainly not thinking about her mother catching her eating chocolate éclairs! A girl like that probably didn't think about her mother at all, but about her own life and the new, wonderful, romantic adventures she would have riding horseback across a vast, dangerous desert into a rosy sunset and the warm, waiting arms of a tall, muscular, tanned man whose soft, melting eyes left no question that he adored her.

"Turn off that light!" Mama's voice startled her. "You'll be dead tired in the morning."

Before Angelica could respond, she heard the sound of her mother's snore. Mama had awakened just long enough to give one more order.

Angelica writhed. "You'll be dead tired in the morning." She mimicked her mother's raspy voice. "You'll be dead tired in the morning. You'll be dead tired in the morning."

I wish *you* were just plain dead in the morning, Angelica thought viciously, sticking out her tongue. Again, moisture formed behind her knees and under her armpits.

She scanned the sheet of copier paper. Why shouldn't she go away to the fitness center and just leave Mama? Uncle Frank would give her the money.

"Abuse in Nursing Home." The headline, which was unintentionally included by the side of the ad when it was copied, caught Angelica's eye. I could leave Mama in a nursing home and hope they abuse her, she thought spitefully.

A partial story about a dispute that BART, the rapid-transit system, was having with someone or another framed the ad on the left. I could push her in front of a BART train, Angelica fantasized, licking her upper lip. The end of the Sea Cliff rapist story ran along one side of the ad, but it was another scrap of a filler story which the copier picked up that suddenly seized all of Angelica's attention. She stared at the words until they blurred. "Dogs Eat Dead Owner."

"Dogs Eat Dead Owner." Angelica read and

reread the words slowly at first, then faster and faster until they whirled and spun through her mind. Round and round they went with dizzying speed until finally the words exploded over her consciousness in a shower of sparks.

She was trembling. Her heart pounded in her ears. Her entire body was damp, and she had trouble catching her breath. She pressed her fists against her throbbing head.

She mustn't even imagine it! It was evil! It was a sin! She should not be thinking about it. She shook her head. She must put it out of her mind, the way the old catechism said to banish an impure thought. But this was worse than any impure thought! No daughter would even begin to do such a thing to her own mother.

Angelica sank down and pulled the covers over her face, hoping to blot out the idea. Yet, somehow, it was perfect. If she starved the poodles until they were fierce, hunting dogs. Until—what had that new paperboy said?—until "them dogs could eat you alive." Angelica giggled. Until they would eat Mama dead!

How would she do it? Not that she would. What harm would thinking do? She shifted in her bed. Angelica was never quite sure when the thought slipped from fantasy to an idea to a plan. Despite her headache, her tired mind seemed determined to work on one. How would she do it? First, Mama must not ever suspect that she was up to something. Angelica's hands felt damp and she wiped them on her sheet. How could she keep Mama from finding out? When they were hungry, Salt and Pepper were snappish, especially Salt. How could she keep the two dogs calm? Angelica mopped the back

75

of her neck, thinking. With Mama's sleeping pills, of course!

She'd mix Mama's sleeping pills with a little dog food, just enough to keep them alive, until she was ready. She could even add some sleeping pills to their water.

What if Mama noticed how drowsy her "babies" were? Angelica's head pounded as she thought the problem through. Why not put sleeping pills in Mama's food, too? What's good for the dogs is good for Mama! She giggled.

Then, just before she left for Utah, she'd slip the down pillow over sleepy Mama's face, the way she'd often daydreamed of doing, and hold it firm until every nasty breath left Mama's body. She'd smother Mother! It rhymed. And when it was done, she'd slam the front door and let nature take its course! How simple! How perfect! She would be free of Mama!

Even though her head pounded, she wanted to shout for joy, to call Uncle Frank and tell him what she was going to do, to tell Mrs. Kenny first thing in the morning and watch her patronizing eyes shoot open in shock, even to wake Mama and to tell her.

Angelica's back and neck were slippery with perspiration. She mustn't tell anyone. She knew that. Oh, no! She must keep it all to herself. It must be her special secret. At last, she would have a secret, just like that thin girl in the fitness ad.

Snuggling down under the bedcovers, happily clutching her own special secret to her heart, Angelica Bowers fell fast asleep.

By the time Kate Murphy fell into her bed, she ached all over. The hot toddies that Mrs. Bassetti had insisted on fixing for the two of them hadn't fazed her. She was wide awake.

The two of them! Even the phrase struck Kate funny. What an odd couple they made!

All day long, Loretta Bassetti had refused to budge from Kate's side until the nursing staff insisted that both women go home. What a tough old bird her mother-in-law was.

Kate shifted on the mattress searching for a comfortable position. Instinctively, she snuggled toward Jack's side of the bed, where his familiar aroma clung to the lumpy feather pillow. She reached out, touching only emptiness, then quickly rolled away, trying not to feel the cavity swelling in her chest.

Even her eyelids ached, as if they were sore from blinking back tears. Kate hadn't yet allowed herself the luxury of a good, hard cry. She had tried to be strong for Loretta, although it hadn't been necessary. Her mother-in-law had held up marvelously well.

The only time Mama Bassetti came even close to losing control was when Mrs. Gallagher had brought the baby home. Watching little John waddle through the house peeking into every room shouting, "Dada, play. Dada, play," had been too much. She had locked herself in the bathroom, and when she finally came out, her eyes were red and puffy.

By then John had climbed into his father's favorite chair in the living room and his big brown eyes were questioning Kate. "Dada bye-bye? Dada come?"

Unable to speak, Kate had scooped him up in her arms, cuddling him, kissing him and rocking him back and forth. The baby had stared up at her pleased, yet puzzled. If anything happened to Jack, how was she ever going to make a two-year-old understand?

Jack's sister Gina had been a welcome interruption. At about seven o'clock, she'd rung the front doorbell armed with an entire chest full of food—green salad, a casserole, French bread, a bottle of Chianti, a small bakery box with dessert, and even a coffee cake for breakfast.

The smell of food had made Kate realize just how hungry she was, how hungry they all must be. John wriggled down from her arms. Running to kiss Gina, he whispered a baby-talk secret to her that no one but he understood. Satisfied that all was moving back toward normal, he began running from room to room returning to show them a stuffed animal or a plastic toy, then busied himself again rushing to whatever it is that toddlers rush to.

"Thank you so much," Kate's eyes had filled with tears as she watched her sister-in-law set out the carefully prepared meal. "You shouldn't have gone to so much trouble, Gina. We could have sent out for pizza."

Mama Bassetti wrinkled her nose at the very suggestion of fast food and pecked her daughter on the cheek. "With her only brother in the hospital and you worried to death, you should have to send out for pizza? Why, when you have a family?"

Gina rolled her eyes at Kate and shrugged. Mama Bassetti was off and running, and they both knew it.

"This is exactly what a family should do." She slipped an apron over her head. "It is the reason we were not all born orphans. Families were invented to help one another. To be there for one another."

She pushed a loose hair back into her bun. "This is how their father, God rest him, and I were raised. This is how we tried to raise our kids. When someone needs you—*famiglia* or no *famiglia*—but especially *famiglia*—you help whatever way you can. You drive them or sit with their kids or you make a good meal. Salad..." Mrs. Bassetti began an inventory of the food chest. Lifting the lid of Gina's casserole, she sniffed it suspiciously.

"Chicken-and-broccoli casserole, Ma," Gina said, accepting a glass of wine from Kate.

"Whatever," Mrs. Bassetti replaced the lid and slipped the dish into the oven. "Where did you get these napoleons?" she asked, peering into the bakery box.

"Fantasia's on California," Gina answered and her mother seemed satisfied with her choice of bakery.

"And tomorrow night your sister better do the same." Mama Bassetti began to set the table.

"I'm sure she will," Gina said calmly.

Unless she never wants to hear the end of it, Kate thought.

In vain, Mrs. Bassetti searched the shelves of the refrigerator for butter and finally pulled out a tub of Jack's latest nonfat craze. "You Won't Believe It's Not Butter," the container proclaimed.

"Anyone with taste buds will believe it isn't," Mama Bassetti said, eyeing the smooth yellow mixture with disgust, then pointing a short stubby finger. "You tell your sister, Gina, that if she can cook for that bozo she tells her mother she doesn't live with, she can cook for her own family. After all, blood is thicker than water."

"Is Mama staying with you tonight, Kate?" Gina had asked, obviously trying to change the subject. Kate had not thought that far ahead. Apparently, her mother-in-law had.

Mrs. Bassetti sniffed indignantly. "Of course, I'll stay in the guest room. That is why people have guest rooms, so other people can spend the night in them. In case Kate needs to leave during the night, I can stay with the baby."

Had Loretta really said that, or just implied it? Lying in her darkened bedroom, Kate couldn't really remember. She was so tired that after they washed up the dishes, she had gone upstairs to bed. Now she was wide awake.

She listened to the late-night silence of the house, wondering if Loretta was asleep yet. If she was tired, her mother-in-law must be absolutely exhausted. All Kate heard was a neighbor's dog barking in the distance. Outside her window, car tires swished on the wet street and, far off, a siren wailed.

Suddenly, without warning, the reality of the day crashed in on her. Despite being surrounded by people who loved her and cared about her, she felt suffocated by an intense loneliness. Overwhelming grief filled her. Tears ran down her face, stinging her eyes, dampening her pillow. "Please, God," she begged the cruel silence. "Please, please, let my Jack live."

Not many blocks away, Tillie Greenwood heard the same siren and shuddered. Somewhere out there in the night, someone was hurt. Perfect strangers were hurrying as quickly as they could

80

to help. Would they make it in time? Tillie hoped so. She knew from experience the hollow panicky feeling of hearing sirens at night, wondering if they were for her child, worrying that something awful had happened to her precious baby.

Thank goodness, tonight her Elvis was home safe in his basement room. She could hear the hum of his television rising up through the floor.

Tillie plumped up her pillow and moved the pink sausage curler that pressed against her ear. Elvis really was such a dear, sweet son. Although, if she were completely honest—and what mother was?—she'd have to admit that during his teens, after Mother died, he had gone through a wild streak. If she had been alive, Mother would have said that he needed stricter discipline, which, to her, always meant a belt on the backside. Tillie had wanted to discipline him, but she could never bring herself to hurt Elvis, despite Mother's claim that a sound spanking never hurt any child.

Boys will be boys, Tillie decided finally. Boys need to sow a few wild oats. And see! She had been right. After that one little incident with that woman. The thought of her made Tillie angry all over again. She would never forgive the old bat for the things she said in court about Elvis—under oath, the liar. And Elvis, with those big, sad eyes being led away.

"Mommy!" he had cried out.

A tear slipped down Tillie's cheek. Thank God, Mother had not been alive to see that. It was a feeling she'd never forget. Such helplessness. And she never wanted to feel that way again.

Poor Elvis. How like him to be so worried

about the police and yet so sensitive and thoughtful that he wouldn't tell on a married woman. It would serve the slut right if her husband *did* find out and set her straight!

After all, Elvis was little more than a boy. Of course, if the police questioned her, Tillie would tell a tiny white lie to protect her son. What mother wouldn't? She hated to see him hurt. She always had. Maybe she should have been stronger and protected him more from Mother's wrath, although poor Mother had done what she thought was best for Elvis.

Tillie rolled over on her side and wondered what time it was. Elvis's television was still on. He'd looked so tired. He'd be worn out in the morning, although there was really no reason for either of them to get up early.

Elvis was—how did he put it?—between jobs. Tillie smiled. He had the cutest way of putting things. He always did have. It was he who had christened the canary "Mr. Cheeps." Once, she remembered fondly, when he was about ten, she'd asked him why he was kept after school. "Because the principal can't get enough of me," he answered quick as a wink.

Another time, when he was little more than a baby, money was missing from Mother's purse. "The not-mes took it," he said with those wide, innocent eyes.

"From the story, I read him," a smiling Tillie had explained it to Mother. But Mother, saying nothing, had dragged the frightened little boy into his bedroom. Tillie had turned up the radio so she wouldn't have to hear his cries.

Her stomach roiled at the memory. She always had a peppermint handy to slip him when

Mother wasn't looking. Funny, now Elvis hated anything that even had a hint of peppermint flavor. Tastes change, she guessed.

Despite Mother's predictions, her Elvis had grown up into a nice young man. And he always managed to find a job. Recently, he had worked for a limousine company driving a string of rich old ladies to parties. "Driving the Misses Daisy," he'd called it and Tillie had giggled appreciatively.

Not really wanting to know the answer, she wondered if he was "between jobs" because he had been seduced by one of them. If so, how unfair it was. Was it her Elvis's fault if some old bag couldn't keep her drawers up? Tillie turned again, trying to get comfortable, and drew in a deep breath.

She had no idea how long she'd been asleep, but when she awoke again, the house was absolutely still, except for the soft sound of rain on the roof. Suddenly she shivered, feeling as if someone were standing over her, staring down at her. She squinted into the darkness. Without her glasses, it was difficult to make out more than shadows.

"Elvis?" she whispered into the darkness. "Is that you, sweetheart?"

No one answered. Nothing moved. I must be dreaming, Tillie thought. She turned over and fell back to sleep.

As tired as she was, Sister Mary Helen's mind refused to turn off and let her drift into sleep. Over and over again, it replayed the day—a day that had started out quite normally. So much had happened since the first thing this morning when she talked to Angelica Bowers, that it seemed as if their conversation had taken place days, not simply hours ago.

At that time, all she'd had to worry about was Angelica's rather odd reaction to her suggestion that the young woman enroll at the the American Institute of Fitness. That was before she called Gemma back.

Was it really possible that her old friend Gemma Burke was dead and Jack Bassetti in St. Mary's Medical Center, barely clinging to life? Or was it all a nightmare from which she would soon wake?

The steady rain gurgled in the gutters and splashed out the spouts, like tears still unshed for her friends.

Gemma was such a gracious lady, so full of goodwill and good humor that it seemed impossible that she should come to harm. If she had any flaws at all, possibly it was her addiction to changing the color of her hair, if that could even be considered a flaw. Mary Helen smiled, remembering Gemma's impish delight when arriving at some social function or another with a bright new shade of hair, and watching her friends struggle not to stare. It had been their private joke.

Occasionally, Mary Helen herself was tempted to put a little something on her own salt-and-pepper bob, just for the adventure of it.

"Life is either a daring adventure or nothing," someone famous had said. To save her soul, Mary Helen couldn't remember whom. Obviously, it was someone more of a free spirit than herself. More like Gemma, whose hair, over the years, had been champagne blonde, Moroccan brown and black cherry which, in Mary Helen's opinion might just as well have been called shoe-polish black.

One season, Gemma had arrived at an alumnae function with pumpkin orange hair. She called it terracotta red. This last season she had favored a soft copper color. Recently, to Mary Helen's surprise and, she suspected, to the relief of Gemma's hair follicles, Gemma talked of returning to her natural color, whatever that was.

A thick lump formed in Mary Helen's throat. Gemma would never have to comb a gray head. Somehow, that seemed fitting and, in a sense, merciful. What didn't seem fitting was the degrading and terrifying way in which she had died. In the distance, lightning crackled and thunder rolled in agreement.

Did the rapist strike his victims like random lightning, or did he have some particular reason for choosing each of them? Gemma seemed to have very little in common with the other victims of the Sea Cliff rapist, at least very little Mary Helen that could glean from the newspaper articles. According to the *Chronicle,* the police, too, were having a difficult time finding a link.

Although all three women lived in the district and were about the same age and build, that was where the similarity stopped. The first victim had been a wealthy spinster living with her cat, a virtual recluse. The second was a widow who traveled extensively and had recently returned, tan and fit, from six weeks in Baja. The third was Gemma.

Had Gemma been in the wrong place at the wrong time? Was it an accident of fate? Perhaps it was from the killer's point of view; yet,

85

in her heart, Mary Helen knew that with God there are no accidents. Each of us is too precious. Nothing happens without a loving God knowing it. But why? What could possibly be the reason? Mary Helen let out a deep sigh. She'd have a great many questions for God when they finally did meet, face to face.

Tears filled her eyes as she relived the truth of the Christian paradox: the way to life is through death. The reason for human suffering is always a mystery that flies in the face of common sense. In the meantime, she must cling to her belief that God loves each of us with such tenderness that "the very hairs on our heads are numbered."

Wind howled around the corners of the convent and sent the rain lashing against Mary Helen's bedroom window. God's unconditional love even embraces the rapist, she marveled, wondering if he were out in the storm tonight, as he had been last night, hunting for another unsuspecting woman.

Instinctively, she prayed to St. Martin de Porres, whose feast was celebrated today. Martin, a mestizo in sixteenth-century Peru, lived a childhood full of hardship and suffering. By today's standards, any psychologist worth his salt would predict a life of crime for the lad. Yet Martin used his misfortunes to become a saint.

"Touch the heart of that wretched fellow," Mary Helen prayed fervently. "Heal him, and, above all, stop him. Someone has to."

Frustrated, she stared into the darkness remembering Kate Murphy's warning not to become involved; remembering Kate's strong conviction that if Eileen and she did, this depraved man might be tempted to harm them.

Mary Helen turned on her side, trying to find a comfortable position, hoping to fall asleep, but her mind wouldn't let go. It kept bombarding her.

Suppose the police were to capitalize on this danger and use Eileen and her as decoys. The idea excited her. However, now was not the time to discuss it with Kate, who was worried enough—and rightly so—about her husband. "Never" was the right time to discuss it with Inspector Gallagher. She knew that. First she must talk things over with Eileen, make a plan. Then, at the auspicious moment, they could present their plan to someone.

Eileen and she might provide a perfect trap that would snap shut on this villain forever. It could be dangerous. She was fully aware of that. But not necessarily. Jessica Fletcher did the selfsame thing time after time on her television show and it always worked out beautifully.

A distant siren wailed. At last, Mary Helen was beginning to feel drowsy.

"Jessica Fletcher is make-believe! This is true life!" she could hear Inspector Gallagher shouting.

Truth is stranger than fiction. Dreamily, Mary Helen readied her rebuttal. It's just not quite so popular!

Wednesday, November 4
Feast of St. Charles Borromeo, Bishop

In the cold light of morning, Sister Mary Helen's plan to serve as a police decoy to help catch the rapist didn't seem quite as brilliant as it had late last night.

In fact, if she were honest, it smacked a little of the melodramatic. But then, she had been desperate.

Over breakfast, she jokingly mentioned her daydream to Eileen, who doused it with a splash of cold sense.

"Every dog is brave in her own doorway," Eileen said.

"What does that mean?"

"That you'd be scared to death!" Eileen speared a grapefruit section.

Mary Helen tightened her lips and straightened her shoulders.

"Not that I blame you," Eileen added tactfully.

"I don't remember saying I'd be frightened." Mary Helen dug into her own grapefruit. "I only said that this morning the idea seems impractical."

Eileen looked up. "That too, old dear."

"On the other hand, if we thought it through, perhaps it could work. We could set something up."

"We?" Eileen's bushy gray eyebrows shot up. "Who's we?"

"I've never know you to pass up the opportunity to do some good."

"Even do-gooders have their limits," Eileen said and looked relieved when Sister Anne asked if she could join them.

Back in her office, it was impossible for Sister Mary Helen to keep her mind on the alumnae Christmas Tree Extravaganza. By mid-morning, Shirley, her secretary, suggested that the best thing she could do for the entire event was to go somewhere else.

Without a second invitation, Mary Helen called Eileen, and the two of them arranged to sign out the convent Nova and pay a sympathy call on Gemma Burke's grieving family.

"Did you call ahead?" Sister Eileen asked when Mary Helen turned off Lake Street and onto 27th Avenue.

"I tried," Mary Helen admitted, "but every time I rang, the line was busy. Maybe it was off the hook."

Slowly, she drove through the stone gates of Sea Cliff, pausing to admire, once again, the verdigrised bronze heads of the seal pups which poked their noses out from the pillars. The pups had been placed just above the carved name and cockleshells which marked one boundary of the exclusive community built on the cliffs above the craggy coastline. Thankfully, there was no traffic. What with the Cadillacs, the Suburbans, and the Lexuses parked on the narrow streets, Mary Helen didn't know what she'd do if she met a car coming the other way.

"You never got through to anyone?" Eileen said in that Irish question-statement way of hers. "What if they don't want company?" A bit of a nervous brogue was beginning to creep into her voice. "There are people, you know, who are very private about their troubles."

"Then we'll just leave the goodies and go home," Mary Helen said nodding toward the basket of freshly baked yeast rolls that Eileen was balancing on her lap.

"We should have called." Eileen chewed on the thought while Mary Helen drove cautiously past the mixture of grand mansions that made up the district.

Luckily, there were several spaces in the municipal parking lot above China Beach. After checking that the No Parking sign referred to Monday-morning street cleaning, she easily pulled into one. Well, actually two. That way, she wouldn't ding any car doors.

Sister Eileen stood rooted by the fender of the Nova and drew in a breath of damp tangy air. "This view is breathtaking," she said at last. Mary Helen had to agree.

For the moment, the rain had stopped, but the leaden clouds already piling up for the next storm had swallowed the towers of Golden Gate Bridge. A black cargo ship made its slow way through the choppy bay while the miniature light station on faraway Point Bonita blinked its warning for all to see.

Below them waves pounded against China Beach, a rockbound cove once used as a campsite by Chinese fishermen who supplied the young city with fresh seafood. A wide path led down to the beach. Under any other circumstances, Mary Helen would have been tempted to take it, but today she had a mission to accomplish.

Gemma Burke's home, a two-story Spanish Colonial mansion, was the last of a row of dwellings on Sea Cliff Avenue. It virtually hung from the cliff, a tangle of boxwood hedges, mirror plants, rhododendrons, cypress trees, and overgrown bushes of white rambling roses. The house itself looked as if it had been backed into the space between a pine and a palm tree.

As the two nuns walked from the parking lot toward Gemma's home, they passed manicured gardens, rows of picture windows with all the shades at exactly the same length and locked wrought-iron gates, but not one human being. Not even a curtain flickered, and the persistent ringing of an unanswered telephone simply underscored their aloneness.

"An Irish yew." Eileen stared at a small scruffy tree. "You find them in all the cemeteries in Ireland." She shivered. "I feel as if I'm in one of those science-fiction movies where everyone's disappeared except us."

"And that cat," Mary Helen pointed to a fawn-colored Siamese sitting in the front window of a Tudor mansion. The animal watched them and yawned.

Approaching the driveway of Gemma's home, Mary Helen noticed that the heavy gate was pushed back into an ice plant. The familiar wide yellow police band cordoning off the estate was fastened to it on one side and to a wind-bent cypress tree on the other.

Her stomach tumbled, then formed an elusive lump somewhere between her chest and her throat. Seeing that yellow band somehow made it official. Her dear friend Gemma was dead, the victim of an unspeakable violation. Unexpected tears of anger burned her eyes.

"Are you all right?" Eileen asked.

"It must be the wind." Knowing full well that Eileen wasn't fooled, Mary Helen took off her bifocals and wiped her eyes.

"We had better come back later, old dear." Eileen shifted the basket of yeast rolls on her arm. "It looks as though they're not allowing anyone in just yet."

Pretending not to hear, Mary Helen studied the wide yellow band. Even on her best day, she could never get her legs over it. Maybe one leg, but two? Never. The thought of being caught on it like a wishbone made her smile. But what about the knot?

"Can I help you, ladies?" The deep masculine voice startled her.

"May I," Mary Helen corrected automatically and looked into the intelligent blue eyes of a young patrolman. "Sorry, Officer," she apologized, "I was a teacher. It's an occupational hazard."

"Yes, ma'am, I understand," he said with a serious face that looked as if it had just been shaved. "Just like mine is being suspicious. This is the scene of a crime. Like I said, may I help you with something?"

To Mary Helen's amazement, Eileen spoke up. "Little John O'Reilly, is that you?"

Mary Helen watched the muscles in the patrolman's jaw tighten and red splotches ride up his cheeks.

"Yes, ma'am. I'm John O'Reilly," he answered, lowering his voice almost an octave.

Eileen introduced herself quickly. Officer O'Reilly's mother, Noreen, was an alumna of the college, and Eileen hadn't seen him since he was "this high," although she'd recognize those big blue eyes anywhere.

"All we want to do," she said candidly, "is bring the family our condolences, our promise of prayers, and these yeast rolls." She offered one to Officer O'Reilly.

Refusing, but trying hard to hang on to both his dignity and his good humor—which from Mary Helen's point, he was doing quite admirably—the young patrolman explained that he couldn't let anyone into the scene of the crime. Not his own mother, not even nuns.

As a matter of fact, he explained, he had strict orders from Inspector Dennis Gallagher whose case this was, to make absolutely sure that nuns, however harmless they looked, were not to enter the premises.

Officer O'Reilly's cheeks colored again. "These are his words, not mine, Sisters. If I do let you through, it's my neck. That's not exactly the part of my anatomy he mentioned, Sisters, but you get my meaning."

"Absolutely, John," Eileen flashed him a generous smile. "I know you'd let us in if you could. Where is Inspector Gallagher now? Is he inside?"

"No, ma'am. Sister. He left here about an hour ago. He was going downtown."

"To the Hall of Justice?" Mary Helen had been silent long enough.

Officer O'Reilly nodded. "To check out some stuff on the computer, I think," he said.

"Inspector Gallagher doesn't look like the computer type," Mary Helen muttered, walking back to their parked car.

"What does the computer type look like?" Eileen asked.

"I don't know, younger maybe, more yuppie looking. Certainly not plump, bald, sixty-fiveish and cigar smoking."

"Do I hear a hint of 'computerism'?" Eileen asked with an impish twinkle in her eye.

"What in the world is 'computerism'?" Mary Helen fit the key into the car door.

"You know. Like sexism and racism and age-ism."

"Corny!" Mary Helen said, glad to be in the car and out of the sharp wind strafing the parking lot with grains of sand.

The two nuns sat in the front seat, listening to the waves pound against the rocky coast-line. Seagulls wheeled and cawed against the darkening sky. A hard gust of wind rocked the Nova. Mary Helen wondered how the two brave fishermen she had spotted on the beach far below were managing to hold onto their rods.

"What are we going to do with all these rolls?" Eileen asked, staring down at the basket in her lap.

"Inspector Gallagher may not look like the computer type, but he surely looks like the yeast-roll type," Mary Helen said with a sudden burst of enthusiasm.

The car engine roared into action, and Eileen fastened her seat belt. "Where are we off to?"

"We'll just drop by the Hall of Justice, as if that's where we were going all along, and give these lovely rolls to the Inspector to share with his people. I'm sure the other homicide detectives will be glad for a snack and we'll have a chance to visit with Inspector Gallagher."

Mary Helen felt Eileen's stare. "I don't believe what I'm hearing," she said. "After all the times Inspector Gallagher has made it clear that he does not want us anywhere near him when he's on a case, you pick this moment to drop in to the Hall of Justice. The instant he spots us, his back will go straight up."

Mary Helen tried without much success to appear that she had missed her friend's point. "We have to give these rolls to someone. It would be a shame to let them go to waste," she said.

"Even if I believed for one moment, which I don't, that your sole purpose was social and your overriding concern was the fate of a few dozen yeast rolls, *he's* never going to buy it.

"And, by the way, my friend, your innocent, confused stare just doesn't make it."

Mary Helen laughed despite herself. "Of course, while we're there, if we play our cards right, we may be able to find out if he's learned anything about Gemma's killer."

"If he's learned anything? He'll never let us know if he's learned anything. If you ask me, old dear, the only thing we'll learn from this trip downtown is that there's nothing to be learned from the second kick of a mule."

Angelica Bowers woke up happy! She could not remember the last time she had. In fact, it was such a foreign feeling that it took her a few seconds to identify it.

She was beginning to wonder whether happiness showed. On her way to work, several people on the Number 31 Muni bus smiled at her. When she arrived at the Hanna Memorial Library a few minutes before the bell, Mrs. Kenny eyed her quizzically.

"Well, good morning, Angelica," Mrs. Kenny said in that put-on pleasant voice of hers that Angelica despised. "You're early." The head librarian put down her coffee cup and studied

Angelica's face as if she were a specimen. "Is everything all right this morning?"

Angelica felt herself flush. "Everything is just fine," she said, stripping off her wet raincoat and that silly little plastic rain bonnet that Mama insisted she wear. She hung them both on the faculty coatrack and watched with satisfaction as moisture ran off her coat and onto the polished parquet floor. Mrs. Kenny, who hated anything dripping on *her* floor, rushed to the cupboard for a bath towel.

"Do you think this rain is ever going to let up?" she asked, as if Angelica should know.

But Mrs. Kenny didn't really want an answer because, after she spread the towel underneath the coatrack, she moved to a library window to stare out at the dark morning.

Huge drops of rain had begun to fall. Angelica visualized them pounding down on the bowls of water she'd put outside the back door for the poodles. She hoped the rain wouldn't dilute the powdered sleeping pills. Maybe she should have left the bowls in the kitchen. Even if the dogs weren't drowsy, they'd be hungry! She smiled.

Before leaving for work, she had carefully cleared the sideboard and the kitchen table of any food they could possibly reach. Smiling to herself, she shoved it all into the back of the refrigerator and the door closed with a cheerful little click. She had even swept the kitchen floor before she left, picking up every single tiny crumb.

"Why are you sweeping now?" Mama had shouted down from her bedroom. "You'll be late for work."

Instead of answering, Angelica had turned

96

on the garbage disposal and emptied the dust-pan into it.

Angelica poured herself a cup of freshly brewed coffee, then settled in behind her corner desk and opened the crisp white bag from the Sugar Bowl. She had stepped off the bus at the bakery on Balboa Street. It had been difficult to choose between the brownies with walnuts and the bear claws. When she finally picked the bear claws, she bought three. She usually bought only two, but today she was celebrating "Smother Mother" week.

Grinning at her own cleverness, she moved her glue pot closer to the scissors, and the stack of books she was to mend, and spread out her napkin.

"It looks as if someone is having a picnic," Mrs. Kenny said snidely.

Ignoring her, Angelica took the first bite. Closing her eyes she savored the taste of its sweet nutty filling.

"You do intend to get to those books soon, I hope," Mrs. Kenny snapped.

"As soon as your baby-kins finishes her itty-bitty, bearsy-wearsy claw," Angelica said, imitating the baby talk she'd overheard Mrs. Kenny using on the phone.

This must be what happiness feels like, Angelica thought, looking up at the head librarian. At first, all the color drained from the woman's face. Direct hit! Angelica thought, watching it being replaced with flaming red, until Mrs. Kenny looked as if someone had slapped both her cheeks, hard.

"You definitely do have a problem, young lady," Mrs. Kenny spat out, then turned on her

Cuban heel and stormed away. All my problems will soon be over, Angelica thought, and it shouldn't take too long.

Today was Wednesday. By the weekend, the poodles should be hungry enough to devour any piece of dead meat, even Mama. When they did, she'd be in Utah.

She took another bite of her bear claw. When the dogs jumped on Mama with their clipped oval feet, Angelica might be getting a pedicure or having a rinse put on her faded auburn hair. Nothing garish. Just something to bring out the highlights. While the poodles straddled Mama and tore at her scrawny neck, Angelica might be enjoying a European facial.

She smiled, thinking of the dogs' teeth like scissors cutting hungrily into Mama's mean brown eyes while she herself was lying on a table luxuriating in a full-body massage.

Before the week was over, Angelica envisioned herself sitting on the red rock next to the attractive young woman in the brochure. Maybe they'd exchange secrets. Angelica giggled, imagining the shocked expression rising on the woman's perfect plastic face when Angelica told hers.

Oh, no! She felt a drop of perspiration meander down her back. She mustn't tell anyone. She must not let on that she knew anything about what happened. She must cry when the police came to take Mama away and when they sent the men from the pound to take the dogs and put them to sleep.

Her problems would be solved. Angelica wiped her fingers on the sticky, white bakery napkin and giggled.

At her ten-fifteen coffee break, Angelica Bowers left the library. Mrs. Kenny looked at her queerly, but Angelica didn't care. She needed to call Uncle Frank, and she didn't want that old busybody listening.

Angelica wedged herself into the narrow, old-fashioned phone booth located in the far corner of the college entryway. She shivered as the cold draft blew in under the door and found its way up her legs.

Dropping her coins in the slots, she dialed her uncle's number.

"Hello," she shouted over the chatter and shuffle of students coming and going.

"Well, hello!" Her uncle sounded surprised, then worried. "What's wrong?"

"I've decided to take that trip after all," Angelica said quickly.

"Well, I'll be damned!"

"Is it still all right?" She leaned her moist forehead against the cold glass of the phone booth.

"Sure, sure," Uncle Frank said. "Where to?"

"Utah."

"Utah? What the hell is in Utah?"

"A fitness center," Angelica said. "I've decided to try to lose some weight....Uncle Frank, are you there? Is it still all right?"

"Sure!" He sounded genuinely happy. "I was just surprised. Good for you, Angel-pie. What does your mother think? Where are you, anyway?"

"She doesn't know." A tightness formed in Angelica's chest. "I'm at work, and I'm calling from a phone booth. You won't tell her, will you, Uncle Frank?"

"Hell, no," her uncle laughed. "Wild horses couldn't drag it out of me. When do you want to leave?"

"Friday." Angelica wiped the palm of her free hand on her skirt.

"And how long do you want to stay?"

"Ten days, if that's all right with you."

"Great!" Uncle Frank laughed again. "Tell me how much and where to send the check. And where in Utah you want to go. If you like, I'll make the reservations, and you can pick them up at my travel agent."

Angelica gave her uncle all the details. "You'll need a ride to the airport," Uncle Frank said.

"No," Angelica interrupted. "No, thank you," she added, remembering her manners. "I'll take the Airporter." A siren screamed its way down Turk Street.

"There is something you can do for me, though," she mopped her upper lip with a matted tissue. When Uncle Frank didn't object, she went on. "If Mama will let me, I plan to board Salt and Pepper at the vet's."

Uncle Frank chuckled. "Those two spoiled mutts won't know what hit them. It'll do them both good to realize they're dogs!"

"One of Mama's friends promised she'd stay over while I'm gone." Angelica lied, hoping Uncle Frank didn't know that Mama had no friends. "But I'd feel better if you stopped over, maybe next Friday, to see how she's getting along."

She heard her uncle swallow. "Sure," he said finally. "For you, Angel-pie, I'll drop in on the old battle-ax. Won't she be surprised when she sees me!"

100

And won't you be surprised when you see her, Angelica thought, replacing the damp receiver.

Tillie Greenwood settled herself down at the breakfast table with her first cup of coffee of the day. Yawning, she pulled her pink chenille robe tightly around her. A draft was coming in from somewhere. She'd get up and investigate as soon as the caffeine gave her a jolt of energy.

Closing her eyes, Tillie savored the delicious aroma and the hot, fresh taste. "The best part of waking up is coffee in your cup." The jingle from the television commercial ran through her mind. Actually, most days it was the only good thing about waking up in this silent, lonely old house.

But this morning was different. She heard Mr. Cheeps. The little canary was warbling and trilling away as if his tiny heart might burst with happiness.

Apparently Elvis had removed the night drape. She must remember to give the little fellow some fresh water and birdseed. And to change that soiled newspaper in the bottom of the cage. For a moment, she thought of asking Elvis to do it, before she remembered how much he always despised the task.

The front door closed with a soft click, and Elvis came into the kitchen clutching the morning paper in one hand and a mug of coffee in the other.

"Did you sleep well, sweetheart?" Tillie asked, noticing the deep circles under her son's eyes. They were so dark that they seemed to reflect the brown of his velvety eyes. His black hair, always thick and coarse, was rumpled, and he needed a shave badly.

Without answering, Elvis flopped into the chair across from her and threw down the *Chronicle* on the table between them. Not sure from the hard expression on her son's face if it was good news or bad that he was showing her, Tillie went to the kitchen stove for the coffeepot and poured them another cup.

The headlines screamed the bad news: "Sea Cliff Rape Attempt Thwarted."

Tillie skimmed the article quickly. Early this morning, an attempt was made to rape a wealthy widow. They gave the house number. Police patrolling area...silent alarm...barking dog...suspect narrowly escaped up the California Street stairs onto the Lincoln Golf Course.

On second thought, this was good news. Her Elvis had been at home last night—all night—right here with her. Tillie smiled over at her son. "See sweetheart, innocence will win out."

Elvis took a cigarette out of his shirt pocket and lit it. Tillie tried not to look reproachful. She did wish that he would stop smoking. There was no telling what it would do to his lungs. Her Elvis might end up with emphysema or, God forbid, cancer.

"See, sweetheart?" She pointed to the bold headline. "Now you don't need to worry about anything," she continued cheerfully. "The police can't possibly think you had anything to do with these horrible rape-murders. Even if they do dig up your old record, and I can't imagine why they would, you have an airtight alibi. You were at home with your mother, asleep."

Elvis gave her that cute crooked grin of his, the one that could melt Tillie's heart. Mother always claimed it looked like a sneer, but Tillie knew better. She knew it meant that he loved her and that he knew she loved him.

Tillie reached over and brushed the back of her hand along Elvis's stubbly cheek. "You look so tired, sweetheart," she crooned. "Why don't you take a little nap?"

Elvis avoided her eyes and did not answer. Tillie hoped that he wasn't getting depressed. She dreaded her son's depressions. He'd sit for hours staring at the television set—unwashed, unshaven, uncommunicative. No matter what she tried to do to lift his spirits, he just sat there brooding.

Suddenly goose bumps ran up Tillie's legs, and she gathered her bathrobe around her. In the background Mr. Cheeps trilled away as if the little canary sensed the mood and was doing his best to alleviate it.

"Do you hear Mr. Cheeps, sweetheart?" Tillie tried to sound upbeat. "He's singing, 'Cheer up, cheer up!'"

Elvis's eyes grew hard, and he gave her that dangerous look which she had grown to dread.

"Enough of that." She rose quickly. "You relax and I'll get dressed and go to the Safeway out by the beach. You look like you could use a decent meal." She touched her son's shoulder, and he flinched as though her hand was scalding.

She put her arms around his shoulders gently, pressed his head to her bosom, and rocked him back and forth. "How about a rare steak and baked potatoes and a veggie? What kind would you like?"

"No veggie," Elvis growled, much as he had as a teenager. "I hate veggies. They taste like hot crap!"

Tillie stiffened. She wished he'd eat better and stop using that language. But now was not the moment to bring it up. Nothing sent him into a black mood faster than her—what did he call it?—her nagging.

Elvis pulled away from her. He had sensed her disapproval. Tillie's stomach pitched forward. She tried to hug him again, but he batted her arms away. Knowing better than to continue, she moved away to a safe distance.

"While I get ready to go, you write down anything you'd like on the shopping list." Tillie said.

"Anything?" Elvis taunted her.

"Anything, sweetheart," Tillie answered with a smile. "Tonight Mommy just wants you to have a good dinner."

Fortunately, the rain had let up. Tillie Greenwood judged from the color of the clouds and a small crack of blue sky that she should be able to get to the Safeway and back before the next storm front hit. At least, she hoped so. She had worn her rain hat and tucked her black umbrella in her wire grocery cart, just in case.

She waited until she was halfway up the block to scan the shopping list. She didn't want to start anything. Elvis was so sensitive to her reactions when he was in one of these moods. She didn't want him to read anything into her face and become upset.

By the time she rode the bus to Ocean Beach,

shopped, and rode it back, Elvis would have slept and be his old self again.

Dragging her wire cart behind her up the 42nd Avenue hill toward Balboa, she ran her eye down the list—steak, potatoes, no vegetables, of course. She wished he hadn't put beer on the list. Beer made him a different person, not the sweet son she knew and cherished. Once, while he was drinking, he had even hit her. Well, maybe twice—not that he really hurt her. And he had been nearly despondent afterward. He was out of his mind, he said. And Tillie believed him. The darling boy had left peppermints for her, just as she once had for him. Wasn't that a precious way of telling her how much he loved her?

Deep in thought, Tillie passed the Bowers home. She was almost to Balboa Street. Now, there's a woman with troubles, she chided herself, without even glancing up at the house.

Widowed young, with a child who still lived at home. Poor thing. Angelica? Is that her name? So overweight that the poor girl is hard to look at. And from what Tillie had heard at the hairdresser, Mrs. Bowers was almost totally bedridden.

Compared to her, I'm a lucky woman. Tillie straightened her shoulders. I'm still healthy and active. And my Elvis is a handsome, hardworking young man who would make any mother proud.

A sharp wind from the beach tore up Balboa Street. It flapped the front of Tillie's woolen coat and ripped at the brim of her rain hat. Her cart rattled in its force and she stopped for a moment to catch her breath.

Nobody's perfect, she reminded herself, still feeling sorry for Mrs. Bowers, but my Elvis is as close to it as any mother could want. Yes, I'm a very lucky woman, she thought. Very, very lucky.

"Does this seem faster to you than the last time we rode it?" Sister Eileen whispered as the crowded elevator shot up to the fourth floor of the Hall of Justice.

Sister Mary Helen shook her head and checked the collar of her navy blue suit jacket to make sure it was straight. "Why do you ask?"

"Because my stomach just turned a cartwheel." Eileen sucked in a deep breath.

More the destination than the ride, Mary Helen thought, glancing around at the carload of tall, well-built, well-dressed and, she imagined, well-armed police inspectors who sandwiched the two short nuns in their midst.

"Are you all right?" she asked, noting Eileen's pale, almost pasty face.

Still clutching the basket of yeast rolls, her companion nodded, but just barely.

Arming herself with an ironclad smile, Mary Helen strode into the Homicide Detail with Eileen at her heels.

"Can I help you?" asked an attractive black woman, whose plastic name plate declared that she was "Gwen Williams." She was trying unsuccessfully to hide her curiosity.

"We'd like to see Inspector Gallagher," Mary Helen announced, all business.

"Is he expecting you?" Not waiting for the answer, Ms. Williams picked up one of the two ringing phones—a tactical error!

"I see him," Mary Helen peeked around the door into the main room. "You're busy, miss. I'll just go right on in."

Before the distracted Ms. Williams could object, she and Eileen maneuvered themselves into the detail room. A group of detectives, including Inspector Gallagher, were huddled around one of the desks.

Being briefed, Mary Helen thought. A shudder of anticipation zigzagging up her spine; she moved closer. Perfect timing! It might be a breakthrough on Gemma's case.

"Did you hear about the old country priest who liked his sauce?" one of them was saying. "The bishop went to see him and noticed a large number of empty beer bottles around the rectory.

"'There are an awful lot of dead soldiers around here, Father,' the bishop said.

"'True, Your Excellency,' said the old man, 'and not one of them died without a priest.'"

Mid-laugh, Inspector Gallagher spotted the two nuns. His face hardened and his eyes shot such fire that Mary Helen feared, if he could manage it, that there would be only a cinder where the two of them now stood.

Except for the insistent ringing of the telephones and the distant hum of the traffic outside, the room was still.

"Inspector," Mary Helen began, ignoring his glare. "Knowing how tired you and the other officers must be, with this Sea Cliff rapist business, we thought we'd drop downtown with a little treat."

On cue, Eileen held out her basket. "Like Red Riding Hood meeting the wolf," she said later.

"Fresh-baked yeast rolls for your coffee break," Mary Helen said. I'm sure none of you has the time for a proper breakfast...." She was dithering, hoping the purple rage on the inspector's face would fade. "I know a coffee break and a little snack always does wonders for me when I'm under pressure, and—"

"What do you two want?" Gallagher strained the words through clenched teeth. His bushy eyebrows met in a straight line.

"Hey, Denny, don't look a gift horse in the mouth," one of the other officers piped up, one Mary Helen knew she'd met before.

"Stay the hell out of this, O'Connor!" Gallagher snapped.

Seeing an opening, Eileen handed the basket to Inspector O'Connor. "There's a small jar of homemade raspberry preserves in there, too," she said, sounding like Martha Stewart. "If you heat the rolls for just a few minutes, it's delicious on them."

Relieved, Mary Helen watched the detective take the basket and pass it around.

"What do you want?" Gallagher demanded, when the others were out of earshot. His color was still deep purple, but at least he could speak civilly. "And don't give me that baloney about passing by with rolls for our health. For all I know, you two mugged some deli delivery boy on your way down the street."

Mary Helen tried to look shocked. "You surely don't mean that, Inspector."

He dismissed her protest with a wave of his hand. "No, I don't. Not that I'd put it past you." He took a deep breath and exhaled it slowly.

"So, Sister," he said finally, "to what does the San Francisco Police Department owe the honor of this visit?"

Paying no attention to the sarcasm, Mary Helen smiled humbly. "We only want to do something."

Obviously, this was not the moment to mention her daydream about acting as a decoy to Inspector Gallagher. Giving him a coronary would not be helpful to anyone.

Looking unusually frustrated, Gallagher rubbed his hand across his bald pate, limped toward his chair, and eased himself into it.

"Sit down, Sisters," he said gruffly and waited until they did. "I know this thing has gotten to all of us."

"Are you all right?" Mary Helen was genuinely concerned.

Gallagher looked up sharply. "Why?"

"I couldn't help noticing that you're limping. Don't tell me you've been wounded, too."

"It's nothing. Just a charley horse." Gallagher rubbed his left thigh. "Last night we thought we spotted the perp. But the guy took off running. I guess we're lucky he didn't stay around to shoot. Anyway, I tried to catch him, but he outsprinted me on the California Street steps. Do you know how steep those damn—excuse me, darn—things are?"

Mary Helen did although she'd never tried to climb them. "I read about it in this morning's *Chronicle*," she said sympathetically. "Did you get a good description?"

Gallagher shook his head. "Young, obviously in good physical shape. Male. White. Slender, about six feet-plus. Lots of dark hair. Leather jacket, jeans. I'm guessing that fits about one-fourth of all the males in San Francisco.

"Knows his way around Lincoln Golf Course. So he could live in the neighborhood. Or he could play golf."

"Or been a caddy when he was a youngster," Mary Helen added, realizing Gallagher's frustration. "Is there anything we can do?" she asked, feeling a little safer.

"Just stay the hell away from anything to do with it," he said blackly. "I don't want to be hovering at your bedside one of these days."

"How is Jack?" Mary Helen asked.

"That's another thing you can do. Pray for a miracle. Pray he pulls through and that he is able to tell us who this guy is. To be shot at such close range, he and Bill Jordon must have seen the perp.

"And if you have any spare prayers left, Sisters..." Unexpectedly, Gallagher's watery blue eyes filled with tears. Taking off his glasses, he wiped them, then blew his nose noisily. He coughed, more to gain control than to clear his throat. "Say one for Liz Jordon, Bill's wife." He checked his watch.

"In about an hour she'll be living every cop's wife's nightmare. The funeral Mass is at St. Mary's Cathedral at noon. I better get going if I want to make it." His eyes flooded again. "And I do. Billy Jordon was one helluva guy."

Assuring him of their prayers, the two Sisters quickly left a now-somber Homicide Detail.

"You were unusually quiet," Mary Helen said, once she and Eileen were back in the convent Nova.

110

"But not idle," Eileen looked as if she had just uncovered the whereabouts of the Holy Grail. "While you were chitchatting with Inspector Gallagher, before he asked for our prayers, I was reading the list on his desk."

"List? What list?"

"If I'm not mistaken, it was a list of possible suspects. Of course, I had to read it upside down and memorize it, as best I could," she said coyly.

"You've got a memory any elephant would envy," Mary Helen muttered while Eileen gingerly found a scrap of paper in her pocketbook and scribbled down several names.

Kate Murphy hurried by a crowded waiting room in St. Mary's Medical Center where a television set blared. Channel 4 was doing a news special on the funeral services for Jack's partner, Bill Jordon.

Kate had seen enough! She had been at the funeral. The hollow clomp, clomp, clomping of the mounted police patrol echoed down the hospital corridor. Over the distant roar of motorcycles, the eerie strains of the bagpiper's lament conjured up the sad scene.

Uniformed police honor guards lining both sides of Geary Boulevard watched in silence as the sleek black hearse inched its way from McAvoy and O'Hara's Funeral Home to St. Mary's Cathedral.

Officers on the cathedral steps saluted the oak box shrouded with golden chrysanthemums and sprigs of vanda orchids which carried their brother officer and friend toward the massive bronze doors.

Mercifully, the rain which had deluged the

city for days had let up. Clouds gathering for a new storm sent dark shadows skittering across the pavement. The single marble spire of the cathedral caught the light as Liz Jordon, beautiful in her somber widow's weeds, stepped out of the limousine.

Straightening her shoulders, she followed the coffin with an expression both brave and bewildered. Their tiny daughter Julie, overwhelmed by the crowd and the pomp, clung to her mother with one hand and reached out to clutch a familiar relative with the other.

Beneath the glittering baldachin of aluminum and gold, the archbishop waited to receive the body and begin the Mass of Resurrection. The ancient ritual, with its familiarity and predictability, gave Kate a strange comfort. She didn't have to pay attention or even think. The chant and rhythm of the sacred words, the aroma of incense, the rote answers to the prayers washed over her and left all her senses free to grieve the loss; free to ponder the eternal, mysterious, unanswerable question: "Why?"

The mayor and the police chief eulogized Bill as a brave cop who had given his life for others. The archbishop praised his moral values and his great sense of fair play. All three offered Liz Jordon sympathy and the comfort which comes from burying a hero.

Could anything really comfort her? Kate pondered whether a hero's funeral could make up for the sharing of small intimate secrets, the pride of watching their child grow, the mutual support of worrying about the mortgage?

Who could Liz tell that the plumbing was backing up or that she'd gotten a great deal on London broil at Petrini's? And how would she get her feet warm during the long, cold winter nights?

At Holy Cross Cemetery, Kate was overcome with deep sympathy and compassion for Liz Jordon and then by an overwhelming sense of guilt at being glad Liz's husband was killed and not her own.

Jack's cubicle in the intensive care unit was warm and still, except for the machines which gave out their reassuring beeps and gurgles. Jack was still alive, still holding his own. In the dim light, his eyelids looked blue. Almost imperceptibly, his chest rose and fell, rose and fell in a steady rhythm. A dark stubble covered his jaws and chin.

Kate bent over the raised rail of the bed and kissed his forehead. It felt damp and soft under her lips. "I'm sure glad you're still here, pal," she whispered, squeezing his limp hand. "Come back to me, Jack. Please come back." She pushed a curl off his forehead. "I promise I'll never lose my temper with you again. Never tell you to get a haircut. Never complain about your snoring. I'll let you and John eat chocolate ice cream for breakfast if you want to...."

The presence of a nurse in the doorway reminded her that they were not alone.

"How's he doing?" Kate tried to sound in command of her emotions.

"He made it through the night," the nurse answered with a reassuring smile. "Every day he makes it, his chances get better."

"Was the doctor in this morning?"

The nurse nodded, but before Kate could ask any more questions, she heard the familiar staccato click of her mother-in-law's thick heels marching down the polished hospital corridor.

"Hello, Kate," Loretta Bassetti shot her a tired smile. "I took little John to the baby-sitter. It nearly broke my heart to drop him off, but to tell you the truth, I think he was glad to get there and see the other kids." Her brown eyes searched Kate's face. "Do you think I was kissing him too much?"

"Don't take it personally, Loretta. He just likes to play with other kids," Kate said and pecked her mother-in-law's cheek.

"Just like his father." She took off her plastic rain hat and folded it into a small rectangle. "I never could keep Jackie in the house if there was one other kid out on the block. I used to swear that he couldn't hear me holler to brush his teeth or change to his playclothes, but he could hear a rubber ball bouncing six doors away.

"When the two girls came along, I thought all three kids might play together at home, safe in our own backyard. But, no! All three of them liked to go…" Her mother-in-law stopped mid-sentence.

"Not that I'm saying you shouldn't have more children, Kate. It's good for a child to have brothers and sisters."

Kate's stomach churned, and she felt her temper start to rise. The topic was bound to come up sooner or later. She knew that. But now? Why would her mother-in-law choose now?

Mama Bassetti's face paled. She must have realized how poor her timing was. "Listen to me going on! *Bocca grande!*" She rolled her big brown eyes dramatically. "How is my son doing this morning?"

114

"You can go in for a few minutes," the nurse, who obviously had not missed a word, smiled at Jack's mother.

Sitting on an uncomfortable vinyl chair, making a charade of paging through a tattered *New Yorker*. Kate thought she heard her mother-in-law crooning a lullaby. If anything will wake him up, that will, she thought.

Deep in her own musing, Kate jumped when a hand touched her shoulder. The faint musty smell of mothballs accompanied the familiar "Hi, Katie-girl." Gallagher!

She turned, glad he'd dropped by. She wanted to know about the case. How close were they to discovering the perp who had shot Jack, killed his partner, and who was making a habit of raping and murdering harmless old women? Nobody was safe until the bastard was collared.

Gallagher was in full uniform. Although she hadn't spotted him in the crowd, he must have been at Bill Jordon's funeral, too.

"How's the old boy doing?" Gallagher asked gruffly and motioned toward the cubicle.

As if to answer, a teary Mrs. Bassetti bolted through the door from the intensive care unit. "His eyelids trembled," she said. "For a minute, I thought he was going to open them.

"Just like him!" Tears ran down her cheeks. "Even when he was a baby, whenever I tried to sing him to sleep, just when I thought I'd done it, Jackie would open those big brown eyes of his and look at me like he'd played a good joke.

"Then I wanted to shake him. Now I'd give anything." Without finishing, she crumpled into a chair across from Kate and Gallagher.

The three waited in a sad silence until the nurse told them it was all right to visit Jack again.

Clutching the bed rail, Kate leaned close to her husband's ear. "You'd do anything to stop her singing, wouldn't you, pal?" she whispered and studied his pale face.

Was it her imagination, or did his lower lip twitch. Was he going to smile, or was it like a baby's smile—nothing but a gas bubble? She stared at him, but there was no more movement.

"Denny's outside," Kate said. Not knowing how much Jack understood, she decided not to tell him that Denny had just come from Bill Jordon's funeral. Instead she said, "He's in his dress uniform. You should wake up just to see that. Poor guy's got to retire soon or get a new one. The thing barely fits!" Kate babbled on, hoping her words or, at least, the tone of her voice would reach the deep recesses of his mind and bring him back.

After her ten minutes, Kate returned to the chair beside her partner. "How are you coming on the case?" she asked, wishing, in one sense, that she could be on it with him.

"Slow, but steady," Gallagher unbuttoned his snug uniform jacket and exhaled in relief. "Got ourselves a list of possible perps."

"Anyone promising?"

"We won't know until we start really looking."

"Who's on it with you?"

"O'Connor. Right now, he's back at the detail making a few follow-up calls. When I get back, depending on what he's uncovered, we'll start making house calls."

116

"Wish I could could help, Denny," Kate squeezed his cold hand.

"Geez, Katie-girl, you sound just like those two goddamn nuns!"

"What do you mean?"

"Those two were at the Hall this morning, bright and early, with rolls and jam, saying exactly the same thing."

"And?"

"And I told them the best thing they could do was pray—pray for a miracle." He shrugged. "Hey! Maybe if Jack's eyelids did tremble, they finally did what I told them."

And maybe pigs will fly, Kate thought, giving her partner a reassuring smile. "Let's hope that praying is all they're doing, Denny," she said.

"What the hell do you mean?" Gallagher's face reddened, and his bushy eyebrows met in a frown. "You don't think they'd try anything, do you?"

"Not if you told them not to," Kate tried to sound sincere.

Unfortunately, neither one of them believed her.

The cafeteria at Mount St. Francis College had already stopped serving lunch by the time Sister Mary Helen and Sister Eileen parked the Nova in the convent garage.

"Let's pick up a quick bite," Eileen said, leading the way to the small convent kitchen equipped with just enough food for these kinds of emergencies.

"I wish I'd saved two of those yeast rolls," she mumbled rooting around until she found some semi-fresh Ritz crackers in a cupboard and a slab of Monterey Jack cheese that was only hard on one end in the refrigerator.

Mary Helen had already put on the kettle for tea.

They were just settling down at the small table when Sister Mary Helen heard herself being paged on the loudspeaker. "Please report to your office," the message repeated insistently.

"Shirley must think I was kidnapped by aliens," Mary Helen checked her wristwatch. "I told her I'd be gone about an hour."

"After all this time, don't tell me she still believes you." Eileen began clearing up their snack plates. "Go! I need to report in, too. Let's meet at"—she looked quizzically at Mary Helen—"say, four o'clock?"

"I can be finished by three-thirty," Mary Helen said.

"Where, then?"

"My office. We can close the outside door and tell Shirley we can't be disturbed."

Like spies from an old thriller, Mary Helen and Eileen synchronized their watches before Mary Helen scurried up the hill to the Alumnae Office.

"There you are at last!" Shirley yelped when Mary Helen cracked open the door. "Thank God." She sighed as if Mary Helen had arrived carrying the cure for cancer.

Mary Helen stared at the virtually unflappable Shirley. Not only had her secretary chewed off most of her lipstick, her impeccably styled hair was mussed and she had shed her high heels and was padding around the office in stocking feet.

"What happened?" Mary Helen asked, astonished.

"What didn't?" Shirley sank into a chair. Shutting her eyes, she made large slow circles with her head. "First of all, the chairwoman of the decorations committee is having a full-scale war with the chairwoman of the Christmas tree committee. The banquet chairwoman is hysterical because we have not firmed up the numbers. The rental company did not receive our deposit check from the college accounting office. The program chairwoman needs the names of the big donors, who are?" She looked accusingly at Sister Mary Helen. "Those are just the major problems. And, of course, everyone is devastated about Gemma Burke's death. The phone has been ringing all day."

At least I was working on that, Mary Helen thought, sitting down to face her phone. Closing her office door, she called until both her ears ached and her index finger was numb from tapping on the number pad.

She was relieved when Shirley knocked and announced, "Sister Eileen is here for her three-thirty appointment."

Thank goodness! One look at her secretary told her that things were back on an even keel. Shirley's lips were a glossy fuchsia and both her shoes were back on her feet.

"Thanks, Shirley," Eileen said as the door closed behind her.

"You look as if you could use this." Eileen put down two Styrofoam cups of steaming coffee.

Sister Mary Helen took a long swallow and savored the warm, comforting flavor. "How was your afternoon?" she asked at last.

"Quiet. But then, libraries usually are. And you know, old dear, despite my initial misgivings, I think you really did the right thing, talking to Angelica Bowers."

Mary Helen raised her eyebrows. "Oh?"

"She's like a new person." Eileen reconsidered. "Well, an improved old person, anyway. She didn't seem as grumpy as usual and when I spoke to her, she almost smiled.

"But now, down to business." She shoved a sheet of paper across the desk to Mary Helen. On it was typed:

1. Mervin Smythe
2. Joseph Mitchell
3. Arturo Dunworthy aka Alan Dunner aka Albert Duvall
4. Elvis Greenwood
5. Humberto Lopez aka Bert the Squirt

Marveling anew at Eileen's phenomenal memory, Mary Helen reread the list.

"What do we do next?" Eileen asked brightly, as if Mary Helen should know.

"The phone book," Mary Helen said, sucking her sore index finger. It was the only idea that came to her. "We can begin by checking if any of these names have addresses close to Sea Cliff."

Eileen's gray eyes lit up. "Brilliant! What's that advertisement on the television? There's nothing you can't find in the phone book. Something like that."

I don't think they meant murderers and rapists, Mary Helen thought, but Eileen looked so enthusiastic that she didn't say anything.

For the next two hours, the nuns searched the San Francisco telephone directory. There was an amazingly short list of Smythes. No Mervin Smythe. One M with no address, and that line was disconnected.

Even the business section was Smythe-less, except for Smythe and Son. A phone call revealed that Father Smythe had gone to God. Son was retired, and granddaughter Smythe ran the repair shop. She never heard of anyone named Mervin.

Two and one-half columns of Mitchells yielded only one Joseph M., one Joe, ten Js, four of whom included a second initial, hoping, no doubt, that it would clear up their identity. Most Mitchells did not list their home addresses. The ones that did were primarily in the Bay View–Hunters Point area, a city—some would say a world—away from Sea Cliff. The Mitchells produced no leads at all.

Alberto Dunworthy, even with two aliases, nearly came up a blank. The only Dunworthy listed was Judith, who claimed not to know any Albertos, Alans, or Alfreds.

No Dunner, Alan. Actually, no Dunners were listed at all, except in the business section. Alfred Dunner, manufacturer of women's sportswear. He didn't seem like a very likely suspect.

With Duvall, they hit pay dirt. Mary Helen's heart was thumping when a young woman at Duvall's Studio Club answered the phone with a hard, sharp, "Hello."

"Yeah," she knew Albert. He was her husband, the no-good lying bum. Yes, she knew where they could find him, not that she could imagine why anybody would want to. He was

121

in Vacaville Prison. He'd been there for three months. She had had him picked up for rape, but not before he had blackened both her eyes and stolen her money.

"By the way," the woman asked finally, "who the hell are you?"

The only Greenwood listed was not Elvis, but Tillie. Her address was on the Avenues, but no one answered when they rang.

The listings for Lopez were only slightly shorter than the listings for Fong in the San Francisco phone book. Mary Helen was so intent on searching it that she waved absently when Shirley popped her head in the office to say, "good night."

The listings yielded two H. Lopezes. Both swore at her in Spanish when she asked if they were, by any chance, "Bert, the Squirt."

A third listing was B & R Lopez. She tried B for Bertie. They turned out to be a pest-control firm, way out on Alemany Boulevard.

"Well, that was a waste of time," Mary Helen placed the telephone receiver in its cradle.

"Not really!" Ever the optimist, Eileen crossed Albert Duvall and his aliases off the list. "We know he's positively not guilty.

"The disconnected phone could belong to Mervin. Just because you didn't pay your phone bill doesn't mean you necessarily moved. And Mitchell could have access to a car. Tillie Greenwood might answer tomorrow and just because a person owns a pest-control company, doesn't mean he can't also be a criminal. Maybe he likes to kill things.

"Anyway"—she rose and stretched—"you look worn out. Let's call it a day and start fresh in the morning." She checked the big electric clock on Mary Helen's office wall. "We don't want to miss dinner, too. Ramon is making party pork chops, and I'm starving."

The very mention of the thick, succulent chops baking in the chef's special sauce of onions and lemon and brown sugar made Mary Helen realize how long it had been since she'd eaten breakfast.

The dinner hour was the most difficult part of the day for Angelica Bowers. Work had actually been fun, especially after she'd imitated Mrs. Kenny.

Angelica enjoyed thinking about the head librarian's face flushing and her small spotted hand flying up to her mouth. Unless Angelica was mistaken, Mrs. Kenny had looked at her and even spoken to her with a new sense of respect and deference. It must be contagious. For some reason, the students had been more polite when they asked for her help. Even Sister Eileen seemed more pleasant than usual.

"What's going on?" Mama asked, her hard eyes narrow, when Angelica finally labored up the narrow staircase with her dinner tray.

"Going on?" Angelica tried to keep her voice steady. "For goodness' sake, Mama, nothing is going on. What makes you think something is going on?" Angelica wished she'd just said, "Nothing," and stopped there.

"I don't know." Mama clutched and unclutched the handle of her cane. "You're acting...I can't put my finger on it." She stuck out one long pointed nail.

Angelica willed her voice not to shake. "Acting

how?" She balanced the heavy tray on the edge of the bed.

"Different." Mama paused while her mean little eyes studied Angelica's face, peering through her forehead and into her thoughts. Angelica tried to make her mind blank.

"You seem more nervous, or restless, or something," Mama said finally. "I don't know. Just different. Is something bothering my angel? Something you want to tell Mama about?" One bony hand reached toward Angelica.

"Is something or someone upsetting you?" Mama asked softly, then rubbed her brittle fingers across Angelica's cheek. Grabbing a large pinch of soft flesh, she twisted it until Angelica winced. "Is there anything you want to talk to me about?" Mama repeated.

"No." Angelica said quickly. "No, thank you." She must remember her manners. The backs of her knees and her armpits were damp again. A vise squeezed her forehead.

"What makes you think something is bothering me?" Angelica pressed, hoping her mother would give her a hint so she could be more clever, more secretive.

"I can't put my finger on it." Mama released Angelica's cheek and shook her head. The long gray hair barely moved over her shoulders. "You just seem different."

"You said that already, Mama. But how?"

Suddenly interested in her dinner, Mama shrugged and smoothed the bedclothes covering her lap. She arranged a towel over them so that Angelica could set down the tray.

Steadying her small rare steak with her fork,

Mama cut into it. Angelica watched the bloody juice ooze over the plate and into the potatoes. She watched it seep under the green beans.

Soon the sharp teeth of the poodles will cut into Mama, Angelica fantasized, and her juices will run bright red over her freshly laundered nightgown.

"You were later than usual tonight." Mama mopped up her plate with a corner of her French bread. "What happened?"

"The library was crowded," Angelica answered too quickly. She wondered frantically if Mama had heard her shove the American Institute of Fitness brochure and her airplane tickets under her mattress.

"Crowded on a rainy Wednesday afternoon?" Mama stopped, her bread poised midway to her mouth. "Why was it crowded today?"

Angelica shrugged and wiped her palms with the corner of her apron. "I guess a lot of students have papers due," Angelica muttered. Then, ducking her head, she busied herself straightening an imaginary wrinkle at the foot of her mother's bed. She hoped the flush she felt spreading up her cheeks didn't give her away.

"That isn't your job," Mama said, her mouth full of bread. "It's just like those nuns to take advantage of someone who can't stick up for herself." She stopped long enough to swallow. "And the dogs. Have you noticed? Something seems to be wrong with them, too." Mama sipped some water.

Angelica's knees felt weak and she sank into the chair beside Mama's bed. "I haven't noticed," she said, hardly able to catch her breath.

"They're snappish. They can't seem to settle down. And they're making a lot of noise. Do you hear them."

Angelica made a pretense of trying to listen, but it was difficult not to hear the fierce sharp barks floating up from the backyard.

"The paperboy will be here any minute, and since he complained, I decided to lock them in the backyard." Angelica willed her voice to stay even. "They're just spoiled."

Mama chuckled. "I guess all my babies are spoiled." She pushed her tray aside. She pulled her rouge pink satin bed jacket over her shoulders. Without checking the *TV Guide*, she pushed the remote control for the television set. A game show roared into action.

With one hand, she grabbed Angelica's forearm. Her bony fingers dug into the freckled flesh. "I guess a person's imagination works overtime when they're alone most of the time." She coughed pathetically and looked at Angelica with her "cow eyes." Angelica wanted to laugh aloud whenever her mother put on that big innocent-victim stare since, no matter how hard she tried, the glint of cruelty never quite left Mama's real eyes. Was it that "coal that comes hissing hot from hell," that Uncle Frank had told her about? Was that what Angelica always saw in Mama's eyes?

"It isn't easy to be bedridden." Mama sighed and coughed again. "I hope it never happens to you, Angel."

Angelica's legs felt like cooked noodles as she carried Mama's dinner tray down the narrow staircase. Two more days, she reminded herself; only two more days until Friday. Then she would fly away to Utah, where she would sit on one of those magnificent red rocks and gaze with the thin girl on the brochure at a brilliant blue cloudless sky.

The lunge of Salt's heavy body against the back door brought her up short. Perspiration formed on her upper lip. She must let Salt and Pepper in. Mama might get suspicious if her "babies" didn't go upstairs to say "good night."

Before she did, Angelica cleared the stove, the table, and the sink. She swept up every crumb from the floor. The poodles must not be able to find anything to eat.

At bedtime, Angelica had a difficult time putting the two dogs back outside. Despite the sleeping pills Angelica had dissolved in their water bowls, the pair circled the kitchen sniffing, growling, jumping up, snapping at her and at one another.

I'd better increase the dosage, Angelica thought, grabbing the broom from the closet. "Out! Out! Get out!" she hissed, swinging the broom handle at the dogs, forcing them toward the back door. Teeth bared, a low, angry growl rattled deep in Pepper's throat as the dog backed away.

"Get out!" Angelica swung the broom a second, then a third time. The dogs snapped at the broom handle. Salt's dark eyes glared at Angelica with loathing. She kicked at the dog's head, but missed. Gasping for breath, she finally forced both animals outside and, slamming the back door, leaned heavily against it.

With savage barks, the thick bodies thudded and banged against the wooden door as though they might break through it.

"What's all the racket?" Mama's voice rose above the din.

"There must be a cat in our backyard." Angelica was pleased that she had thought of an answer so quickly.

"It sounds like they're ready to eat it," Mama complained.

Sounds as if they're ready to eat just about anything, Angelica thought. Stifling a giggle, she sat down to her own dinner.

For some reason, this evening the drive from St. Mary's Medical Center out Geary Boulevard to her home seemed longer than usual to Kate Murphy.

Maybe it was because the six o'clock traffic had turned the wide street into a virtual parking lot. Or maybe it was the unrelenting rain which made it difficult to see even the car ahead of you, or the fact that Kate seemed to hit every stoplight along the way. Whatever the reason, the minutes dragged by.

The windshield wipers beat a steady, friendly rhythm trying to clear her view. "Cheer up. Cheer up," they repeated over and over.

Kate's shoulders slumped as she waited at the corner of 25th and Geary for the light to change. Closing her burning eyes, she realized just how tired she was.

Tension alone had kept her alert all day, waiting for some sign of improvement in Jack's condition. Now her shoulders and neck ached.

When the doctor finally did come by in the late afternoon, he had been optimistic.

"Vital signs are good," he said in his best

Marcus Welby voice, "and under the circumstances, Kate, Jack is doing very well."

What does that mean? Kate wanted to shout, but didn't. None of this was the doctor's fault. The poor guy was doing the best he could. He was only human. What Jack needed was a first-class miracle.

The impatient toot-toot of a horn behind her reminded Kate that the light had changed. Moving slowly across the intersection, avoiding a group of sauntering teenagers who felt the lights were not for them, Kate hoped that the nuns were praying for a miracle. Miracles were their stock in trade. She hoped just as fervently that her partner, Dennis Gallagher, had grabbed onto a good solid lead.

When Kate had talked to him earlier in the day, he was going slowly, methodically through the known felons in the area. He had made a list of all those who had been convicted of— or even arrested for—sex crimes. The list was short and, of course, did not necessarily contain the killer's name; still, it was a start.

All day Denny had been calling, talking to neighbors, following each and every lead doggedly and thoroughly. This was the way good police work was done. Kate knew that, despite the fact that she often wished homicides were solved as quickly and easily as they were on the television cop shows: The murderer was caught and booked in sixty minutes, minus commercial breaks.

When Kate last talked to her partner on the telephone, Gallagher was back at the Hall of Justice and had not yet come up with anything solid.

"A couple of things are needling me, though," he confided to Kate.

Her heart quickened. "Such as?"

"Rapists don't usually kill their victims, unless there's a reason."

"Right," Kate agreed.

"So either this guy was known by these old ladies, or they saw him and could finger him later, or maybe he has some identifying feature—"

"Like what?"

"Who knows. A deformed hand, or a tattoo, or some distinguishing physical factor like a limp." Gallagher let out a deep breath. "Or he could just be a plain psycho who murders for the hell of it."

"What about them all recognizing him? What could he do that all his victims would use?" Kate asked with the part of her which was aching to track down and stop this perp. "Did they use the same gardener? He could be on the crew. A delivery boy from the grocery store? Or the drugstore? Did he work at the cleaners? Was he a rug shampooer?" She searched her tired mind. "What else do elderly women use? A hairdresser?"

When Gallagher didn't answer, Kate went on. "You said a couple of things were bothering you. What else?"

Gallagher hesitated. "Maybe it's just a coincidence, but the perp got into all these homes through an unlocked window. And it was the only unlatched window in the place."

He lowered his voice. "Wouldn't you think that an old lady who lives alone would check all her windows before she went to bed? Especially once she knew there was a rapist loose in the neighborhood?"

"You'd think so," Kate agreed. "Do you suspect someone like a window washer might have left one open on purpose?"

"I don't know, but it's worth a look. How's Jack?" Gallagher seemed eager to change the subject.

Kate knew her partner was superstitious about his intuitions. He was afraid that if he voiced them, they would somehow dissipate into the air.

"Jack is holding his own." Kate tried to sound positive. "I think his color is a little better today, although that might be just wishful thinking."

Mercifully, Gallagher did not comment. "Maybe tomorrow he'll be able to tell us something," he said.

"Maybe," Kate agreed, refusing to add, "and maybe not."

The traffic was thinning out by the time Kate passed George Washington High School. Absently, she noted that the shrubbery on the Geary Boulevard side of the campus badly needed a trim. It was probably too wet for the gardeners to work.

She checked her wristwatch. By now her mother-in-law had picked up little John from the baby-sitter and was at home with the heat and lights on.

Tonight Kate was glad for Loretta's company. She dreaded going into the cold, dark house. It was bad enough on a normal day, when she knew Jack and the baby would be there soon. But now!

Her throat filled and her eyes stung. For a moment, she was afraid she wouldn't be able to breathe around that lump of sadness that was forming.

When she drove past 34th Avenue a line of

131

customers was already queuing up outside The Pacific Café, waiting to be seated for a fish dinner. Making a somewhat-illegal U-turn at the corner, Kate parked in the one spot left in front of her house. At least something went right.

The lights from her living-room windows glowed out and across the wet sidewalk like sparkling fairy paths leading to an enchanted cottage. In the lower right-hand corner of one rain-streaked window, she spotted a small curly blond head, two big brown eyes and a pug nose pressed against the pane.

Little John was home, all right, waiting at his favorite lookout, waiting expectantly for her and for his father to come home.

Kate's heart dipped like a ship in a stormy sea. Unexpected tears rushed to her eyes. At least my baby's father will come home eventually, she thought. The lonely picture of Liz Jordon clutching her daughter loomed in Kate's mind. Anger bubbled up inside her. How dared anyone kill another human being so callously? And cause so much sorrow!

Despite all the theories and sad circumstances—which she knew well—that made some men rapists, at the moment Kate Murphy felt no sympathy. All she felt was loathing.

Someone, she raged, dashing across the wet sidewalk, someone must stop the bastard. And soon!

A few minutes after nine, Sister Eileen led the last trump card, and Sister Mary Helen added the score quickly.

"Our game," she said, pushing back from the card table. "That's enough pinochle for me."

She stifled a yawn. "I think I'm ready to call it a night."

Sister Cecilia, the college president, nodded in agreement, but her partner, Sister Anne, groaned. "You two can't quit while you're ahead," the young nun complained.

"That's the time to quit," Cecilia commented wisely, leaving Mary Helen to wonder if there was a hidden meaning.

"It's been a busy day altogether," Eileen began chattily, "what with Gemma Burke—"

Mary Helen kicked Eileen's leg, but it was too late. She knew from the look of horror on Cecilia's long, thin face that the damage was clearly done.

Cecilia peered over her rimless glasses. Whoever the wag was who said the woman had a face like a frosty morning must have seen this expression, Mary Helen thought.

"I surely hope," Cecilia whispered dangerously, "that neither of you will become involved in that sordid—"

While she searched for a dignified way to say "rape-murder," Eileen jumped in. "How can we not get involved?" Her gray eyes stared accusingly at Cecilia. "Gemma Burke was an alumna, a generous supporter of this college, and a good friend!"

Cecilia's face colored. "You know very well that I didn't mean that kind of 'involved,'" she said, each word cut and crisp. "What I mean is that you aren't going to become involved with the police and do something dangerous that will end up on the front page of the *Chronicle*, are you?"

She turned her powerful gaze on Mary Helen

who, luckily, had just helped herself to a handful of See's bridge mix. No one—especially not Cecilia—expected her to answer with a mouthful of chocolate and nuts.

Uncomfortable silence covered the card table. Sister Anne fidgeted while Eileen worked at getting the pinochle deck back into its box. In the distance, an aging movie star touted the advantages of Sprint long-distance telephone service. Why doesn't the blasted thing ever ring when you need it, Mary Helen thought.

Cecilia's eyes were now an icy blue. "After that last affair at the priests' retreat, I thought we had a clear understanding."

Still chewing, Mary Helen returned the stare. What is clearly understood by one party is not necessarily clear to all parties, she wanted to say, but thought better of it. What was that old saying of Eileen's? "Don't let your tongue cut your throat!"

Satisfied that she had made her point, Sister Cecilia rose with presidential solemnity from the table and excused herself.

"Poor loser," Anne quipped nervously when the college president was clearly out of earshot.

After taking a hot bath, Mary Helen read a few chapters of the latest Dick Francis mystery, which was almost too thick for her prayer-book cover. Despite the book's tension, she was scarcely able to keep her eyes open. She reached over, snapped off the bed lamp, and snuggled into her pillow, confident that she'd fall asleep immediately.

A deep night silence hung over the convent. Outside, the rain had stopped, but water still dripped from the rain gutter and from the leaves of the eucalyptus trees. In the distance, tires swished on wet pavement. A cat yowled.

The events of the day crowded in on Mary Helen's sleepy mind—dear Gemma and the fruitless trip to her home, the meeting with Gallagher, the Christmas Tree Extravaganza, the series of phone calls leading nowhere.

And finally, Sister Cecilia's clear injunction so directly opposed to the strong call Mary Helen felt to become involved. Is that what was keeping her awake, or was it Ramon's party pork chops?

Her mind drifted back to the morning Mass, Feast of St. Charles Borromeo. Now there was a young man who was really up against it! He became Cardinal of Milan at twenty-five and felt a strong call to reform the medieval clergy, which he began with dispatch. Battling both the plague and the Medici family, he plugged away and managed to pull off the famous Counter-Reformation council, the Council of Trent.

There's opposition for you, Mary Helen mused, not surprised that he had died at forty-six. She really did wonder if it had been from natural causes, as her "Saint for the Day" book claimed. Next to St. Charles's opponents, Cecilia seemed almost an ally!

"You have not chosen me; I have chosen you," this morning's communion antiphon declared. Mary Helen drew in a deep breath, reflecting for a moment on Jesus's words, so applicable to St. Charles. She searched for their meaning in her own life.

Your words are true for all of us, Lord, she

prayed with a new sense of peace, no matter what we may be chosen to do. And what was the end of that antiphon? "Go forth and bear fruit that will last."

Tomorrow, she hoped fervently, her efforts would bear some fruit, or at least offer a small fragile bud of truth on the heinous murder of Gemma Burke.

Thursday, November 5
Feast of St. Zachary and St. Elizabeth,
Parents of St. John the Baptist

Right after breakfast, Sister Mary Helen headed for the alumnae office. For once she wanted to arrive before Shirley did. She hoped the shock would not be too much for either of them.

She made her way slowly across the nearly deserted campus, passing only two students on her way. Both were so bundled up in jackets and scarves and woolen caps that it was difficult to tell who they were.

Mary Helen was glad that she had worn her heavy Aran sweater and remembered to bring a woolen scarf. She pulled it up around her ears.

The rain had stopped and the wind, hurling clouds across the sky, made rolling shadows on the asphalt. Small puddles filled the potholes.

It felt good to stretch. Mary Helen took a deep breath. The air smelled of wet earth. A bold blue jay with a large acorn in its beak perched on the edge of an overflowing bird-bath. Cocking his eye first at Mary Helen and then at the plaster statue of St. Francis, he dared either of of them to challenge him. Chrysanthemums bordering the driveway were full with tight blossoms of gold and white and grape purple.

In the distance, beyond the spires of St. Ignatius Church, Sutro Tower rose like an immense orange and white cocktail pick stuck atop Mount Sutro in a base of parsley-size trees.

The three top spikes of the controversial landmark were hidden by ragged black clouds. To her left, a band of gray fog blotted out the East Bay hills.

Mary Helen's breath formed little white puffs and she rubbed her cold hands together. Grasping the ornate handle of the heavy front door, she pulled it open.

Inside, the college building was still dark and chilly despite the comforting hiss of the steam heat. She made her way down the narrow concrete steps to her basement office.

The basement, once a storage area, now housed not only the alumnae office, but the campus-ministry office, the athletic department, the communication center, the development office, and all other departments which had emerged since the college was built in the 1930s.

Although the administration had done its best, no amount of renovation and interior design was able to disguise the cold, dark fact that it was still a basement.

A web of shadows grew out from the corner. Mary Helen switched on the lights and a stark white fluorescent glare filled the empty hallway.

The sweet fragrance of sandalwood escaping from under Sister Anne's campus-ministry door mingled with the acrid stench of gym socks, damp towels and the sharp antiseptic smell of janitors' Lysol.

Locked in overnight, the odors, were much more pungent than they would be during the day, when the hallway was filled with laughing, bustling students.

It was funny about odors, Mary Helen mused, closing the office door behind her. The light gentle smell of lavender always reminded her of Gemma or of Eileen, while the scent of roses brought Cecilia instantly to mind.

Already the light on the answering machine is flashing, Mary Helen thought, glad she rarely came in early. Much to her surprise, Shirley arrived right on her heels.

The two of them stood together listening to the sad, yet controlled, voice of Gemma Burke's oldest daughter telling them that her mother's funeral—both the wake and the Mass—would be held that night at St. Monica's Church at seven o'clock. The burial service at Holy Cross Cemetery on Friday morning was to be for family members only.

"Isn't that unusual?" Shirley asked. "Isn't the rosary always at night and the Mass on the morning of the burial?"

"It's getting more and more common to combine the two and have them in the evening," Mary Helen explained. "It's easier on friends, especially those who work, and certainly on the family members."

Satisfied, Shirley went to make a pot of coffee and Mary Helen called Eileen in the library to tell her about Gemma's arrangements which

Eileen had already read in the *Chronicle* obituary column.

"Are we still on for one o'clock?" Eileen asked furtively.

"Of course," Mary Helen said. "I feel sure I can get this Christmas-tree business completely done by then."

"And, as planned, we'll work this afternoon on the project?" Eileen asked.

"The project?" For a minute Mary Helen was taken aback. "Is someone listening?" she whispered.

"Yes, Sister," she trilled.

"Mrs. Kenny?"

"No, Sister."

"Then who?" Mary Helen detested guessing games. Mentally, she ran through the names of the library staff. The only person, besides Mrs. Kenny, who might logically be near the phone was Angelica Bowers. But Angelica always just beat the bell. "Not Angelica?"

"Yes, indeed, and you don't know the half of it!" Eileen chirped.

Mary Helen didn't have the time to chew on Eileen's comments. As soon as she hung up the receiver, she went ahead, full throttle, diving into lists, approving menus, reviewing plans, making at least a dozen telephone calls, checking and rechecking the details of every aspect of the Christmas event.

In fact, at ten-thirty, it was Shirley who suggested that they call it quits for twenty minutes and take a well-deserved coffee break.

On Thursday morning, Tillie Greenwood slept in. Actually she wasn't really asleep. She had dozed on and off, but for the most part, she lay in her bed with her eyes closed and the covers pulled up over her ears.

During the night the rain had stopped, but water still dripped from the gutters. The morning was dark and the wind howled around the corners of the house like a portent of disaster.

Tillie shivered and tugged the bedcovers tighter. The heater roared on. Elvis must be up, poor baby, and freezing to death, she thought from her cocoon of covers.

Tillie could hear her mother's voice. "Why, any good mother would be up by now and have the house warm and her child's hot breakfast made, instead of lollygagging in bed like a lazy good-for-nothing, weak-willed, ne'er-do-well, irresponsible nitwit, poor excuse for a mother." She could see the look of contempt on her mother's face, feel the prickle of her own shame.

Slowly, as she had done so often before to silence the nagging, strident litany, Tillie put one foot on the cold bedroom floor and forced herself into a sitting position.

For a moment, she felt queasy. Was it the wine? She and Elvis had had such a nice dinner last night—steak, baked potatoes, Caesar salad, which Elvis didn't even realize was a vegetable. Tillie felt it needed red wine, so she had bought a bottle of merlot, and they had finished it. There was no point in leaving a few inches in the bottle to go to waste, now was there?

They had not talked much during the meal, but Elvis had eaten everything. Tillie was thrilled when he ate so well. She was so delighted, in fact, that she ignored it when he flicked his cigarette ashes onto the dinner plate and then ground out the butt on it.

There was nothing like a good meal to raise a person's spirits, her mother always said, and for once Tillie agreed with her.

Poor Elvis certainly needed his spirits raised. When she had returned from grocery shopping yesterday afternoon, Tillie still felt the tension in the house even after his nap. A large serving of apple pie a la mode had failed to dispel it completely, although they had watched a re-run of *Roseanne* in companionable silence.

Mother would have made short work of Roseanne's sassy youngsters, Tillie had wanted to remark, but she knew better. She never mentioned his grandmother to Elvis. Tillie hoped that someday he'd appreciate her and all she'd done for them.

"Good morning, sweetheart," Tillie called cheerfully when she reached the breakfast nook.

Barefooted and wearing only his old, ill-fitting flannel bathrobe, Elvis was crouched in a chair near the heating vent. "Good morning, Mommy," he mumbled without looking up.

Tillie felt that familiar surge of love. She crossed the small room and ran her fingers through his tousled hair. Such a nice thick head of hair, she thought, placing a kiss on the top of his head. Elvis smelled faintly musty, as if he—or at least the basement room—should be aired out.

"Where are your slippers, sweetheart?" she asked and saw his tattoo ripple as the muscles in his arms tensed. Tillie's stomach roiled. She must not nag. Elvis hated her to nag. And, who could blame him? Everyone hated to be nagged. She did herself.

With one finger, Tillie lifted up her son's chin. He was badly in need of a shave. After all, it had been two days since he had one, but now was not the time to bring that up.

At first Elvis refused to look at her. For an uncomfortable moment, she thought he might pull away.

"Mommy's sorry for being an old nag, sweetheart," she said softly and kissed the tip of his nose. It was cold. "How did you sleep last night with all that wind? Were you warm enough down there in that old room?"

She wished he'd move upstairs to the vacant room across from her bedroom, but she knew better than to mention it. Elvis wanted his privacy, and who could blame him? What grown man wants his mother knowing every move he makes?

Tillie studied her son's long, thin face. Circles like bruises ringed his velvet brown eyes, which had a vacant look as if his mind were miles and miles away. What in the world was he brooding about? Tillie wondered, but knew better than to ask. His mouth—such a pretty mouth, Tillie thought—almost like a girl's, drooped down at the edges.

"Why so glum, chum?" she joked, hoping to cheer him up, but his nostrils flared and he pulled away from her.

Knowing better than to continue, Tillie padded into the dining room to the birdcage and removed the night drape from Mr. Cheeps. In a few minutes, the little canary would be hopping around, warbling, brightening up the mood.

Opening the front door, Tillie retrieved the *Chronicle* from the top step. She must give that new paperboy a good tip for getting it so close to the door on these wet, cold mornings. What a nice little boy he was. His mother must be very proud!

On her way down the entry hall, Tillie caught a glimpse of herself in the old wall mirror. What a sight! Her hair was all standing up on end as if she'd been shocked. She ran her fingers through it examining the gray roots which were quickly invading the copper rinse. She needed a touch up soon. Maybe she'd make a appointment with Lynette, her hairdresser. Going to Lynette always gave her a boost.

Tillie heard the chair scrape back. The refrigerator door opened and closed, followed by the familiar pop of the tab on a beer can. She checked her watch. It was only ten o'clock in the morning. She wished Elvis would at least wait until afternoon before he started.

"No self-respecting person drinks before four in the afternoon," Mother always said.

"It's four o'clock somewhere!" Tillie's husband used to answer while Mother seethed. Tillie smiled. For all his faults, Elvis's father was such a card. It was too bad he'd left them so soon.

Slowly, she removed the plastic sleeve protecting the *Chronicle* from the rain and opened the paper. She'd stall here in the entryway until Elvis had finished his beer. There was no sense making a scene so early in the morning, especially when Elvis was so close to falling into one of his sulky moods.

Tillie had seen and felt the results of Elvis's sulks. She knew that no good could come from starting something at ten o'clock in the morning. If she walked into the breakfast nook now, even if she didn't actually say anything, he might look at her face and think she disapproved.

Poor Elvis was so sensitive to her face. He always had been that way, ever since he was a baby. Even then, if Tillie frowned and said, "No, no," ever so gently, his little lips would turn down and big tears would roll down his sweet face. It broke her heart.

"Spoiled rotten," Mother had said when she had taken them in. And Tillie was too desperate and too grateful to argue.

Tillie glanced at the newspaper. This morning, like yesterday morning, the headlines screamed up at her about the Sea Cliff rapist and his victims.

Reading it again, Tillie's heart froze with a new thought. They were all widows, living alone, just as she was. Sea Cliff was not many blocks away. What if this rapist decided for some reason to move out of the neighborhood? Raw panic washed over her. It could happen to her! Right here in her own home.

Goose pimples ran up her legs and down her arms. Tillie moved over in front of the hall heating vent. The warm air blew up under her chenille bathrobe.

"Mommy?" Elvis called from the kitchen. "Where are you, Mommy?"

She heard him crush his beer can and drop it into the trash can in the cupboard under the sink.

"Coming, sweetheart," she called cheerfully, giving her hair a final pat. "You must be starving."

Tillie refolded the newspaper and left it on

the hall table. There would be plenty of news about the Sea Cliff rapist on the radio and television. There was no point in bringing it into her own kitchen. Elvis was so upset about it the other night that she could not bear to upset him further.

She stopped at the kitchen door. Elvis was back in his chair, as though he'd never left it, huddling near the heater. But now he was smiling.

Tillie's heart swelled. Mr. Cheeps was trilling. If the sun would only come out and shine in their back windows, the house would be the beautiful, tranquil scene she always wanted their life to be.

"Shall I make you a big breakfast," Tillie asked. "Bacon? Eggs? Pancakes?"

When Elvis nodded at each suggestion, Tillie giggled. Unable to help herself, she crossed to him. Bending over, she cupped his cheeks with the palms of her hands and kissed his forehead tenderly. Then, bursting with motherly love, she hugged his face close to her bosom.

Much to her surprise, Elvis nuzzled against her and took a deep breath. "I love that smell," he mumbled.

Tillie felt his warm breath against her flesh. "Do you?"

He nodded. His coarse hair was rough against her skin.

She had no idea that he liked the smell of her lavender. She'd make sure to get some more and wear it every day. "Let me fix your breakfast now, sweetheart," she cooed softly. "You must be starving."

"I am," he said, but instead of pulling back

as she expected, Elvis put his thick arms around her waist. His large hands grabbed at her hips, and he squeezed her until she wondered if he'd ever let go. And he might not have either, she thought later, except that the phone rang.

Kate Murphy was sitting on a lumpy vinyl chair in the waiting room of St. Mary's Medical Center intensive care unit, wishing she'd never given up smoking, when Inspector Dennis Gallagher arrived.

"What are you doing here?" she asked, trying not to sound too glad to see him. "Aren't you supposed to be out solving a homicide?"

"How you doing, Katie-girl?" Gallagher asked with a crooked smile. Clearly he was not put off by her greeting. "I thought you might need some company."

Abandoning any pretense, Kate gave her partner an enormous hug. "Am I glad to see you, Denny!" She forced the words around the now-permanent lump in her throat. "Even though you look awful."

"Geez, Kate, you really know how to hurt a guy." Gallagher ran his palm over his head in an attempt to smooth down his brittle fringe of gray hair. "What's wrong with the way I look?"

"Well, for one thing, your face is gray green. Your eyes, watery blue at the best of times, are red-rimmed with fatigue. Your glasses are clouded with fingerprints. That tie is full of spots, and you need a fresh shirt. All in all, you look like a guy who hasn't had a hot shower, a night's sleep, or a decent meal in days. Wait till your wife sees you!

"Furthermore, you're limping." She watched

him cross to the window of the small room, check the street below, and walk back again. "What happened to your leg?"

"I'm out of shape is all." Gallagher let out a little groan when he sank down next to her on the couch. "I tried to catch a guy on the California Street steps. I bet he's not limping this morning. He sure as hell wasn't limping last night."

"Do you think he was the perp?" Kate's heart quickened.

Gallagher shrugged. "We may never know. I lost him." He stared at a snag in the blue tweed carpet. "Geez, Kate, it's hell to get old."

"It beats the alternative," Kate said.

Wisely, Gallagher changed the subject. "Where's the mother-in-law?"

"The nurse suggested we take turns for a while. It's her turn to be in with Jack." Kate sighed. "It breaks my heart, seeing the way she looks at him. Listening to the way she talks to him." Kate cleared her throat, trying to keep her voice steady. "I was just sitting here wondering how all this happened. One minute everything is normal, and the next..." She extended the pause until she was sure she could go on. "Or maybe I should say I was wondering why it happened."

Gallagher's eyes filled and he scratched his bald pate. "Whys are always mysteries," he said. "Best we can hope to do is to discover who. And that's the other reason I'm here, Kate."

Kate was puzzled. She should have suspected that her partner had more on his mind than keeping her company. She waited for an explanation.

A few large drops hit against the glass and

then, as if a cloud had actually burst, torrents of rain blurred the windowpane. The lights in the waiting room dimmed, but remained on.

"The other reason?" she prodded, when Gallagher did not speak. "Do you suspect who did it?"

"Hell, no! Not even close. To tell you the truth, I can't get a damn thing done down at the Hall of Justice. The place is thick with press. If they could, they'd follow you into the john with those cameras and ask you how things were going. When they couldn't get anything from us downtown, they flocked over to Sea Cliff like a bunch of seagulls."

"Isn't that vultures?"

"Whichever. Anyway, they're parked all over the place with those vans, driving the neighbors crazy. If we didn't have a police guard posted at the bank of elevators, I wouldn't put it past one of them to try to get in here to see you or even Jack!"

Gallagher cleared his throat. He was so hesitant to get to the point that Kate wondered what in the world he was working up to.

"I need someone to knock this case around with," he admitted finally.

"What about O'Connor? Didn't you tell me he's on this with you?"

"I left him up to his ass in reporters and ringing phones." He lowered his voice almost to a whisper. "Besides, Kate, he's not you."

"That's the nicest thing you ever said to me, Denny." Kate was genuinely touched and eager to do something, anything to help catch the maniac who shot her husband.

Gallagher squirmed and loosened his tie.

"Besides, the devil you know is better than the devil you don't," he said gruffly. "Now can we get down to business?"

Without wasting any more time, Kate and Gallagher fell into their well-tested brainstorming routine. They were so intent that even Mama Bassetti passed them without speaking.

"Do we agree that in some way the perp must know all of his victims?" Kate asked. "That there has to be some common denominator? Especially, if he is a serial rapist, as we suspect."

"Agreed." Gallagher said. "We've checked out the victims' gardeners, their hairdressers and manicurists, their doctors, their banks, their stockbrokers, their cleaners. So far only the cleaners match, probably because it's the closest one to Sea Cliff. They didn't even go to the same churches. But we'll keep digging."

"What else do most older women have or use?" Kate wondered aloud.

"A paperboy, a favorite restaurant and, of course, relatives," Mrs. Bassetti said, unable to resist any longer.

"Good ideas!" Gallagher grinned at the older woman, who settled back in her chair, looking extremely pleased with herself.

"And the known sex offenders and rapists in the area? Are you still working on them?" Kate asked.

Gallagher pulled the computer printout from his jacket pocket and spread it on a small magazine table in front of Kate. "If the guy I was chasing was one of these, where did he disappear to? He is either very familiar with all the hiding places on Lincoln Golf Course or he has a friend or relative in the area."

Kate skimmed the list. None of the names were familiar to her, which only proved that none of them had ever been a homicide suspect. That wasn't unusual. Actually, it was unusual for a rapist to commit murder.

"There's got to be a reason," Gallagher said, when she mentioned it. "Fear of recognition or panic."

"Or fear of going back to jail if he's caught," Kate speculated. She glanced again at her partner's list of names. "What have you found out about any of these guys so far?" she asked.

"I spent a good chunk of the morning calling next of kin, girlfriends, known acquaintances. You know, nosing around anywhere I could."

"And what did you come up with?"

"Nothing much, except on this guy." He pointed to Elvis Greenwood's name. "The phone at his apartment was disconnected. When I went over there, the manager said he'd thrown him out because he was months behind on rent. So, I called the next of kin, his mother, who, by the way, lives in the outer Richmond."

"And?" Kate knew better than to get her hopes up. She twisted a piece of her red hair into a tight curl. Having a mother in a neighborhood not far away from Sea Cliff does not necessarily make a man—even a convicted rapist—a murderer.

"The mother says she doesn't know exactly where he is. She hasn't heard from him in a couple of days, but that on the night in question, he had dinner with her and was feeling drowsy afterward. He decided to spend the night, which he did."

Kate studied Gallagher's face. "You look as if you don't believe her. Any reason?"

Gallagher shrugged. "None, except that she offered the alibi before I even asked for it. Almost like she'd been thinking about it or rehearsing it or something."

"It could just be her motherly instinct to protect," Mrs. Bassetti muttered.

Kate had nearly forgotten that her mother-in-law was there. The two detectives gave her their full attention. Mama Bassetti's soft, round face colored. Self-consciously, she pushed a straggly piece of hair off her forehead.

"We all protect our children, especially when we think they're guilty," she explained with her own brand of logic.

"So you're saying that you think he's our perp because his mother made up an alibi?" Kate asked.

"I'm not saying he's guilty." Mama Bassetti's large brown eyes shot open. "How would I know that? All I'm saying, Kate, is that his mother probably thinks he is. Or at least, she thinks he might be."

Kate frowned, and her mother-in-law felt the obligation to explain. "I remember when Jackie was just about two, and one day, out of the blue, he bit another little boy.

"He was my first child, and I didn't know at the time that lots of children bite and that he'd outgrow it. Anyway, the little boy was screaming. The mother was upset. I was so ashamed. I thought I had failed as a mother.

"I did everything it said to do in that Dr. Spock book. I was firm. I put my hand over

151

his mouth. I tried to look firm, but not disapproving.

"When he bit my mother, she swatted his little behind. She had never read Dr. Spock. And, he was cured. At least, I wanted to believe he was.

"One day, I'll never forget it, at Billy Brady's birthday party, I heard one of the kids let out a bloodcurdling scream. 'He bit the birthday boy!' one of the mothers hollered. I was so ready to defend my Jackie, make excuses for him, swear that he was at my side the whole time, that I barely heard her say, 'Tommy bit him.'"

Kate's head was reeling.

"I get your point," Gallagher said, "and it's a good one." He scratched a note in the margin of his printout.

"See the mother in person," Kate read.

A self-conscious smile played on the ends of her mother-in-law's lips. "For whatever it's worth," she said, then checked her wristwatch. "You two must be hungry. While you are talking more, I'll go down and get us some good hot soup. Everybody thinks better with something hot inside."

Mama Bassetti's short staccato footsteps echoed down the polished hospital corridor, and Gallagher's stomach growled in anticipation.

"How long since you've eaten anything decent?" Kate asked.

"A couple of days, but who's counting? What about you?"

"With Mamma Mia for a roommate, I've never been able to have one hungry moment. If anything, by the time Jack wakes up"—a chill ran down her arms—"I'll be so chubby, he won't recognize me. Where were we?"

Gallagher turned his attention back to the printout. "Arturo Dunworthy alias Albert Duvall. When I called Duvall's Studio Club, I had the pleasure of talking to his wife. His soon-to-be ex-wife. She would love to have him guilty of murder, but he's doing a little time in Vacaville at the moment. Unless he's Houdini, that's where he was when all three victims were killed. A funny thing though…"

"Yes?" Kate asked eagerly. Sometimes funny things turned into concrete leads.

"This woman—this Mrs. Yolanda Duvall—acted like she'd had a call like mine before."

"What do you mean?"

"Only that she acted like somebody had already called her about her husband."

"Could it have been O'Connor? Maybe you guys somehow overlapped. It happens."

"That was my first thought. But when I asked her about it, she said it was a woman who called."

"A woman?"

"Yeah. Seems it was an older woman who didn't identify herself or leave a number to call back."

"Strange," Kate said with a sinking feeling.

She watched Gallagher's face tighten like a fist. Obviously, they were both having the same thought.

"She wouldn't," Kate protested with more conviction than she felt.

"The hell she wouldn't!" Gallagher catapulted from the couch. "That nun—no, those *two* nuns—are going to drive me to drink without a cent in my pocket."

"I went into minute detail, explaining just how dangerous it could be," Kate said.

"Like dangling a carrot in front of a horse."

"I *warned* her."

"Water off a duck's back."

"We'll have to stop them before they get themselves or someone else hurt," Kate said, struck with the enormity of the problem that their "do-gooding" might create.

Gallagher yanked the waist of his trousers up to cover his paunch and tucked in his shirttail. "I say arrest 'em," he demanded, so loudly that the nurse in intensive care looked through the small window in the door and frowned in his direction. "Handcuff the two of them together, book 'em, and throw away both keys!"

"Don't you think that's a little extreme, Denny?" Kate said. Secretly, she was not too sure that he hadn't hit on the perfect solution.

Actually, the only thing that stopped him was the arrival of Mama Bassetti carrying a tray with a pyramid of sliced sourdough bread, butter, and three bowls of steaming chicken-noodle soup.

Angelica Bowers spent the full half-hour before her lunch break perusing the yellow pages in the phone book. She noticed Mrs. Kenny giving her a few sour looks, but Angelica simply ignored them. Once she smiled back sweetly, which seemed to rile the head librarian even more than being ignored.

Fortunately, Mrs. Kenny knew better than to say anything to Angelica about getting some work done. Angelica almost wished she would. She was ready for her.

Angelica squirmed in her chair. She loved this new feeling of power. She'd marched into the hushed library early this morning and announced, in a voice loud enough to disturb the handful of students who were at the tables studying, that she was taking the afternoon off for "personal reasons."

"I hope it's nothing serious," Mrs. Kenny had said.

Angelica knew she was only pretending to care. Actually, she was just curious.

"Whatever is wrong is personal. That's why I'm taking time off for personal reasons," Angelica had said, and watched Mrs. Kenny's mouth snap shut like a gigantic turtle's.

Actually, Angelica had decided when she woke up to spend the afternoon shopping for new clothes to take with her to Utah. Before leaving home, she had emptied all the cash from the emergency-grocery-money jar in the kitchen into her purse. Then while Mama and the poodles snoozed, she took Mama's credit card out of the special drawer where she hid it. Now that she was all ready to shop, Angelica wasn't really sure just what she wanted to buy.

The woman pictured in the fitness-center brochure wore slacks and shorts and tank tops. But the photos all seemed to have been taken during the summer. This was November.

Angelica was nearly at the end of the yellow pages when she came upon the heading Western Apparel. In one of the advertisements, she spotted a trim, glamorous woman complete with boots and a cowboy hat. Something in the nonchalant way the woman posed, one hand on her hip, appealed to Angelica.

Utah was the West, wasn't it? Western garb might be perfect. She checked the address. The shop was on Taylor Street near Fisherman's Wharf. Angelica had no idea what buses to take to Fisherman's Wharf.

What should I do? She fought down her panic. How will I get there? The familiar perspiration formed on the back of her neck. One drop trickled down her backbone before she remembered the grocery money. This is an emergency and, besides, Mama will never notice it's gone, she thought, counting out nearly fifty dollars. Pretty soon, poor Mama won't be noticing much of anything at all. Angelica chuckled at her own wit and used the library phone to call for a taxicab.

The cabdriver dropped Angelica in front of Golden Gate Western World and waited impatiently while she doled out his fare and a tip. Her hands were slippery with nervousness. She hoped he wouldn't realize that this was the first time in her adult life that she'd ever taken a cab anywhere.

"Too expensive," Mama always said.

That's over now, Angelica thought, watching the taxi streak away. After this, she'd take cabs whenever she pleased.

Aware of someone standing behind her, Angelica turned slowly and stared into the blank eyes of a life-size wooden Indian chief guarding the entrance.

He smiled at her benignly. At least, Angelica imagined he did until she noticed a tomahawk in his hand. The neon boot and Stetson hat in the front window assured her that she was in the right place. The store itself was long and narrow and stuffed to its high ceiling with merchandise.

Angelica pulled herself up the entrance steps painstakingly and stopped to catch her breath. It had been so long since she'd bought anything in a store, she wasn't sure what size she wore. For several years now, Mama had ordered her clothes from one of those full-figured women's catalogs.

She'd ask one of the salesgirls to help her. Surely they wouldn't mind. But the only one Angelica saw from where she stood was talking on the telephone.

She glanced around the store furtively, trying to get someone's eye. The only eyes she seemed able to catch were the glassy ones set in a hairy buffalo head hanging high on the wall. A price tag dangled jauntily from one of his enormous horns.

Not knowing what else to do, Angelica began to wander down the aisle that stretched from the front to the back of the store. As she moved along, her hips touched the glass showcases on one side and the display of boots on the other. Boots of ostrich hide, elk, and lizard aimed their pointed toes at her. Boot boxes filled every available floor space.

A wall of cowboy hats rose to the ceiling while string ties, bolo ties, the sign said, and beaded belts on hooks swayed as she passed. She edged forward cautiously, careful not to knock anything.

From behind a display rack of cowboy greeting cards, a pale young man with what looked like an earring in his nose popped out. "May I help you?" he asked, his face blending in with the beige of his shirt.

Angelica felt herself flush. "I'm looking for women's clothes," she whispered.

"Women's wear is in the far back," he called out cheerfully.

Angelica cringed.

"Next to the dressing room." He pointed with one thin finger to a cubicle covered by a flimsy burlap curtain.

Even from where she stood, Angelica knew she could never try on clothes comfortably in that cramped space. It was just too small. Everything was too small for her. What had she been thinking? How could she possibly have imagined she could buy clothes at Western World? She belonged in Fat World.

Tears blurred the display of cowgirl blouses with frilly lace at their necks and the ones embroidered with red roses. The bright brass buttons ran together, and the colorful fringe faded.

"Are you finding everything you need?" the pale young man asked.

His voice startled her. Turning away quickly, Angelica wiped her eyes and forced herself to smile.

"There are several beaded jumpsuits on sale over here." He pointed to a rack against the wall.

Next to the "Sale" sign, a black-and-white photograph of a young Dale Evans grinned down at her. She was caressing her horse, Buttermilk, and even the horse seemed to be grinning.

"But, you know, madam, if you don't mind my making a suggestion…"

Angelica's whole body stiffened. It seemed like an eternity before he continued.

"I think you'd look stunning in one of our specialty hats. Would you like to try some on?"

His remark was so unexpected that Angelica didn't even nod. Chatting pleasantly about the rainy weather and its effect on the tourist trade, he guided her to the front of the store.

Carefully, he selected three felt hats from the hundreds of pegs on the wall and placed them, almost reverently, on the glass countertop. One was turquoise with a feather band, one a vibrant purple, and one black and made of the softest wool. He turned the face mirror toward Angelica and watched with interest while she tried on each hat.

"You really have a face for hats," he said when she was trying them on for a second time. "Not everyone does, you know."

Please, please don't spoil it all by saying I have a pretty face, Angelica pleaded silently, and the young man didn't.

"Which one do you think?" she asked timidly.

"I think the purple is lovely with your hair, and the wool is excellent quality. You'll get a lot of pleasure from it, I'm sure."

Without even asking the price, Angelica put the hat on Mama's credit card, forging her name with practiced ease.

"We have some deliciously comfortable moccasins that would be perfect with your new hat," he said. His earring—or was it his nose ring?—Angelica wondered—vibrated slightly when he spoke.

Angelica giggled. She had never heard any-one call shoes "delicious" before. He steered her gently to a long bench along one wall. Angelica's knees were beginning to feel weak. She was glad to sit down.

Her young man—she'd begun to think of him as hers—knelt before her, measured her foot, and brought several pairs of soft leather moc-casins for her to examine. As she slipped her foot into the first one, she felt like Cinderella after the ball. Was he Prince Charming?

The strident voices of a group of German tourists broke the quiet of the shop. "Excuse me"—her young man rose from the floor—"let me just see what these people want, and I'll get right back to you."

Left alone on the bench, Angelica fingered the soft shoes, rubbing the toe of one against her cheek. One pair had an intricate beaded pattern. Another fastened at the ankle with a long, graceful fringe. Closing her eyes, she smelled the leather.

"Do you see something you like?" She hadn't heard her young man come back.

"Which ones do you think?" she asked coyly.

"If they feel comfortable, these seem to be a natural with your new hat." He held up a pair of white leather moccasins with a beaded purple eagle on the instep.

Angelica put the shoes on Mama's credit card. She felt her young man's hand brush hers when he handed her the pen for her signature.

Reluctant to leave Western World, she searched for something else to buy. She noticed a small wooden contraption which looked like

160

a large napkin holder. "What's this?" she asked her young man.

"That's a hat holder," he said. "It would be perfect for your new chapeau. To keep it in shape and all."

The hat holder, a large bandanna with a lone coyote howling in its center, and a scorpion-enclosed-in-plastic paperweight for Mrs. Kenny all went on Mama's credit card.

"Enjoy your purchases," her young man called as Angelica, balancing her bags, stepped back onto Taylor Street.

Crazily, she noticed that the tomahawk she'd thought the wooden Indian at the entrance held was really a peace pipe. Angelica sauntered down the tourist-clogged street, admiring the shop displays as she passed.

She studied ropes of pearls and moons of jade. She watched clothes lines of T-shirts snapping in the wind. She delighted in a life-size wooden bear dressed in a 49er football jersey and helmet. He smiled at her. What bear wouldn't smile if his jersey number was 8? she thought, reluctantly moving past him to make room for a gawking ten-year-old. The number belonged to all-star quarterback Steve Young.

The rain had started again, but somehow it seemed softer. The crowd was thick and their languages and accents mixed, rose and fell, and bumped against her in a symphony of sound. In the distance, the clang of the cable car sounded sweeter.

This must be what love is like, Angelica thought, standing at the corner of Beach Street. She juggled her packages, trying to free one hand. When she did, she raised it and hailed a taxicab.

Avoiding a broken spring, she wedged herself in the backseat. "Home, James," she said. She had always wanted to say that. "Home, James, and don't spare the horse," Angelica giggled.

"What are you, lady, some kind of nut?" the cabdriver snarled and slammed down the meter. "I ain't got time for this. Where do you want to go?"

Meekly, Angelica gave her home address. As the taxi pulled away from the curb, she suddenly felt as crushed and as weighed down as the battered old seat on which she sat.

Sister Mary Helen and Sister Eileen were just finishing lunch when it began to rain again. They scarcely noticed the soft quiet drops tapping like small fingers against the windows of the Sisters' Dining Room.

"Are you ready?" Mary Helen asked, trying to curb her impatience.

The two nuns had decided to eat early in order to avoid the usual crowd and anything else that might delay them from working on their "project," as Eileen called it surreptitiously.

"Ready?" Mary Helen repeated, shoving her bifocals up the bridge of her nose.

Sister Eileen nodded and, quickly gathering up both their dishes, fed them to the conveyor belt making its way steadily toward the dishwasher.

"What's our plan?" Eileen's gray eyes were wide with excitement. Not waiting for an answer, she rushed on. "I had some free time in the library this morning."

"Not many students?" Mary Helen wondered aloud, following her friend out of the dining room.

"About the same number of students as usual for a Thursday morning. It wasn't the students who made the difference, it was the staff. Do you remember when you called me this morning?"

Of course I remember, Mary Helen wanted to growl. I may have lost a decibel or two of hearing, but nothing whatsoever is wrong with my memory. Instead, she simply nodded while Eileen wound her way into her story.

"And, I couldn't speak freely because Angelica was right next to me?"

Mary Helen nodded vigorously, hoping her friend would hurry and get to the good part.

"Well," Eileen paused, her eyes wide, "she was not only next to me, she was everywhere. And talk, talk talk! Actually, she was so out of character that she was making me uneasy. It was almost as if she was a bit manic. Raving about the trip to Utah. I'm not so sure you did her a favor."

Eileen rushed on before Mary Helen could protest. "She talked incessantly about the new clothes she was going to buy for the trip. To tell you the truth, she moved around the office more this morning than she usually does in any given month. Not that she did any real work. Her whole purpose seemed to be to annoy Mrs. Kenny which, for Angelica, isn't difficult. She also spent a great deal of time informing the student aides that she intended to cut her mother's apron strings once and for all. Honestly, Mary Helen, the vehemence with which she said it was almost frightening." Eileen gave a little shudder.

"She proclaimed for all to hear that she intended to begin a new life. To be like a butterfly breaking out of a cocoon."

"Butterfly out of a cocoon?" Mary Helen found it difficult to visualize Angelica in those terms.

Eileen smiled. "Yes, indeed! And that isn't all. She said she would rise from the ashes like a phoenix. She would become the beautiful swan from, of course, the ugly duckling. She was quite enthused and articulate about her expected transformation."

"I hope she won't be too disappointed." Mary Helen moved closer to Eileen to let a harried-looking professor hurry past. "One can hardly expect that much change in a lifetime, let alone ten days," she said, ignoring the ominous feeling elbowing its way into her mind.

"To Angelica's credit, she was pleasant and friendly right up until the moment she left before noon with barely a by-your-leave.

"On the other hand, the whole morning, Mrs. Kenny was uncharacteristically silent. In fact, you could have cut and served the tension around her. I didn't have to be Sherlock Holmes to figure out they'd had some sort of row. And as we say back home, 'Red-hot ashes are easily rekindled,' so I just avoided the fireplace. By staying out of everyone's way, I was able to busy myself digging up information, taking notes which I've stowed away in my office where we can go now, shut the door, and get down to business!"

"What kind of information?" Mary Helen

asked, beginning to feel like Eileen's straight man. Or was it straight person?

The two nuns followed the dimly lit hallway away from the dining room toward the main section of the college building. As they walked, the rhythmic clink, clink of the tiles punctuated Eileen's words.

"I read as much as I could find on serial killers." She turned toward Mary Helen. Her bushy eyebrows arched. "Actually, I read as much as I could stomach. We're dealing with a rare breed, you know."

"Thank God," Mary Helen sighed.

"Statistically, they are one in five million of the overall population. Serial killers are so detached from the concept of guilt and consequences that they become anesthetized to the possibility of getting caught. What makes them so dangerous, of course, is that in most ways, they appear to be just like the rest of us. Some serial killers even take photographs of their work to preserve the moment and save it for future fantasies!"

Mary Helen's stomach roiled at the very thought. "Imagine being the person who develops such a thing!"

"That's how one fellow was caught," Eileen explained. "The killer had his pictures enlarged! Now, if that isn't being detached from reality, I don't know what is!"

"It sounds as if you've had your share of unrealistic behavior this morning, what with your research and Angelica Bowers's antics."

Eileen stopped, her eyes wide. "You can't be putting Angelica Bowers in the same category as some insane killer?"

"Of course, I'm not!" Mary Helen protested, but even as she did, she was aware of an inexplicable, unsettling sense of dread spreading over her like a shadow.

Turning the corner, the two nuns met a small knot of students, head-on. The group smelled faintly of wet wool and muddy sneakers.

Eileen glanced up at the wall clock. "Classes will be over any second." She pointed to a bench positioned against the wall. "Let's sit here out of the way until the stampede is over. Pull in your feet, Mary Helen," she cautioned.

No sooner were they seated than all the classroom doors flew open as if a switch had been thrown. Young women spewed out into the corridor, laughing, talking, rushing, waiting, filling the high-ceilinged hallways with exuberance and life.

Sister Anne appeared, followed by a string of sophomores. "What are you two doing here?" Anne asked, looking surprised to see them. "I thought you'd still be at lunch."

"We ate early," Eileen explained too quickly. "We both have work to do this afternoon."

"What kind of work?" Anne asked. Behind her purple-rimmed glasses, her hazel eyes narrowed suspiciously. She was actually expecting an answer.

"Oh, good, we've run into the work police!" Mary Helen said. She'd heard that line, or something like it, on one of those silly new half-hour sitcoms on television.

Even though it sounded flippant, it seemed far kinder than saying what she wanted to say: "It's really none of your business, Sister, dear."

"Work police! Good one!" Anne said. Then,

with a wave, she hurried on down the hall. "See you two later," she called back over her shoulder.

"She means no harm," Eileen said when the young nun was out of earshot.

"What is it you always say? 'A silent mouth does no harm'?" Mary Helen quoted, hoping to make her point. "Let's give her nothing to let slip, even accidentally."

The Hanna Memorial Library was nearly deserted when the two nuns pulled back the heavy door. Mrs. Kenny was on her lunch break. Angelica Bowers was gone, of course. Only two students remained at the long study tables. At least, that was all that were visible from the doorway.

The steam heat hissed pleasantly, and one of the students appeared to have fallen asleep bundled up in a down jacket. A student aide sat behind the check-out desk.

"We are not to be disturbed unless it's an emergency," Eileen instructed the young woman as they passed.

"Or Shirley," Mary Helen added with a twinge of guilt. With the Christmas Tree Extravaganza only a month away, she did not want to leave her secretary in a lurch.

The top of Sister Eileen's desk was strewn with papers. "My research," she said, offering Mary Helen a comfortable chair.

Eileen plugged in the old-fashioned coffeepot. With the steady perk of the brewing pot and the delicious aroma filling the warm room, the two nuns began to pore over the data.

Although reading through the profiles and

case studies that Eileen had unearthed made Mary Helen a little nauseated, it made her more determined to catch this man.

Before long, the two nuns had developed a profile of their own. According to the data and statistics they uncovered, the man they were looking for was probably a white male, between twenty-five and thirty years old, who had been an aggressive, hostile youth, filled with rage, probably against a neat, orderly, compulsive, conservative and punitive mother figure.

Most likely, he had not intended at first to kill his victim; but fear, or perhaps an accident, had caused the death of his first victim, and he'd strangely enjoyed it.

While Mary Helen poured them each a second cup of coffee and invaded Eileen's bottom desk drawer for a fresh package of Girl Scout cookies, Eileen went into the main reading room to gather up the recent *Chronicle*s.

For days the paper had screamed for the apprehension of the Sea Cliff rapist. Columnists had written on every aspect of the crime, even resurrecting Jack the Ripper and the Boston Strangler. Gun sales in all parts of the city had risen.

"In every one of the cases we've read about, a common thread usually runs through the victims," Eileen noted, setting the copies down in a pile on the side worktable. Mary Helen agreed.

The nuns dragged over their chairs. Eileen cracked open the small window. "I could use some fresh air," she said. Mary Helen understood the feeling.

Trying as hard as she could to distance herself from the painful reality, Mary Helen read the *Chronicle* accounts of the murders of each of the Sea Cliff matrons. To be of any help to the victims, Mary Helen knew it was important to remain objective, simply to look for similarities.

Determined to treat the murders like a huge puzzle, she managed to numb herself to the revulsion and rage she would ordinarily experience.

Eileen seemed to be doing the same. The two nuns studied each account diligently, taking notes.

Mary Helen broke the silence. "Isn't it strange?" She held up a page from Monday's *Chronicle*. "I didn't notice this before, but the continuation of the Sea Cliff rape story runs along one side of the fitness ad we gave to Angelica Bowers."

"*You* gave," Eileen corrected without looking up.

"Whatever." Mary Helen shrugged. "My point is, little did I know when I gave it to her, that we'd be involved." A sudden chill zigzagged up Mary Helen's spine. It must be the open window, she thought, studying the page reflectively. "What's one person's misfortune is another person's hope," she said softly.

"And you accuse me of making up sayings, old dear!" Eileen harrumphed and rattled the sheet of newsprint.

When both had finished reading and refolding the last paper, Eileen sighed. "It's hard to imagine the terror these women must have felt." Her large gray eyes brimmed with tears.

Pensively, Mary Helen listened to the rain, now turned heavy, lash against the building. A eucalyptus branch scraped against the window-pane. The smell of wet earth filled Eileen's small office.

"Let's try to make sure no one else feels that terror," she said around the lump swelling in her own throat.

Systematically, with more detachment than Mary Helen thought possible, they drew up a common list of similarities which, unfortunately, turned out to be short.

The first, of course, was the location. All three attacks had taken place in Sea Cliff.

"There was no sign of breaking and entering," Mary Helen said, "so the women must have known and trusted whomever he was."

Eileen agreed. "A delivery man, a gardener, someone all three of them had no fear of. And all three were shot. Most rapists, I read, stab or strangle. So this fellow must have an affinity for guns."

"No conscience and a gun! A horrendous combination," Mary Helen muttered.

Eileen scanned her notes. "For their ages, all three women were in very good health," she said, "and that's the last similarity I have. How about you, old dear?" She looked at Mary Helen hopefully.

"This may not count," Mary Helen said, "but I noticed that the reporter refers to the second victim, the widow who traveled, as a 'copper-haired socialite.'"

Eileen looked puzzled.

"Recently, Gemma's hair could be called copper-colored. It makes me wonder about the hair color of the spinster with the cat."

"Can we find that out?" Eileen asked.

Her sudden frown told Mary Helen that her friend realized the answer. "Not Inspector Gallagher," she whispered. "I have the definite impression that he's quite serious when he says he'll brook none of our interference."

"How can asking the color of a victim's hair possibly be misconstrued as interference?" Mary Helen asked innocently. "If you're afraid we'll bother him, I'll simply put a call into the coroner's office. Surely, that can't be confidential information."

"Please God, whoever answers the phone in the coroner's office doesn't mention the call to Inspector Gallagher," Eileen muttered.

Mary Helen pretended not to hear. This selective deafness really has its advantages, she thought, watching the long evening shadows steal across the office floor. Had she stumbled onto something? Only time and a call to the coroner's office would tell!

Eileen flipped on a lamp. A gentle tapping at the office door sounded above the ripple of the rain against the small window.

A flushed-faced Mrs. Kenny stuck her head around the doorjamb. "I'm about ready to leave," she said.

"Where did the time go?" Eileen asked, knowing the answer full well. "We'd better get over to evening prayer and dinner if we intend to be at Gemma's funeral by seven."

Mary Helen glanced up at the wall clock. It was just past five o'clock. Too late to call the coroner's office today. And they hadn't tried the Greenwood woman again, either. Maybe it would be better to call both of them first thing in the morning, when everyone was fresh.

Reaching up, she rubbed the back of her neck, then rotated her head slowly. Was it the hours of concentration that made her neck and shoulders stiff and prickly? Or was it because all afternoon Angelica Bowers's strange behavior had stuck in her mind like a familiar tune that would not be shaken?

Back at the Hall of Justice, Inspector Dennis Gallagher stared out the rain-streaked window at the traffic already clogging the James Lick Freeway. Or at least the small sections of it he could see around the new jail the city had thrown up to block the view. Most drivers had flipped on their headlights because of the rain and the early dusk.

Gallagher checked the time. It was not yet four o'clock. Goddamn, he hated this time of year! The short afternoons made him feel morose. It was bad enough looking for a nut cake of a rapist-murderer, let alone looking for him in the gloom.

The Homicide Detail was nearly empty. Long shadows spread across the linoleum floor. The two detectives who were there were both on the telephone. From the looks of things, O'Connor was out, too.

Gallagher studied his desktop. He's probably left a note somewhere in this mess, Gallagher thought, rifling through the paperwork strewn across it. While he was at it, he dumped four days' worth of half-full Styrofoam cups in the wastepaper basket, ignoring the coffee that splashed on the floor.

Geez, he missed Kate. Not only was she great to bounce ideas off, she also kept the tops of their adjoining desks halfway clean. He'd better never say that to her. She'd have his head. Call him sexist or chauvinistic, or something. But he couldn't help it. Women just were tidier than men. That's the way God made them. He tossed a stale, partially eaten jelly doughnut into the trash.

Goddamn, without Kate he was lucky he didn't have cockroaches, or at least ants. It must be too wet outside even for bugs. It sure as hell was too wet for humans, he thought glancing up at the darkened sky. All this dampness was making his corns hurt. He glanced up at the framed group picture of the Homicide Christmas party which hung on the wall. Kate and John were right in front. He wondered glumly whether or not they'd be at this year's doings.

Gallagher plopped down in his swivel chair. The springs groaned and creaked as he searched the desktop for anything that resembled a note from O'Connor.

Kate always left messages in that clear, precise printing of hers on a piece of yellow legal pad, Scotch-taped to his telephone receiver. He moved some files to uncover the phone, but there was no note. Systematically, or as systematically as his impatience would allow, Gallagher combed the top of his desk.

O'Connor would probably be back by the time he found the damn message. A folder slid off the side of his desk. Gallagher dove to catch it, but he was too late.

Only when he left his chair to pick it up did he realize that he had been sitting on O'Connor's note. O'Connor had written on the slip of a telephone message pad and left it on the seat of his chair. What a helluva place to put a message! Gallagher fumed, flattening out the crumpled slip of paper.

"Gone to Sea Cliff," the note read. "Checking out neighbors again. See if they forgot something the first time. Going through Gemma Burke's address book. Will talk to merchants. See if I can come up with a link. May drop by Greenwood's old apartment. Someone might be hanging around."

In a second paragraph, O'Connor had jotted down the telephone number and address of Elvis Greenwood's mother—as if I might have lost it, Gallagher fumed. "Maybe you can pay this lady a visit," O'Connor had written.

Gallagher was reaching for the telephone to check if anyone was home at the Greenwood house when the blasted thing rang. "Homicide. Gallagher," he growled into the receiver. He was surprised to hear O'Connor's voice.

"Denny, it's me, O'Connor," he said almost timidly.

"Yeah," Gallagher barked. "I know it's you. What's wrong with your voice? You sick or something? You don't sound like your usual cocky self."

"Right." O'Connor gave a short empty laugh. "Could you do me a big favor? I'll owe you one, big time."

"Depends," Gallagher said, letting him twist a little in the wind. It was good for the guy. "What kind of favor are we talking about?"

"I just realized that tonight is parent-teacher conferences at Our Lady of Lourdes. I promised the wife that I'd be there to go with her. She says that the kids take after me, and she

174

doesn't know why she's the only one who has to listen to their behavior problems. She got the teachers to give us late appointments so I'd be sure to be home." He snorted. "If I don't show, you'll be investigating *my* homicide."

"*Your* homicide," Gallagher grumbled. "We'd have so many suspects, she's liable to get away with it."

O'Connor forced a laugh. "Denny, could you cover for me at the Burke wake? Please, Denny?" He was almost begging. "I'll owe you one, anything. With all the kids you had, you must remember how it is."

Gallagher did and he was glad that the parent-teacher aspect of fatherhood was over.

"Okay," he mumbled finally, "but only for your wife's sake. She's got a tough enough life putting up with you."

A relieved O'Connor hung up. Gallagher dialed Tillie Greenwood's home. He listened to the steady hollow rings counting ten, twelve, fifteen.

Even if you lived in goddamn Buckingham Palace, you could pick up the phone in that many rings, he thought, slamming down the receiver after counting twenty-five rings.

Stretching, Gallagher yawned and stared out at the leaden sky. Tomorrow was another day. He hitched up his pants and checked his watch again. He felt dog-tired. In fact, any dog worth his salt would have too much sense to let himself get so beat.

If he left now, he'd beat the traffic and be home in time for a shower, a catnap, a decent meal and maybe even a few minutes with his wife before he had to go to the Burke funeral.

After a quick call to tell Mrs. G. that he was on his way, Inspector Gallagher left the Homicide Detail.

The telephone was already ringing when Tillie Greenwood put her key in her front-door lock. As usual the door stuck in all the dampness. Try as she might, Tillie was unable to push it open until the ringing stopped.

Maybe Elvis answered it, she thought, setting her dripping umbrella into the bucket she had remembered to leave by the front door. She hoped it wasn't that policeman again.

"Elvis," she called his name softly, hoping that he was home although she could tell he wasn't. The house felt dark, cold, deserted. Suddenly Tillie wanted to cry, to sit down and bawl like a baby who's found herself left all alone.

Don't be silly, she thought, removing her plastic rain bonnet carefully so as not to muss her brand-new hairdo. Tillie admired herself in the hall mirror. The old thing seemed to be getting more black spots every time she looked in it. Yet, it was still good enough to tell her that, as usual, Lynette had done a wonderful job.

The color was just the way Tillie liked it, a nice soft copper, not brassy looking, and the hairdresser—beautician, Tillie corrected herself, set it in a good tight curl that would last for a week, at least.

She pirouetted, checking her neck which was clipped nice and clean. Satisfied, she switched on the heater and stood over the vent until she felt the first faint breath of warmth blow up her goose-pimply legs.

All dolled up and no place to go, she thought. A sudden melancholy moved like a late-afternoon shadow across her being. Shake it off, she told herself, frantically turning on the lights in the hallway, in the living room and in the kitchen, until the house glowed as if it were full of life. She even switched on the dining-room light, although she couldn't remember the last time she'd actually dined in it. Only Mr. Cheeps really used it. The lovely old mahogany table was a catchall for unopened junk mail, old newspapers, and unpaid bills.

She opened the basement door. "Elvis," she called hopefully down the basement steps. "Are you there, sweetheart?" No sound came from below.

Surely he'd leave her a note if he'd gone out so she wouldn't worry. Time and again she'd asked him to do that when he lived at home. Honestly, it was the least he could do!

Tillie caught herself. There was no sense getting annoyed so quickly. She hadn't even looked!

"Right, Mr. Cheeps?" she trilled at the little canary who was hopping from his tiny swing to the floor of the cage. "Do you need your paper changed?" she chirped, then puckered her lips in the space between the bars of the cage and made quick kissing noises. The silly bird cocked his head nervously and studied her with one wary black eye.

A note! Tillie remembered, her eyes darting across the breakfast table, then along the kitchen sideboard. Next to the phone. They swept over the fireplace mantel in the living room. Across the table in the front hall. Everywhere she thought Elvis might reasonably leave a note. But Tillie found nothing.

Perhaps he wrote one, then forgot and left it in his bedroom. Of course! She chuckled tolerantly. As far back as she could remember, he was always forgetful. Leaving his toys outdoors to be stolen, losing the change when she'd sent him to the store, forgetting to give her notes his teachers sent home from school. It was not that he did it on purpose, as Mother had claimed. He was just a very bright, sensitive child and easily distracted.

Tillie would just march right down to her son's room, and surely she'd find out when he'd be home.

With an inexplicable surge of uneasiness, she swung open the basement door. It wasn't as if she were prying, she told herself. After all, this was her house. Elvis was her son. She had every right to know what time to expect him home.

A stale, damp chill floated up from the basement. Tillie flipped the switch and a single dusty lightbulb glared onto the wooden steps. Deep shadows filled in all the corners and ran down the rough two-by-fours along the walls.

Clutching the banister, Tillie slowly descended. The steady roar of the gas furnace lit up one corner of the basement, giving the place a clammy feel.

The concrete floor sloped a little toward the makeshift bedroom. From where she stood, Tillie could see that Elvis's door was shut. A plastic "Do Not Disturb" sign hung from the door handle. How silly! But no matter. She was his mother. He had nothing to hide from her.

After all, it was not as if she were snooping. She was simply looking for a note.

She crossed the floor where a canal of rust ran toward the drain. Something must have leaked, she thought absently. Her ears were alert for even the slightest sound, but there was none.

She turned the door handle cautiously and stepped into Elvis's bedroom. A musty odor filled the space. His blankets and bedspread were in a heap in the middle of the bed, and the corner of one sheet brushed the floor.

Clothes were strewn everywhere, dirty underwear mixed with socks and jeans that looked as if he had just walked out of them. The dresser drawers were all catawampus—some bulging with old sweaters and sweatshirts, some empty and off the runners.

If I didn't know better, I'd swear we'd been robbed, Tillie thought, picking up a soiled T-shirt and dropping it into the clothes hamper which she had set in one corner.

It was a shame the room had only one small window. What it needed more than anything was a good airing. Despite the rain, Tillie struggled with the corroded window frame until she raised it three or four inches. The salt air just eats away everything, she thought, brushing her hands together until all the little chips of enamel were off them.

Tillie bustled around the room, throwing dirty clothes in the hamper, folding clean ones, putting them into straightened drawers.

With a tug, she pulled the bottom sheet taut, made up the bed, and pumped life back into the mauled pillows. She rinsed out the small bathroom sink and doused a little Pine Sol in the chipped old toilet, giving it a swish and a flush.

With feelings of satisfaction, she dust-mopped the floor, threw the dirty laundry into the washing machine, and started it. Tired but content, Tillie went back into her son's room to shut the window.

The place looks 100 percent better, she thought, surveying her handiwork. It even smells better. He'll sleep much sounder in a clean, fresh room. Anyone would, she thought, remembering how this morning his velvet brown eyes had looked so flat and tired, ringed with those bruising circles. Yes, she assured herself, he'll sleep much better tonight.

She had been so busy with the cleaning that she almost forgot she had come down here looking for a note. It was just as well, really, since she hadn't found one.

Tillie was about to switch off the light and close the bedroom door when she heard the sound of water. Not the drip, drip, drip of a faucet, more like running water. Not gushing, just a small, steady leak.

She followed the sound into the bathroom. The sink and the makeshift shower were fine. The sound was coming from the toilet. The old thing never did work right, Tillie fumed, heaving off the heavy porcelain tank top. Mother had hired some two-bit amateur to install it, probably to save money and they'd been paying for it in water bills ever since.

The black rubber bulb inside never seemed to hit the hole dead center. Tillie stared into the empty tank. The corner of something which glistened like a wet plastic Ziploc bag was stuck in the opening.

Her heart lurched. She blinked and bent closer to the tank, examining its watery bottom. She gripped its porcelain sides until her hands cramped. It can't be. The sickening sensation of bile rose in her throat. It just cannot be! But it was. Someone had put a funny-looking little black gun with a short barrel and and a thick handle inside the bag!

Kate Murphy stared out a narrow window of the intensive care waiting room, at the backs of the homes bordering the entrance to St. Mary's Medical Center. She watched the soft rain soak the shrubs in their backyards and flatten the heads of the purple hydrangeas.

Suddenly, in one house, a kitchen light flipped on. Someone was getting an early start making dinner, or maybe it was a child just home from school fixing a snack.

A sudden rage filled Kate. How dare life go on so normally, so unconcernedly, she fumed, when not one hundred fifty feet away, her life was falling apart? How could anyone peel potatoes or fix a peanut-butter sandwich while her Jack fought for his life?

Kate wasn't aware of anyone else in the room until she felt a hand on her shoulder. She must have jumped because a gentle voice said, "I'm sorry, Kate, I didn't mean to startle you."

Kate whirled to face Melinda, the duty nurse. "What's wrong?" she asked, fighting down the sudden metallic taste of fear.

"Nothing's wrong," Melinda assured her. "Your mother-in-law just asked if you'd come in."

"My mother-in-law?" Kate steadied her voice. "Whatever for?"

Melinda shrugged somewhat helplessly. "I didn't ask her. She just told me to come and get you, and here I am."

Kate knew the feeling. When Mama Bassetti commanded, all but the most obdurate obeyed.

Trying to ignore her swelling dread, Kate followed Melinda through the double doors and down the corridor to the intensive care unit. She struggled to think of nothing but the sound of Melinda's soles squeaking on the highly polished linoleum and the bounce of her blond ponytail. The few short yards seemed endless. Kate forced herself not to push Melinda aside and run to her husband's bedside.

As soon as they entered the unit, Kate caught her mother-in-law's distorted reflection in the round security mirror high in the doorway of Jack's room. Like a grotesque image in the Hall of Mirrors at the Fun House, Kate thought crazily.

Standing on tiptoe, Mama Bassetti peered over the rail of the high bed. She examined her son's face with intense, critical scrutiny.

It's the same expression she uses when she's cleaning spinach, Kate realized, a little lightheaded. "What is it?" She moved to her mother-in-law's side.

"Look." Mrs. Bassetti pointed at Jack's eyelids. "What do you see? Movement!" she announced triumphantly.

Grabbing the bed rail, Kate bent over and studied her husband's face. His eyelashes seemed almost glued together. Was the dying light playing tricks, or did his eyelids tremble slightly?

182

"Did you see it?" Mama Bassetti asked expectantly. Kate didn't have the heart to tell her that she wasn't sure.

The two women stood together in silence while the monitor beside Jack's bed kept a steady impersonal record of his vital signs. The wall clock measured time in seconds, reminding those who watched that every single one of them was precious.

Still gripping the rail, Kate felt Mama Bassetti's pudgy hand cover hers. It was oven warm. Kate turned toward her. Her mother-in-law's cheeks were flushed and her brown eyes were dull with weariness. One wisp of hair had escaped from her usually neat bun, and she pressed her lips together so tightly that Kate wondered if she were afraid that if she loosened them, she might scream and scream and never be able to stop.

"How are you doing, Loretta?" Kate asked softly.

Her mother-in-law only shrugged.

"You look exhausted. Why don't you go home and rest for a while?"

Loretta Bassetti straightened her shoulders and gave Kate's hand a quick squeeze. "I'll stay right here with you if you need me."

"I don't know what I'd have done these last four days without you," Kate whispered, realizing, as she said it, how true her words were.

Mama Bassetti's eyes glistened with unshed tears. "You're a good woman, Kate Murphy," she said, self-consciously searching her purse for a tissue. "My Jackie was very lucky to find such a good woman."

Without warning, Jack moaned. Both women

183

leaned forward on the railing and watched his head move ever so slightly. Kate fought back the urge to laugh out loud. If anything at all is going to wake you up, pal, she thought, staring down at her husband's pale stubbly face, it's hearing your mother and me saying nice things to each other. You poor guy—she bent to kiss his forehead—you probably think you've died and gone to heaven. I can hardly wait to tell you. She felt the frozen fear that had clutched at her heart over the past few days and nights begin its slow thaw.

"Wake up, Jackie! Time to get up, sleepyhead! Jackie, do you hear me? Wake up!" Mama Bassetti called, stroking his hair. Kate watched a large tear escape from her eyes and run down her nose.

"You've been asleep long enough," she insisted. "Now wake up!"

Slowly, as though it took great effort, Jack opened his eyes, then, with a flutter, shut them again.

Why didn't his eyes pop open? Why didn't he start to talk, like people do in the movies? Kate stormed to herself. She grabbed her husband's hand and kissed it. "Come on, pal," she begged, "come back to us."

"How," Jack mouthed, his eyes still closed.

"How?" Kate asked. "How what, pal? How to come back?"

Jack frowned. "Hound." His words were jumbled.

"Hound?" Kate puzzled. "How end? How did you end up here?" she asked, hoping to unravel his meaning.

But Jack simply knit his brow, then was still.

"Nurse." Kate heard her mother-in-law calling for Melinda. "He opened his eyes. He spoke," Mama Bassetti announced proudly. "He's better."

Melinda moved around the bed noiselessly, checking all those things highly trained nurses check while the two women stood by expectantly. Finally she faced them with a broad smile. "Looking good!" she said. "Looking real good."

With a whoop, Kate Murphy and Loretta Bassetti threw their arms around one another. Laughing and crying, they rocked back and forth until Melinda firmly suggested that they go to the cafeteria for a cup of hot coffee.

By the time Angelica Bowers's taxicab reached the corner of 42nd and Balboa, it was nearly dark. "Pull over, driver!" Angelica shouted from the backseat. "I want to get out."

The cabbie studied her in his rearview mirror. "Here?" he asked incredulously. "You sure you want me to pull over and drop you at the corner in the rain?"

"I'm quite sure," Angelica said primly. "I've only a few doors to go."

"Suit yourself, lady!" He maneuvered his cab to the curb.

After she'd paid him and given him a generous tip, Angelica watched the cabbie drive away. She yearned to be driving off with him to a new house, a new city, a new anywhere except where she was going.

As she stood on the wet, dark corner, she realized the enormity of what she had done. A numbing fear ran down her legs, then down her arms to her hands clutching her purchases.

Her whole body began to tremble. Mama would never find out about the money she'd spent, but where was she going to hide all the packages?

Without thinking, Angelica peered down the block at Mama's bedroom window. Her heart leapt. The room was dark except for the dim shadow of a flickering television screen. Mama must still be dozing!

The pills are working, Angelica thought. Ducking her head against the drizzle, she made her way down the block. "Don't go on! Don't go on!" she chanted, hoping the light would hear and obey.

She opened the front gate carefully and mounted the slick wooden steps, praying with each one that Mama wouldn't wake up. She opened the door as quietly as she imagined a good cat burglar would.

Stepping inside the entry, she cringed, expecting the poodles to trot down the stairs and bombard her with their familiar yipping and snapping. But the house was absolutely still.

Angelica's spirits rose. The sleeping pills in the dogs' drinking water were working, too, she thought; afraid to hope lest, if they had worked, her hoping would undo them.

After stashing her purchases carefully in the dark back corner of the hall closet and covering them with an old afghan, Angelica pulled herself up the stairs and peeked into her mother's bedroom. Mama lay on her back, looking as peaceful and as pale as an embalmed corpse in a casket.

Flanking her on the large bed, Salt and Pepper snoozed contentedly. Angelica stifled a giggle.

The whole scene reminded her of the stories she'd read about Egyptian royalty being entombed in pyramids with the things they loved.

If Mama were an Egyptian queen, Angelica watched the sleeping woman, she would be buried with her dogs, her *TV Guide*, and her television set. And what else? Not me, Angelica thought, relieved. Hard as she tried, Angelica could think of nothing else her mother loved, unless it was rocky-road ice cream.

What would I take? Daydreaming, Angelica descended the steps slowly. My new hat and moccasins, chocolate éclairs, my young man from the western-wear shop. She giggled. Wouldn't he be surprised to find himself sealed off forever with me?

Still enjoying her reverie, Angelica popped a small roast in the oven and smothered it with potatoes, carrots, and onions.

Finally, she set out a tiny portion of food for each of the dogs. Mama might get suspicious if they began to look too thin. There would be plenty of time for them to starve while she was gone.

Pleased at the way her plan was developing, Angelica placed two bowls of drinking water next to the dogs' dishes. Then, without spilling a gram, she emptied the contents of a sleeping capsule into each one.

"Lullaby and good night," she hummed, watching the powder dissolve. She stirred the mixture with her index finger, making sure all of it disappeared. She nearly licked her finger clean—until she remembered.

Satisfied, Angelica moved into the living room, turned on the floor lamp, and sighed. Mama and the dogs were dozing. Dinner was in the oven. Her packages were hidden successfully. Now she had a few minutes for herself.

Stealthily, she removed the travel section of Sunday's *Chronicle* from under the sofa cushion where she'd stashed it, and sat down.

The rich aroma of roasting beef began to fill the small house. The living room was warm and cozy. Rain hit like popcorn against the window pane and Angelica felt almost content.

Slowly, with a sense of reverence, Angelica opened the paper. Above her she heard her mother's bed creak. Angelica's stomach churned. Had Mama heard the crinkle of newsprint? Or had one of the dogs?

She listened, the familiar dampness gathering behind her knees, but all was still again. Taking a deep breath, Angelica studied the paper. Mama didn't approve of her reading the travel section.

"It's bad enough your Uncle Frank fills your head with this nonsense," Mama had fumed when she discovered Angelica with the paper. "Now you're doing it on your own. I forbid you to read that garbage! Do you hear me, young lady?"

Angelica had heard and chose to disobey. If God thought she was committing a sin against the Fourth Commandment, Angelica didn't much care. When she got to heaven, she'd have plenty of time to explain her side of the story. She just hoped she wouldn't land up too close to Mama. Of course, if Mama were near her, it wouldn't be heaven, now, would it?

This Sunday the travel section was filled with stories of exotic islands with peach and gold

188

sunsets, romantic hideaways full of fragrant jasmine, luxurious accommodations with spectacular views, and gala banquets fixed by leading French chefs.

Angelica's eyes cut to a piece on Hawaii. The paradise of the Pacific, the travel writer called it and described it as more luxurious, more romantic, even more economical than ever. Angelica licked her lips, picturing the clean white sand, lush tropical flowers, majestic waterfalls, and tall muscular beach boys wrapped only in loincloths of tapia, their warm brown eyes beckoning her....

Maybe when she returned from Utah and spent a respectable amount of time mourning for Mama, she'd fly to—

"Angel? Are you home?" Mama's voice startled her and Angelica felt her heart pounding.

"So, sleepyhead, you're awake," Angelica said when she'd pulled herself upstairs. The two poodles stared at her groggily. "What finally woke you up?"

"The smell of roast beef!" Mama snapped. "We're starving." The poodles whimpered in agreement.

Angelica glared at the dogs. "Your dinner is downstairs," she said and began to descend the steps. The poodles followed, rushing against her legs, urging her to hurry until she clutched the banister, fearful that they'd push her over. In their haste to reach their bowls, their muscular bodies slid on the polished linoleum floor. They attacked their food greedily.

Mama was right. They were starving. Angelica wiped her damp palms on the corner of her apron. Watching the poodles devour their food, tumbling over the bowls in an effort to lick them clean, lapping the water, she began to giggle.

"What's so funny?" Mama shouted above the canned laughter of her television set.

"Nothing," Angelica called.

"You're down there giggling at nothing?" Mama demanded.

Angelica felt hot rage fill her stomach like a black creature full of claws and fangs. "I was just watching the dogs eat, that's all, Mama," she said, despising the whine in her voice.

"Well, stop it—" Mama sounded peevish— "and for heaven's sake, get me my dinner!"

After Mama and the dogs had fallen back into a drugged sleep, Angelica pulled the brochure from the American Institute of Fitness from under her mattress. She studied it. By tomorrow night her life would change. She giggled, then covered her mouth and listened. How would she explain her giggle if it awakened Mama?

She heard her mother move in the bed and give a little snort. Finally, the slow, rhythmic breathing began again, and Angelica released her own breath.

Smiling at herself in the dresser mirror, she studied her face. "A face that can wear hats," her young man at Western World had said. A pretty face, an angel face, a shining morning face, the face that launched a thousand ships, the face that drove men mad.

She stared at her reflection until it blurred before her. Soon that face would change its life.

The telephone rang like a scream. Angelica

jumped, then snatched up the receiver. It was that Sister Eileen from the library—Mrs. Kenny would be absent tomorrow. Things were going right.

"Angelica!" Mama's shout startled her. "Do you know what time it is?" Mama did not wait for an answer. "It's almost ten, missy! Get to bed! I need my sleep. Do you hear me? Tomorrow is another day."

Angelica covered her mouth and bit her cheeks, afraid she might giggle again. Tomorrow is another day all right, she wanted to taunt her mother. Tomorrow is the day I will change my life and your life, too, dear Mama. Soon you'll get your sleep. You'll get all the sleep you'll ever need. I'll make sure of that. Soon, Mama, you will sleep a sleep that is deep and dreamless and absolutely eternal.

Sitting stiffly at the kitchen table, Tillie Greenwood stared at the flowered plastic tablecloth without really seeing it. She scarcely heard the rain, like fingers tapping against her window.

A gun! She traced one of the yellow daisies numbly with her finger. It can't be! It just cannot be Elvis's gun. My Elvis would never hide any such thing in his toilet tank. Never! He's not that kind of boy. Her thoughts tumbled. There has to be a very logical and very reasonable explanation. Is he hiding it for a friend?

Mother always said Elvis didn't have very good judgment in picking friends, but Tillie knew that was not true. It was simply that Elvis's sensitive nature was always at work. He couldn't help it. He just went out of his way to be kind to the kids no one else paid much attention to.

191

"Losers," Mother had called them. Tillie had watched Elvis's face tighten with anger. Not that he said anything, God love him. He was always very respectful to Mother.

But hiding a gun? Elvis *hated* guns—Tillie was sure of that. Her memory rushed back to one Christmas when he was about eight. He had begged her for a cap gun. "All the other kids got them," he said. "All the kids who got dads."

When he said that, Tillie thought her heart would break.

"A cap gun! Whatever for?" Mother had asked. "It seems to me that no good can come from giving *that* child a gun."

Something about the way her mother had said "that child" had enraged Tillie and made her more determined than ever to buy her Elvis the gift he had set his heart on.

Sadly, however, as her mother predicted, the gun had been a disaster. Elvis shot caps at everything that came into his path: gangsters on the television, passersby on the street, the pictures on the wall, the paperboy.

The last straw came when he covered his little face with an old dish towel and pretended to rob the members of Mother's bridge club. Only dear Mrs. Wilde thought it was funny.

Mother, of course, was livid and had seen to Elvis after her lady friends left. When she finished, she marched to the curb and threw his cap gun into the old metal garbage can. Tillie still remembered the cruel thud it made when it hit the bottom and the ache in her own heart as she watched Elvis's small, tight face burn with shame and resentment.

"How could you do that?" Tillie had asked Mother after Elvis was in bed.

"Actually, you are the one who should have taken care of it!" Mother snapped, and Tillie wished she had. Then she wouldn't have had to see her small son bursting with such raw hatred.

"Do you want Mommy to buy you another gun?" Tillie had whispered, bending over to give Elvis a good-night kiss.

"Who wants an old gun anyway?" he shouted, turning his face to the wall. Tillie's heart throbbed with his pain.

To her knowledge, Elvis had never touched a gun since that night. So surely that gun in the toilet could not belong to him.

Tillie moved around the kitchen woodenly. Why his tank? Why him? she wondered, peeling the potatoes. Whose gun is it? She scraped and cut the carrots. Why is my Elvis hiding it? Who did it really belong to? She dredged several pieces of chicken absently.

Only when Mr. Cheeps stopped singing did Tillie realize that her house was dark. She flipped on the light. There is nothing to do but ask him, she decided, washing the flour from her hands and drying them on her apron. I know he'll have a perfectly good explanation. All I have to do is ask.

While dinner cooked, Tillie went into the front room and turned on her television set. The local news exploded with stories of the Sea Cliff rapist. Fear jabbed her. Was anyone at all safe with this man stalking the streets?

The regular commentator introduced a thin, scholarly looking expert on serial killers who gave a rundown on their characteristics. As if anyone cares! Tillie thought.

"Domineering and abusive mother," he droned.

I've never been that, Tillie thought.

"Flat, expressionless eyes." The expert's own hooded eyes stared out from the screen.

Elvis has beautiful tender eyes, Tillie dithered. How could anyone possibly think it's my Elvis? She switched to another news channel.

"Services will be held at seven o'clock tonight at St. Monica's Church in San Francisco for socialite and philanthropist, Gemma Burke," this newscaster began, then gave a brief, but moving account of her life. When the woman's weeping grandchildren appeared on camera, Tillie switched again—this time to a rerun of *Murder She Wrote*.

Although she had seen most of the episodes and remembered the killers, it was preferable to hearing about real-life murders. Jessica Fletcher had just raised her eyebrows and said, "Oh, my!" when Tillie heard Elvis on the front steps.

"Come in, sweetheart." She swung open the front door. "You must be drenched!"

With a grunt, Elvis came in. All hunched over like a pretzel, Tillie thought. She wished he would throw back his shoulders. She knew from the tight set of his mouth that it was better not to mention his posture, nor the fact that he had not left a note. Elvis was so sensitive to criticism, especially hers. Although she had told him a thousand times, he never seemed to understand that the only reason she ever said anything negative at all was because she loved him.

"Let Mommy have your coat." She helped him remove his dripping peacoat. "Sit down and take off those wet shoes. Dry your feet by the heater while I get you something hot."

"Make it a cold beer," Elvis said, his eyes avoiding hers.

"A cold beer?" Tillie caught herself. "If that's what you want, sweetheart." She hurried into the kitchen.

"Dinner will be ready in just a few minutes," she called. "Are you famished?"

Elvis grunted again. An unpleasant sound, really, that made a menacing shiver zip down Tillie's spine.

The television was switched to what sounded like a prizefight. She marveled at how Elvis could always find a wrestling match or boxing or mud wrestling or a war movie on TV. How he loved action, especially when he was feeling restless.

Tillie turned up the burners on the stove and the oven. She'd serve dinner as quickly as possible, then go to the memorial service at St. Monica's for that woman. What was her name? Gemma Burke?

That way she'd be out of the house when Elvis went down to his bedroom. While he was in one of his moods, she was never quite certain just how he'd react to her help. Sometimes he was so grateful, hugging her, kissing her, telling her that she was the best mommy in the whole world. How her heart soared when he said that.

Then, at those other times, he would frown and shout and call her a nosy old busybody and worse! At those times, Tillie, holding back her tears, would thank God, Mother wasn't alive to hear him. Not that his rages lasted all that long. And he was always sorry afterward.

Tillie put a lid on the potatoes. She actually had no idea how he would react tonight. Although she knew, just from the way he'd slumped into the house, that this was not a good time to ask about anything, especially about a gun. Nor to tell him that that policeman had called.

"I'm dying of thirst in here!" Elvis hollered over the roar of the fight crowd on the television set. "Where the hell did you go for the beer? Alaska?"

"Coming right up, sweetheart," Tillie trilled. "Mommy's coming!" Ignoring the sudden chill that wrapped her when she opened the refrigerator door, Tillie Greenwood carried a cold can of beer and a bag of corn curls into the front room.

Inspector Dennis Gallagher set out for Gemma Burke's funeral service feeling like a new man. Well, almost! His eyelids were still sandy from lack of sleep, but there was nothing like a long shower, a good hot meal, and Mrs. G. to make him feel that at least he was in the land of the living.

An added bonus was Kate Murphy's telephone call. When his wife had said it was Kate on the line, Gallagher's heart took a dive. Even the receiver felt heavy when he took it from her.

But the moment he heard Kate's voice, he knew it was good news. And, God knows, they could all use some about now!

"Jack opened his eyes," Kate nearly sang.

"And he said something, although I couldn't make out what he really meant. And the nurse is optimistic that he's on the mend."

Kate's voice caught, and Gallagher knew she was fighting back tears. For that matter, so was he.

Thank you, God, he thought, clearing his throat. "Now, Katie-girl, why don't you and his mother get the hell out of there and leave the poor guy in peace so he can get a good night's sleep."

"Yes, boss!" she barked, but Gallagher could tell she was much too relieved to be annoyed at his suggestion.

"I'm on my way to the Burke funeral," he told her. "I want to see if anyone unusual or suspicious turns up, although with the size of the crowd that promises to show up, I don't know how in the hell I'll be able to tell.

"Anyway, first thing in the morning, I'll meet you at the hospital. Jack might be able to give us a lead or, between the two of us, we might be able to figure out something."

"Right!" Kate agreed, her spirits still soaring. "See you then, Denny, and thanks."

"For nothing," he muttered.

Hunched over in the car, Gallagher turned on the ignition, the heater, and the windshield wipers all at once. Rubbing his hands together to keep warm, he waited for each of them to do its work.

Although if he thought about it, he was still bone tired. His little respite at home, coupled with Kate's good news, had renewed his energy. Besides, he had a hunch that tomorrow was going to be his lucky day.

Tomorrow they'd nab the bastard, get the mayor's office and the commissioner, the media, and the general population of the city off their backs.

Gallagher took a deep breath and let it out slowly. He couldn't wait to wrap up this case and get back to routine homicides. Actually, he couldn't wait to get back to life as usual.

"Go back inside before you catch your death of cold," he called to his wife, who was still in the doorjamb waving to him, looking much too appealing for a woman her age. She blew a kiss. You're a grandmother, for crissake, he thought, his whole body filling with desire.

"Get back inside, before I get out of this tub and go back inside with you!" he called, throwing his car into drive.

"Pure luck!" Eileen said, when Sister Anne pulled into what seemed to be the last parking space in St. Monica's schoolyard. Behind them the line of cars stretching from the yard ran down 23rd Avenue to Clement Street in one direction and to Geary Boulevard in the other.

Mary Helen was delighted that Sister Anne offered to drive to Gemma Burke's services. What with the traffic, the dark, and the rain, tonight she preferred being a passenger.

Since Mary Helen detested backseat drivers herself, she didn't want to be one. On the way from the college to the church, she tried hard not to step on an imaginary brake or draw in any sharp breaths. But she had to point out that red light. From the way Anne was barreling down Geary, Mary Helen was sure she just didn't see it!

The heavy rain had been replaced by a cold, penetrating drizzle. The moment Mary Helen stepped out of the car, before she could open her umbrella, it had frizzed her short gray hair, fogged her glasses, and dampened the shoulders of her good black suit.

The three nuns mixed with the crowd of mourners hurrying down the darkened avenue. The lights coming from inside the church set the stained-glass window of St. Margaret Mary and the Sacred Heart ablaze.

Careful to grip the banister, they made their way up the steep slippery front steps and entered the vestibule. It was packed with people signing the mourners' book. I'll come back later, Mary Helen thought, pulling open one oversized wooden door.

Inside, St. Monica's long, narrow center aisle was filled with women who looked as if they had just stepped out of a window at Neiman Marcus. Men with forty-dollar haircuts and handsome children shook hands, talked softly, introduced one another.

Sister Mary Helen had taken only a few steps up the aisle when she spotted Inspector Gallagher. She was surprised to see him, although she knew she shouldn't have been. He was undoubtedly on duty.

"Why, Inspector." Mary Helen shook his hand. "How nice of you to come." She leaned close. "I hope you find whoever it is you're looking for."

Gallagher scowled. "I hope you're not looking for whoever I'm trying to find," he hissed back into her ear.

Taken aback, Mary Helen simply gave him

a cold stare and moved on. Imagine! she fumed, waving across two pews to an old college chum of Gemma's. One would think that he'd be happy for the help! The old...old...poop! The word just popped into her head from nowhere. Amazingly, it seemed a perfect fit for Inspector Gallagher.

The old poop, she repeated to herself, greeting a group of alumnae and their families.

Mingled with their sadness, Mary Helen sensed their feeling of horror and disbelief at what had happened to a woman as genuinely good as Gemma Burke.

"Why?" They asked the age-old unanswerable question. The answer, Mary Helen knew, would always be shrouded in mystery. The only possible answer to suffering—difficult as it was to hear—was to embrace it with faith and with courage and hope.

The three nuns were walking up the aisle to view the body and to offer their condolences to Gemma's family when Mary Helen remembered that she hadn't signed the mourners' book.

Feeling like a salmon swimming downstream during spawning season, she made her way to the back of the church. In the vestibule, the crowd had dispersed. Only one woman stood in front of the book, staring at it.

Mary Helen's heart jolted, then began to thud. She squinted. In the dim light, she looked like Gemma. But she couldn't be! Gemma was dead.

When the woman lifted her head, Mary Helen knew she was mistaken. But there was something about her size, her posture, the copper-colored hair.

Her heart still pounding, Mary Helen stood behind the woman, trying to catch her breath. With a nervous smile, the woman handed her the pen and slipped quietly into the church.

Stepping up to sign the book, Mary Helen couldn't help noticing the woman's name. She stared at the scrawled letters in disbelief. Tillie Greenwood!

For a moment, she felt light-headed and clutched the sides of the stand to steady herself. That was the name of the woman she and Eileen had tried to telephone yesterday to ask if she knew an Elvis Greenwood.

How many Tillie Greenwoods could there possibly be? This was too much of a coincidence to be a coincidence! Someone's guardian angel was working overtime.

Sister Mary Helen could not sleep. Despite the fact that before going to bed, she'd deliberately soaked in a hot tub until her fingers shriveled like prunes, and drunk a cup of hot chocolate, she just could not relax. She had even eaten a piece of toast spread thick with peanut butter. That usually did the trick, but not tonight.

Tonight her mind continued to roll, full of faces and feelings, like the credits at the end of a film. St. Monica's Church with its white marble altar protected by golden seraphim...The organ's solemn tones...The brilliant stained-glass windows turned black by the darkness outside...Christ and the four evangelists staring down from the behind the altar with blank eyes while the priest blessed what remained of Gemma Burke.

"Death is not extinguishing the light," he had

quoted the Indian poet Rabindranath Tagore, "but blowing out the candle because the dawn has come."

The dawn had come, cruelly and violently to Gemma at the hands of a serial rapist. Numbly, Mary Helen pondered this faceless man. Why had he chosen good, generous Gemma? Why had he chosen any of his victims? There was a reason. Somewhere there was a logical, reasonable explanation why he had picked these particular women.

Some secret hatred—which probably stretched back to childhood—caused him to humiliate and degrade these women. A sight, a sound, even a smell might rekindle his rage and set him off. If sleuths could only discover the similarities in the women or the circumstances, maybe they would discover the link.

She felt sure Inspector Gallagher was spending his every waking moment trying to do just that. From the color of his face at the funeral tonight and the exhaustion in his eyes, she guessed that he had been awake quite a lot recently.

Sister Mary Helen plumped up her pillow and turned over on her side. The rain and even the drizzle had stopped. A strong wind flung a tree branch against her bedroom window, and fallen pieces of eucalyptus bark rattled along the ground.

If she didn't get to sleep soon, she'd be useless tomorrow. And tomorrow promised to be a very full day.

When the three nuns arrived home from St. Monica's, there had been a note on the bulletin board for Sister Eileen to call Mrs. Kenny. When Eileen returned the call, the woman sounded dreadful. She was nursing a sick headache, and her ulcer was kicking up again. She would not be in tomorrow.

"She asked me to fill in for her." Eileen raised her bushy eyebrows. "She wants me to call Angelica Bowers and make sure she is coming in. I had better do that before it gets much later."

While Eileen hurried to make the call, Mary Helen measured out two cups of milk. "Hot chocolate?" she asked Sister Anne.

"Too much fat," Anne said, "but thanks anyway."

Turning on the burner, Mary Helen pondered, once again, one of life's great mysteries. Why is it always the slender who watch their figures?

Several minutes later, Eileen returned with an odd expression on her face. "That was really very bizarre," she said, stirring two more heaping tablespoons of ground chocolate into her cup.

"What do you mean, bizarre?"

"To begin with, Angelica answered on the first ring. It was as if she were sitting by the phone expecting someone to call."

"Maybe she has the phone near her bed so that the noise doesn't wake up her mother," Mary Helen offered sensibly.

Eileen blew on her hot chocolate, then took a small sip. "And her voice was excited. No, animated is a better word, really. High and cheerful. A party voice! Yet there was no noise, not even a television set in the background."

"What did she say that was so bizarre?"

"That she'd be happy to come in. Now, you know as well as I do, old dear, that Angelica Bowers is never really happy to do anything pertaining to work. And she let me know quite clearly, mind you, that she is only staying half the day. She plans to begin her trip tomorrow evening, and she has to pack."

Eileen stopped and studied Mary Helen. "I wonder if we did the right thing giving her that advertisement."

"Maybe she sounds happy because she is going to do something to improve her life."

Eileen frowned. "Toward the end of our conversation, she really began to sound strange—almost...almost manic."

Despite the warm chocolate, Mary Helen felt a chill.

"She kept repeating over and over that tomorrow night her life would change. Things would never be the same. That a new day would dawn. She went off on something about her face. Her 'angel face,' she called it. A face that can really wear hats.

"I'm afraid she is expecting too much from ten days at a spa. They can steer her in the right direction, of course, but they are not going to perform a miracle. I surely hope that we haven't set her up for a terrible letdown!"

Suddenly Eileen yawned. "I am exhausted," she said and left the kitchen before Mary Helen had a chance to mention Tillie Greenwood. Now, hers was the one face that kept rolling through Mary Helen's mind.

She hadn't told Eileen about bumping into Mrs. Greenwood in the vestibule while they were still at St. Monica's because Anne was never far from earshot. The less said about their plans, the better. Not that Anne would say anything on purpose, but...

Mary Helen had fully intended to tell Eileen when they arrived home, but with the phone call and all, at least, one of them should get a good night's sleep. Although Mary Helen wondered whether Eileen really was asleep. Perhaps she, too, was replaying the evening. If I knew for sure that Eileen was awake, she thought crazily, we could get together for a quick game of gin!

Instead, she tried rolling over on her other side to get comfortable. The Development Office would be a zoo tomorrow morning. Undoubtedly her secretary, Shirley, would have a zillion questions about the Christmas Tree Extravaganza. Who would fill the holes left by Gemma's death? Mary Helen had no idea. Some holes just cannot be filled.

The convent heating system roared into action. The temperature must have dropped. Mary Helen wondered whether the Sea Cliff rapist was out in the cold, stalking yet another victim.

Watching the headlights from a lone car climbing the college road skitter across her ceiling, she was filled with a goading sense of urgency. The first thing tomorrow, she must tell Eileen about meeting Tillie. They had to talk with her, to try diplomatically to ask her why she attended the funeral. To ask her if she thought her son Elvis might be the one responsible.

Mary Helen's stomach churned. Would a mother sense that something was terribly wrong with her child? Would she believe it? Would she admit that her son was a serial rapist-murderer? Did they dare ask?

With a sigh, Mary Helen decided to put the problem squarely where it belonged—in God's hands. Centering herself, she remembered that today was the feast of the sainted parents, Zachary and Elizabeth. Their only son, John the Baptist, had been *different* from his birth. Had they suffered to hear him called a madman? Were they concerned when he chose to live in the desert, clothed in camel hair and eating only locust and wild honey? Did they realize that he was destined for greatness, or had they secretly wished that he would grow up to be an ordinary rabbi like his father?

Even though it must have been very difficult for Elizabeth to be the mother of a prophet and nearly unbearable to hear of her son being beheaded for declaring the truth, how much more difficult it must be to be the mother of a rapist-murderer.

Friday, November 6
Feast of St. Leonard of Noblac, Monk

Friday morning dawned clear and cold and much too early for Sister Mary Helen. Overnight the wind had swept away the rain clouds, leaving the whole city sparkling in clean, crisp sunlight.

The leaves of the deep blue hydrangea bushes beside the college walkway glistened in the cold air. The border of gold and white chrysanthemums looked none the worse for wear, which was not the case with Sister Eileen.

"You look exhausted," Sister Mary Helen said when the two nuns met after Mass.

Eileen shot her a sideward glance. "If that isn't the a classic case of the pot calling the kettle black, I don't know what is," she muttered. "Did the wind keep you awake, too?"

"Don't I wish that was the only thing." Mary Helen steered Eileen toward a wooden bench near St. Francis's fountain and wiped the slats with a tissue so they could both sit down safely.

Without any preamble, Mary Helen recounted her discovery of Tillie Greenwood in the vestibule of St. Monica's Church.

"That is too much of a coincidence to be a coincidence," Eileen observed when she finished.

"My thought exactly." Mary Helen stared out across the rain-washed campus, across the choppy gray water of the bay to the campanile at the University of California which stood out against the East Bay hills. "Out of the shadows of night, The world rolls into light"; the words of Longfellow's last poem came crazily to her tired mind.

"It is daybreak everywhere." Eileen finished it, then went on as if she hadn't. "Maybe we should call Inspector Gallagher and tell him about Mrs. Greenwood." Her bushy eyebrows rose. "He may have missed her in all that crowd."

"How will we explain knowing her name?"

Eileen's pale face became even paler. "Kate Murphy, then. Shall we give Kate a ring?"

"I'm sure she has her hands full what with Jack so sick."

"One of them does need to know." Eileen

made a circle on the wet ground with the toe of her shoe.

"Certainly." Mary Helen cleared her throat. "And we will tell them both everything we find out about Mrs. Greenwood, which we can't do until after we've found something out, right?"

Eileen narrowed her eyes. "Inspector Gallagher will be furious, you know."

"Think of how furious he'll be if we send him on a wild-goose chase. Why, she may not even be related to this Elvis character."

Eileen considered this for a long moment— much too long a moment to suit Mary Helen. "I suppose, then, that we should be the ones who pay the first visit to Mrs. Greenwood?" Her words curled into a question.

"Good idea!" Mary Helen agreed, amazed that Eileen had given in so easily. She hurried on before her friend changed her mind.

In as few words as possible, Mary Helen outlined the plan she had hatched at dawn, and in the bright light of day, found really very simple.

"First, we both need to go to our offices. That is a given. We surely don't want to draw any attention to ourselves by being absent this morning." She pushed her bifocals up the bridge of her nose. "What time do you think you can be free this afternoon?"

Sister Eileen frowned and thought aloud. "Mrs. Kenny is not coming in. Angelica is leaving at noon. I wouldn't be a bit surprised if she disappears even earlier. We have good student aides today, and it is Friday." Her face brightened. "I'm sure I can safely leave about one."

"Perfect!" Mary Helen felt that familiar rush of assurance that comes from knowing she was on the right track. "And, for heaven's sake, let's not sign out the convent Nova. No one need know we're out." Particularly Sister Therese, she thought, who was an avid car-calendar reader! "We can ride the Muni out to 42nd and walk down the hill. It can't be too far from the corner."

"Fine," Eileen said, but Mary Helen noticed she was beginning to look wary. Obviously, she had not talked quite fast enough.

"What do you suggest we do when we get there?" Eileen asked, her gray eyes blinking. "We can't just ring the front doorbell and ask the woman if her son is the Sea Cliff rapist. If she's even home, that is."

"Not at all." Mary Helen felt annoyance color her face. "We can say we are just dropping by for a visit. I can start by saying that I'd seen her at Gemma Burke's funeral last night and...I...we..." She hesitated, realizing with cruel clarity, that Eileen was right. There really was no plausible explanation for dropping in on a perfect stranger for a visit. Somehow the holes in her plan were not quite so apparent at dawn after a long restless night. Even a few minutes ago, it seemed to make perfect sense.

"You have a point," Mary Helen admitted finally.

Eileen looked surprised. "Do you mean about having no excuse to pay Mrs. Greenwood a visit?" she asked.

Feeling her confidence escaping, drip by drip, like a leaky faucet, Mary Helen nodded.

"For heaven's sake, old dear," Eileen said with the grin of a devil's advocate, "when has that ever stopped you before?"

Mary Helen laughed, realizing yet again, why they had been such good and true friends for over fifty years. "We're on then?" she asked and Eileen gave her a thumbs-up sign.

After deciding on a time and a place of meeting, the two stood silently and watched a sassy blue jay splashing in the fountain.

"I can't get Angelica Bowers off my mind," Eileen said. "Something is just not right." She skimmed off some pine needles from the fountain while the statue of St. Francis, ankle deep in rainwater, looked on benevolently. "I can feel it in my bones." Eileen's eyes shone with apprehension as the two nuns started for the Sisters' dining room. "Perhaps hers is the home we should visit."

"Perhaps," Mary Helen said. "When is Angelica leaving for Utah?"

"Tonight."

"Well, after we visit Mrs. Greenwood, if it will make you feel better, we can drop by the Bowerses. If I'm not mistaken, they live in the same neighborhood."

"On the same block," Eileen said. "I checked the addresses." She swung open the dining room door.

"Come join me," Sister Anne called from a nearby table.

"Remember! Not a word to anyone," Mary Helen warned.

Eileen's worried face crinkled into a smile. "No one would believe me even if I told them," she teased.

"I still think we are wise not to say anything," Mary Helen insisted.

"As they say, 'A wise head keeps a shut mouth.'"

"Now don't tell me that's one of those old sayings from back home."

Eileen's gray eyes twinkled. "Well, if it's not, old dear, it most certainly ought to be!"

Despite the sun streaming in through her breakfast-nook window, Tillie Greenwood sat shivering in front of the heating vent. Rather than warming her and cheering her, the brightness of the room depressed her.

Under its relentless glare, every old crack in the ceiling showed up, every coffee stain on the plastic tablecloth, every worn spot in the linoleum. It put a hard edge on the ancient toaster and highlighted the chipped china in her cupboard.

Its rays changed Mr. Cheeps, perched in his cage in the dining room, from golden feathered to tawny yellow. Tillie hoped, though it was early in the day, that already a band of gray fog was hovering over the ocean, just waiting to roll in and cover her world in the gloom she felt.

Rummaging in the pocket of her chenille bathrobe, Tillie pulled out a wad of old napkins, blew her nose, and fingered her left cheek gently. It was sore to the touch, and she was afraid to look at herself in the mirror. She was sure her left eye would blacken.

Fresh tears blurred Tillie's eyes and all the flowers on her plastic tablecloth swam together in a mishmash of faded colors. Trying not to press against her cheek, she brushed them away.

She hauled herself up from the chair wearily, crossed into the kitchen, and poured herself another cup of coffee. Its strong, fragrant aroma only made her feel more miserable. Even Mr. Cheeps's trills sounded plaintive in the silent empty house.

"Poor little sweetie-bird." Tillie made kissing noises toward him. "You must have been scared to death with all the shouting and cursing and banging last night."

Last night! Tillie felt her muscles cramp with tension, and she sank miserably into the chair. The kitchen seemed to be moving around her, just as it had then. Her eyes filled and she closed them trying to blot out the memory. But she couldn't. Even with both eyes squeezed tight, she could still see Elvis when she'd come home from church.

He was standing there, waiting for her. She knew something was wrong the moment she opened the front door. Everything was too quiet. And Elvis had just stood there, blocking her way into the kitchen. Just stood there like a statue, with his fists clenched, the muscles in his arms bulging, and his whole body swollen with rage.

"What is it, sweetheart?" she had asked, struggling to keep her voice calm. "What is wrong?" She raised her hand to caress his face, hoping to soothe him, but he had pushed it away and stared at her. Tillie felt the raw, unblinking hatred burning in his eyes. Her mouth went dry.

"You cleaned my room." Not a question, but a statement. His voice was low and dangerous.

"Yes, sweetheart." She had given him a loving smile. "Mommy picked up after you because Mommy doesn't want her sweet boy living in a pigsty."

Tillie's whole body began to tremble and she had to steady her coffee cup with both hands. She didn't mean to call him a pig. She loved him. She'd told him that.

What had she done, she wondered, to deserve the filthy, vile names that he called her? Thank goodness Mother is gone, she thought, watching motes of dust twirl in the sunbeam. It would have killed her to hear all that gutter talk coming out of Elvis's mouth.

"Mommy's sorry, sweetheart," she had cried into his fury, but he didn't stop. He just kept bombarding her with horrible names and ugly words. She couldn't imagine where he'd heard them. She could only guess the meanings of some words.

Fresh tears stung her eyes, and she fought back a sob. When she had put her two hands over her ears, trying to block out the loud, mean sound of his voice, her Elvis raised his arm. With one fast blow, he had backhanded her.

Tillie had tumbled against the doorjamb, her ears ringing, the room spinning. She tasted the blood in her mouth.

For a terrifying moment, Elvis stared at his hand as if he didn't recognize it. Then—without warning—he ran his open palm along the kitchen counter, overturning canisters of sugar and flour and coffee, flinging them into a heaping mess on the floor.

"Stay out of my room," he said very quietly, then pounded down each step into the basement.

It was like a nightmare, Tillie thought, except it didn't go away when she woke up this morning. Her left cheek was still sore. Small grains of sugar which had escaped her broom still crunched when she walked across the kitchen linoleum. And when she had crept quietly out of her bedroom, Elvis was still there, pale and strained now, sorry he had hurt her, she was sure, but too ashamed to say so.

Instead, he just sat in the front room, staring out the window, watching that poor Bowers girl waddle past the house up to the bus stop. He watched her every labored step with that strange fire burning in his eyes.

"I need to get me some fat meat," he mumbled in a low, mean voice that Tillie hardly recognized.

Tillie shuddered. About an hour ago, Elvis had left the house, without saying a word.

"Sweetheart," Tillie had called out to him, afraid that her throat might close, "where are you going? What time will you be home?"

But he acted as if he couldn't hear her. It was as if a giant plastic soundproof shield covered him, a shield that her voice was unable to pierce.

In the stillness of her empty kitchen, Tillie heard the clock tick away endless seconds. Where was her son, her Elvis? A sickening panic flowed through her body. He wasn't going to hurt that Bowers girl, was he?

Surely not! Tillie took another sip of her coffee and tried to think sensibly. Her Elvis was a good boy! A sensitive boy. He always had been. He had a quick temper; that was all. He always did have, ever since he was a small child.

But he was always sorry. She felt a pang of love. No, her Elvis wouldn't hurt a fly. Not on purpose. Not a fly, not a girl, not a rich old stuck-up lady. Certainly not his own dear Mommy. No, he wouldn't.

"No! No! No!" Tillie screamed into the silence. Listening to her voice echo, she circled her arms on the breakfast table, buried her face in them, and wept.

"Hi, Melinda." Kate Murphy waved to the duty nurse in the intensive care unit of St. Mary's Medical Center. "How's our boy doing this morning?" Suddenly her stomach felt empty.

Melinda looked up from a computer screen behind the long white central desk and gave Kate a big encouraging smile. "He's hanging in there," she said with a wink.

Kate exhaled the breath she didn't even realize she was holding and tiptoed into Jack's cubicle. Pulling back the short white drapes, she flooded the room with warm, bright sunshine and watched a tiny rainbow dance against one wall.

For a moment, she stared down at narrow Stanyan Street, where horns honked at a garbage truck maneuvering the corner while a Muni bus swallowed up six passengers, then pulled away from the curb. Life as usual, Kate thought, wondering if her life would ever be "as usual" again.

Careful not to disturb any of the tubes, Kate slipped her hand into her husband's. His fingers were warmer this morning, or was that her imagination? She squeezed and was sure she felt a pressure in return.

"Hi, pal," she whispered, studying his pale, thin face. "I'm here." She leaned forward to plant a kiss on his forehead, then waited expectantly, hoping, praying that he would open his eyes.

Although his eyelids fluttered and it seemed as if he were struggling to open them, the effort was too great.

One corner of his mouth turned up into a lopsided grin. "How...self?" Jack's words were slow and deliberate and slurred, but they were real words. He was responding!

Kate wanted to shout and laugh and hug him. Unexpected tears rushed to her eyes and spilled down her cheeks, running off her chin onto Jack's hand.

"How...self?" he repeated, his eyes still closed and Kate wondered if she would ever again hear words that sounded so sweet.

"Fine, my darling." She tried to steady her voice. "Just fine, now. I love you. I love you so very, very much!"

Behind her she heard a familiar clearing of throat and smelled the odor of cigar. Dennis Gallagher was here. Kate straightened up. She hadn't heard him come in. She wiped her eyes quickly. "Hi, Denny," she said, wondering how long he'd been standing there. "You're early."

"Lucky for Jack," Gallagher growled, putting one arm around her shoulder. "Much later and you'd have drowned this poor guy."

"Hound!" Jack's voice was loud.

Gallagher looked startled.

"Hound!" Jack repeated.

"He heard your voice." Kate studied her husband's frowning face. "He is trying to tell us something. I'm sure it has to do with the perp. He said the same word yesterday. His mother and I thought he was saying 'how' and 'end.' But when we repeated that, it was obvious by his face that it was not what he meant. When we finally said, 'hound,' his face relaxed. I'm sure 'hound' is what he is saying."

Kate stared down at her husband, who looked troubled again. "And he's trying to tell us something about it, but we're too stupid to get it." She glanced over at her partner. "It's not for lack of trying, I assure you. First thing this morning, Mama Bassetti was at it again. She coupled 'hound' with everything she could think of. She even went through *Bartlett's Book of Familiar Quotations.*

"Actually she nearly drove me crazy. *The Hound of the Baskervilles,* run with hounds...I think she was really thinking of *Dances with Wolves*...fit for hounds, barking hounds, fox and hounds. Is one of your suspects named Fox, by the way?"

Gallagher shook his head and loosened his tie.

"Hound," Kate repeated, suddenly frustrated at her inability to decode Jack's message. She moved to the window and stared out. A lone, lost seagull wheeled counterclockwise against the brilliant blue sky—a sure sign that it would rain again. A desperate caw rattled from the bird's throat.

Above the quiet hum of the intensive care unit, short staccato steps, like machine-gun fire, hurried down the polished linoleum hallway. "Mama Bassetti," Kate explained, glancing at her wristwatch. "She took little John to the baby-

217

sitter for me. Then she must have shot down Geary Boulevard like a cannon."

"Hound dog!" Mama Bassetti shouted when she reached the doorway. "What about hound dog?"

Gallagher's watery blue eyes snapped open and he hit his forehead with his palm. "Bingo!" he bellowed and, whirling around, scooped up a surprised Mrs. Bassetti and hugged her. "Hound dog!" he shouted, looking at the older woman as if he wondered what she was doing in his arms. "Hound dog! I'll be damned. Sure! Sure as hell, that's what it is! It's our boy Elvis! Elvis! You ain't nothing, but a hound dog now, fella! I'll bet you a month's pay, Katie-girl, that Jack is trying to tell that Elvis is our perp! Ready or not, Mrs. Greenwood, here we come!"

"What in the world?" Melinda appeared at the door with a head-duty-nurse frown on her face.

A low moan escaped Jack's lips. Immediately everyone's eyes were on him, except Melinda's. She was checking the monitor. Slowly, deliberately, he nodded his head and gave a tired, but satisfied, grin.

"Did we get it right, pal?" Kate ran her hand down his rough cheek. "We finally got it right, didn't we?"

As they all watched, Jack's breathing slowed down. He slipped into an exhausted—but relaxed—sleep.

Angelica Bowers left the Hanna Memorial Library long before that noisy old clock finished chiming twelve. In fact, she'd sat at the table closest to the door for fifteen minutes with her coat on, just to make sure that she could!

218

She let the heavy wooden door bang behind her. What a wonderful feeling to let the old thing go. The only feeling that she would have enjoyed more was to slam it against the wall and listen to the beveled glass break and tinkle into a thousand pieces. Unfortunately, one of those skinny, snooty young aides had caught it first.

Angelica felt that nun's deep gray eyes piercing her back when she left. "She's probably wondering what I have to do that is so important that I have to take a half-day off to do it, Angelica grumbled.

"I'm getting packed early so I can kill my mother, Sister." Angelica mimicked a high, innocent voice. "Please, may I be excused?"

Wouldn't that old bag faint if she knew, Angelica thought, picturing Sister Eileen's round wrinkled face turning from red to white before she crumpled into a round heap on the library floor.

Outside the college's main entrance, Angelica paused, grabbed the banister, and took a deep breath.

What a gorgeous day! Her small blue eyes swept the panorama. During the night, dry, cold polar air had stolen in from the bay and left everything sparkling! St. Ignatius Church, the choppy granite water of the bay, Sutro Tower, the small homes nestled against Twin Peaks—everything shone under a brilliant sky.

That's how the world looks when you're happy, Angelica thought, carefully managing the steep steps one at a time. A wiry young girl brushed past her with scarcely a "pardon me," and Angelica clung tightly to the handrail. This was not the time to fall and hurt herself. This was the eve of her emancipation. Free at last! Free at last! God almighty, I'll be free at last! Angelica wanted to shout, but she needed all the breath she had for the steps.

On Turk Street, Angelica leaned against the bus-stop pole, waiting for the Number 31 Balboa. She checked her watch, ignoring the bulging flesh on either side of the stretch band. She had never taken the bus at this time of the day before, so she had no idea how often they ran, not that it mattered. She had plenty of time—all afternoon. One day soon, she'd have all night, all month, all a lifetime.

Luckily, when the bus did arrive, she found a vacant double seat and filled most of it. On what remained, she placed her purse and her canvas tote bag. Most of the other passengers realized that Angelica intended to keep the seat vacant and passed right by.

Only one man who boarded the bus at Tenth and Balboa stopped. First he eyed the seat. Then those same heavy-lidded eyes fastened on her face before moving up and down her entire body. Angelica felt her face grow hot. Turning her head quickly, she stared out the window at a long block of houses with their small cramped front yards.

She was thinking about the man. This was the second one today who had looked at her that way. The first one was that sloppy-look-ing boy with all the hair whose mother lived up the street. He didn't think that she saw him there in his front-room window leering at her, but she did. Being leered at was an odd feel-ing, Angelica thought. Not that she really minded. It was so much better than having people look away quickly, embarrassed by what they saw, or worse yet, to pretend that they didn't see you at all!

Soon, when she came back from Utah, everything would be different. She would be thin and attractive, with a beautiful face and fancy hats and men friends whom she would not be afraid to bring home. She examined her turquoise ring. She would be able to slip it off and replace it with Mama's rings to wear at dinner parties. Maybe her first dinner-party guest would be her young man from the western-wear shop. Why not? When she got home from Utah, there would be no dogs and no Mama.

Angelica squirmed in her seat. The bus was warm, but she didn't really mind. The doors opened every few blocks to take on or let off passengers, so it was pleasant enough. In fact, she might ride all the way to Ocean Beach.

Sitting on one of those benches gazing out over the Pacific Ocean to the horizon, seemed a perfect place to run through her plan again. She needed to be absolutely certain that she hadn't slipped up anywhere. Dead certain! Angelica giggled at her own little joke.

The woman across the aisle shot a quizzical look in her direction. You better be careful, old lady, Angelica thought, staring back until the woman averted her eyes. If you aren't careful, tomorrow you might be dog meat! Angelica giggled again, but by now the woman was staring fixedly out her window.

Suddenly the bus stopped. "End of the line," the driver called cheerfully. Opening both doors with a swish, he was the first one off.

Angelica struggled out of the Number 31 Balboa. A sharp wind off the ocean twisted her hair and her clothes, while tiny grains blew up to sting her face and her legs.

Deciding against crossing the Great Highway, which seemed much wider than she remembered, Angelica walked into a small sheltered patio built between two apartment buildings. A homeless woman was perched on one of its low walls, guarding her bulging cart. Angelica smiled, but the woman eyed her suspiciously and seemed relieved when she moved on to a vacant bench and settled there.

Hungry pigeons bobbed around her feet, picking at small bits of spilled popcorn. She wished that she had more to throw down for them. She loved to watch their short, shiny necks bouncing up and down, up and down, until they had eaten everything.

She closed her eyes and felt the noonday sun warm her feet. Angelica checked her watch again. I have to recheck my plan. I can't have any loopholes. The plane leaves at six. The Airporter will pick me up at the house at about four-thirty. I have to be outside. Before then, I need to eat, to pack, then to kill Mama in just a little less than four hours.

Maybe coming to the beach was not such a good idea after all. I'd better head for home soon, she thought, wondering if the sleeping pills she'd given Mama and the dogs had worn off yet. She hoped not.

Mama had only four pills left. Angelica hadn't wanted to raise suspicion by reordering too soon. She'd seen it happen on those mystery shows on television. Those pharmacists kept too-good records. Heavens, no! She couldn't do that.

If Mama were awake, she'd dissolve two of the remaining pills in a cup of hot tea and put one pill in each dog's bowl of water. Then, sweet dreams and adios!

On the ride back, the Number 31 Balboa was nearly empty. Angelica was the only passenger getting off at 42nd Avenue. She labored down the hill, relishing each step, knowing this would be the last time she would go to Mama's house. With Mama gone, she realized with sudden clarity that the house would be hers—hers alone. In just a few days, a new improved Angelica Bowers would begin a new improved life in a new improved home.

Buoyant, she swung back the front gate and mounted the steps, turned the key in the front door lock and listened. Hearing nothing but silence, Angelica pushed open the front door and went inside.

"I feel like something right out of *Get Smart*," Sister Eileen said when she finally joined Sister Mary Helen at the Number 31 Balboa bus stop on Turk Street.

It took Mary Helen a second or two to remember that *Get Smart* was an old television spy spoof. "I thought you'd enjoy a little intrigue in your life," she said, balancing on the second step inside the college entrance gate to see if the bus was in sight yet.

"A little intrigue, maybe," Eileen pulled the collar of her black winter coat up over her ears. "But this is absolutely crazy. At this very moment, we could be sitting in a heated convent car instead of standing here freezing."

"We're getting soft," Mary Helen said, hoping Eileen didn't notice her own shivering. "And with today the Feast of St. Leonard!"

Eileen gave her a "so what?" stare.

"That rugged little hermit rode his donkey all over the Frankish Empire helping women in labor and King Clovis's captives. And we're complaining about the cold."

"You made that up, didn't you, old dear?" Eileen's breath came out in a cloud.

Mary Helen sniffed. "Of course not! Besides the bus should be here any minute."

"And imagine us walking to the bus stop, one at a time!" Eileen rolled her gray eyes heavenward. She was not going to give it up! "Honestly! Who in heaven's name is paying any attention to us?"

"You never know." Mary Helen adjusted her bifocals. Moving forward she put the toes of her black pumps in a patch of sun to warm them. "Even the walls have eyes."

"You know very well that's ears." Eileen grinned.

Mary Helen was relieved to see the nose of the bus edging over the crest of the hill.

The driver waved them in with a cheerful "Hi, Sisters." It had been so long since Mary Helen had actually ridden the Muni that it had slipped her mind that in San Francisco all nuns ride free, a privilege granted them by a grateful city after their ministry during the 1906 earthquake.

"I wonder how he knew we were nuns," Eileen said, when they were settled in their seats. "Is it that we are wearing black coats with the crosses on the labels and no makeup?"

Mary Helen shrugged. "Could be. Besides, we were standing right in front of Mount St. Francis College." She dropped the change back into her black leather pocketbook. "He wouldn't need Hercule Poirot's 'little gray cells' to put those clues together."

As the bus rounded the corner onto Balboa, Eileen clung to the bar on the back of the seat ahead to keep from sliding. "Now that we're on our way to see Tillie Greenwood, have you thought of any plausible excuse for our visit?" she asked.

Mary Helen shook her head. "I thought something would come to me, but it hasn't. Besides, when all else fails, what's wrong with the truth?"

The two nuns stood on the sidewalk of 42nd Avenue studying the Greenwood house, double-checking the address to make sure that they had the right place.

"Everything seems pretty quiet," Eileen whispered. "She may not even be home. Should we have called ahead?"

Then she certainly wouldn't have been home Mary Helen thought. She took the lead up the steps and pushed firmly on the front doorbell.

A raspy ring echoed through the rooms. Mary Helen was sure she caught the high, quick trills of a canary coming from somewhere inside. Out of the corner of her eye, she noticed the edge of a curtain flicker. Surely they were being scrutinized.

After several minutes, she rang the bell again.

Almost instantly, the door was pulled open. "What do you want?" Tillie Greenwood asked, her eyes sharp, her voice unfriendly.

Mary Helen was startled at how much the woman had changed since just last night. Her hair, which had been fixed so nicely, spread like an unkept halo around her pale, drawn face. One cheek was bruised and above it her eye looked swollen and sore. Her face was red and bloated as if she'd been crying, and her hastily thrown on housecoat had its label sticking up at the nape of the neck.

"Are you all right, Mrs. Greenwood?" Eileen's voice was concerned.

The woman's eyes flickered nervously from Eileen to Mary Helen. "Of course, I'm all right!" She bit her words. "And, how do you know my name? What do you want? Who are you, any-way? Are you from the probation department?" Her voice rose with each question.

Mary Helen explained gently who they were and that she had noticed Mrs. Greenwood in the vestibule of St. Monica's Church during Gemma Burke's funeral. "May we come in for just a moment?" she asked. "We'd like to talk to you about Gemma."

"I didn't really know the woman." Tillie's face colored. She wore an expression of pained in-decision. "What can we possibly have to talk about?"

"We won't stay more than a few minutes," Mary Helen insisted.

Looking as if this was definitely against her better judgment, Tillie swung open the front door. She led her visitors down a short hall, past an unused-looking front room and an equally-unused-looking dining room with a large birdcage in the corner into a sunny, old-fashioned breakfast nook.

"You know I am a fallen-away Catholic," Tillie declared, as if it were a challenge.

"Oh," Mary Helen said, sitting squarely on the wooden chair Tillie offered.

"Last night was the first time I've been inside a church in nearly twenty years." Fidgeting, Tillie studied her thumbnails with great care.

"Oh?" Mary Helen repeated, figuring the "why" was on its way. Sure enough, she was right!

"One Saturday afternoon, I was so upset. I—I went to confession. That old monsignor, instead of being kind and fatherly, was so nasty to me. He hollered so loud, I'm sure everyone else in the line must have heard. I was so humiliated and angry"—Tillie's face reddened with the memory—"that I just ran out of the box—I don't know what everybody else must have thought and I didn't care—I just ran down the aisle crying."

Mary Helen only half-listened. The story was a familiar one; only the villain changed—a gruff old monsignor, a strict or unfeeling nun, an indifferent parish housekeeper. She wondered, as she always did, why people allowed imperfect ministers to drive a wedge between them and the source of such great grace and comfort. During her long life she'd never found any priest or religious or layperson, for that matter, whom she thought was important enough to cause her to leave the church. To her it made no sense, which didn't make it any easier to listen to.

"That's unfortunate," she heard Eileen say

227

when Tillie finished her tale. Indeed it was, and particularly unfortunate if Tillie had let herself be deprived of a relationship with a loving and compassionate God. However, that is not the reason we're here, Mary Helen reminded herself.

"I've a fresh pot of coffee just perked," Tillie offered, balancing self-consciously on the edge of her seat.

The two nuns assured her that despite the sunshine, a hot drink would definitely hit the spot. Watching her fuss with cups and saucers and sugar and cream, Mary Helen thought that Tillie was beginning to relax, but the moment everyone was served and she sat down, that strained expression returned to her face.

"What exactly do you want to ask me about Gemma Burke?" Her chin rose, and there was an "I dare you!" glint in her eye.

Taking a deep breath, Mary Helen plunged ahead. "If, as you said, you didn't know Mrs. Burke, it makes me wonder why you attended her funeral."

Tillie's face froze and her lips turned down. Their eyes locked. Mary Helen waited for the explosion.

To her surprise, it did not come. She watched Tillie's nervous face as the woman struggled with just how much to say. The breakfast nook was quiet, the only sound was Eileen's spoon stirring her coffee.

Bowing her head, Tillie hugged herself. "It's my Elvis, isn't it?" She asked in a low, sad voice. "You're here about my Elvis." You think he has something to do with this...this..." Tillie's voice cracked as she reached for the word and missed it.

"But he's innocent." She looked up, her eyes pleading with Mary Helen to believe her. "He is really a good boy! A good boy and a loving son. It's just that he's so sensitive. So kind-hearted that he gets himself into things that aren't his fault."

Mary Helen couldn't believe how easily the subject of Elvis had come up. All at once, she was filled with an overwhelming compassion for this desperate woman who must have been aching to share her lonely burden with a willing ear.

A tear slipped from Tillie's eye and ran unheeded down her bruised cheek. "My poor Elvis!" She sniffled. "He warned me that people would suspect him because of what happened before."

"Because *what* happened before?" Mary Helen prodded gently.

Tillie's eyes shifted. "Don't tell me you didn't know that my poor Elvis was accused of"—she hesitated before saying the word, as if the thought of having it in her mouth made her a little sick—"He was accused of rape," she said so quietly that Mary Helen had to strain to hear.

"He was just out of high school. His grandmother had just died. They were very close, Elvis and Mother. She really raised him, you know, because I had to work. My mother was strict, but in her own way, she really loved that boy." Tillie stopped to blow her nose.

"He was high-spirited, I admit. But what twenty-one-year-old isn't? And if you ask me, that woman must have egged him on." She stared at Mary Helen. "Do you understand what I'm saying? My Elvis never would have done such a thing on his own...."

She continued in a monotone, retelling the story as she must have retold it to herself hundreds of times before, always ending with Elvis's innocence.

"He was just a boy, after all. She was old enough to be his mother. Cheap tart! You know the kind of woman I mean. But no one would believe him over that biddy. She had money, you know. And so my Elvis went to jail. I thought my heart would break when—when they led him away and him looking at me with those big brown hurt eyes of his and—and calling, 'Mommy.'" Tillie stopped to dab at her brimming eyes and to blow her nose again.

"He was a model prisoner, just like I knew he would be." Tillie raised her head and smiled proudly. "Never gave a moment's trouble. He learned his lesson, too. 'Mommy,' he said"—Tillie repeated his words earnestly—"'I'll never let another woman put me in that position.' That's what he said, and I believe him."

Mary Helen's heart lurched. Of course, he would never be put in that position again. He would simply kill his victims. She drained her coffee cup, hoping that her face did not give her away.

"Why, then, did you go to Gemma's funeral?" She placed her cup back in its saucer.

Startled by the unexpected question, Tillie searched for an explanation, one they both knew would not ring true. "Well, I"—she sputtered—

230

"I just felt—" Suddenly her eyes sparked. "It *is* a free country, you know."

"It is, indeed," Mary Helen agreed. "But I doubt that you went to the funeral to exercise your freedom. More likely you went because you aren't quite as sure as you'd like to be that Elvis is innocent." The words hung brutally between them. "In fact, you may think that your son is guilty."

The breath went out of Tillie Greenwood as if she'd been punched. Mary Helen expected a fresh surge of anger, righteous indignation, at least some bravado. Instead, Tillie seemed to sputter and shrivel like Oz's Wicked Witch of the West into a sobbing heap. Her heartbroken wail filled the sunny nook.

Mary Helen patted Tillie's heaving shoulders tenderly, while Tillie Greenwood cried as though she might never stop.

"He's got a gun," she hiccupped, all her defenses finally gone. "I saw it in his toilet. A funny-looking little black gun." She tried to catch her breath. "He hit me, Sister. His own mother. He hit me and called me terrible names and said that everything was my fault and that he hated me. He's my baby." Her whole body shook. "I don't want anything bad to happen to him. He's all I have." Her face was pinched with pain.

"Where is he now?" Mary Helen asked urgently.

"Out. Gone. Didn't tell me..."

A sudden thud and the sound of running feet rose from the alley beneath the breakfast-nook window. Eileen glanced out. "It's a man," she said, straining to see clearly.

231

Trembling and sniffling, Tillie struggled to the window and stared down. "Oh, sweet Jesus!" Her face was a white mask. She swayed. "It's my Elvis. It's my baby."

Without looking up, the figure vaulted the back fence of the house next door. Tillie let out a harsh sob. "He's on his way over the fences to the Bowers house." She grabbed at her throat. "No, please, God, no. He wouldn't hurt that poor fat girl. Not my Elvis. He doesn't mean any harm, Sister. He's a good boy. I should have stopped him this morning when I saw that look. It's not too late, is it?" Her eyes studied Mary Helen beseechingly.

"Of course not!" Mary Helen snapped. "Lead the way."

Without stopping for a coat, Tillie Greenwood hurried out the front door and down the steps, the nuns at her heels.

Three abreast, the women marched purposefully and swiftly down 42nd Avenue toward Angelica Bowers's home.

"What the hell is that?" Inspector Gallagher pointed out the front window of the unmarked police car at the three women hurrying down the front steps of the Greenwood house.

Inspector O'Connor squinted against the glare. "Looks to me like those two nun friends of yours," he said, "and if I were a betting man, I'd say that one in the lead, the chubby one with that wild red hair, is our suspect's mother, one Mrs. Tillie Greenwood."

"How the hell did they get here ahead of us?" Gallagher stared accusingly at O'Connor, who only shook his head. Frustrated, Gallagher ran his hand over his bald pate and loosened his tie to think.

After leaving Jack Bassetti's room at St. Mary's, he had driven back to the Hall of Justice as fast as was legal. Well, maybe even a little faster. Picked up O'Connor on the run, told him on their way out to the Avenues about what Jack had said...about what he suspected. They hadn't wasted a minute.

Now, just after they pulled up to the curb and were about to get out of the car and go up to the front door to ask the woman a few questions, the door swings open and those two nuns come out!

"How the hell did they know to come here?" Gallagher asked.

O'Connor shrugged. "Sacred revelation?"

"Sacred revelation, my ass!" Gallagher grumbled. "If you ask me, something is very rotten here. And I intend to find out what it is. I'll get to the bottom of this if it's the last thing I do." His blue eyes boiled like water in a pot.

"If I had my druthers, I'd lock those two up for obstruction of justice and throw away the key. I'd throw the book at them! Except maybe being in jail with those two might constitute cruel and unusual punishment for the rest of the population."

"Lock them up for what?" O'Connor asked sensibly. "For visiting a woman on 42nd Avenue? For walking down a public street?"

"See?" Gallagher jabbed a thick finger at O'Connor. "They fooled you, too. They look like a couple of old sweethearts, right? What harm can they possibly get into, right? Wrong!

Underneath, they're nothing but arsenic and old lace!"

"Look, Denny," O'Connor pointed to the trio. "Looks like they're going into another house. Maybe they were all three invited for tea. Or bridge. My mother-in-law plays lots of bridge with her cronies. Maybe the whole thing is just a coincidence."

"That'll be the day," Gallagher grunted, straining to watch the three women. He couldn't see anyone open the door. All he saw was that they went in quickly.

"What do you want to do?" O'Connor asked.

"Move the car down the hill."

O'Connor coasted along the curb.

"Stop here," Gallagher ordered. "Let's just wait. I don't know whose house this is, but I can guarantee that those two are up to something and that it's no good. Hot damn, I'm going to find out what it is if we have to sit here all day!"

Angelica Bowers pushed open her front door quietly and listened to the flat silence. Relief flowed over her like warm water and she closed the door behind her carefully, stifling the click with the palm of her hand.

Sunshine the color of pale cheese shone down the hall from the kitchen windows. Angelica took her first real breath.

Climbing the stairs, she avoided the ones that creaked and stopped every few steps to make sure nothing was astir.

She crept to Mama's bedroom door and stole a glance. Mama lay in the stifling bedroom, her gray hair fanned out on her pillow, her thin face, sharp as an ax, pointing straight to the ceiling. Her breath made little rhythmic snorts as the bedcovers moved up and down.

Her dog-eared copy of *TV Guide* had fallen to the floor beside her bed. "Soon you'll have no more need for that," Angelica whispered, giving it a kick.

Like bookends, Salt and Pepper lay on either side of Mama, asleep, too. Those pills really carried a punch, Angelica thought, rightfully proud of her plan.

While Mama slept, she would pack and eat. She checked her wristwatch. That would give her ample time to—to—a tingle ran down her spine—to kill her mother and be outside to meet the Airporter.

Angelica opened the old suitcase on top of her bed, ignoring the faint odor of mothballs and dust. With Mama gone, she'd soon put an end to that. Before long, her old suitcase would smell of Utah and Hawaii and who knew where else.

Moving as quickly as she could, she gathered the things she planned to take on the trip. She folded her underwear, her nightgown, her dresses, her blouses and skirts carefully. She planned to wear her new hat and moccasins. She placed them on the chair so she could slip into them just before she left the house.

Suddenly famished, Angelica went down to the kitchen, opened the refrigerator, and decided to make a big Dagwood sandwich. She piled ham, cheese, salami, and some leftover roast beef on one slice of sourdough bread. Then she slathered a second piece of bread with butter and mayonnaise, adding tomatoes, lettuce, and dill pickles for garnish. She stacked a mound of chips on the side of her plate and poured herself a large glass of milk.

Closing her eyes, she bit into the sandwich, relishing its taste and its texture. Soon she'd be thin and would be able to eat this whole thing without ever worrying about a pound.

She was just savoring the last chip and debating whether to get another helping when she heard her mother's bedsprings creaking overhead.

"Angelica"—her mother's voice was groggy— "is that you?"

Angelica took a long swallow of milk.

"Yes, Mama," she called, hurriedly putting a tiny portion of dry food in each dog's dish. Not enough to satisfy hunger, but just enough to distract them while she dealt with Mama. She put the dishes out on the back porch.

"What are you doing home so early?" Mama called, and Angelica covered her mouth so Mama wouldn't hear her giggle. If you only knew, she wanted to shout, but didn't. Soon it would all be over.

"Do you hear me?" Mama demanded. "I have a splitting headache, and I asked you a question. Why are you home so early?"

Humming, Angelica rinsed her dishes and pulled herself up a few stairs.

With heavy eyes, Salt and Pepper watched from the top landing.

"Come down," she commanded. To her amazement, the two animals made their careful way down. She heard their sharp black toenails click across the kitchen linoleum.

She followed them, deliberately slamming the

back door behind them. It would be safer to have them outside until she was ready to leave. They were so hungry—so busy licking their bowls and sniffing for more—that they scarcely noticed.

Don't worry, doggies, she wanted to sing out. Soon you'll be satisfied.

Struggling to keep her breathing even, Angelica climbed the narrow staircase.

"Angelica!" Mama's voice was sharp now. "Come in here this minute and answer me. What is wrong?"

Instead, without saying a word, Angelica turned and went into her own bedroom. She flipped on the radio to the rock-music-station, turned up the volume in honor of Mama's headache, and closed her suitcase. Sitting on the lid, she snapped shut the lock.

"Did you hear me, young lady?" Mama was shouting now. Turning up the sound still louder, Angelica began to sing along, shaking her hips in time with the music, clapping her hands and wiggling. She felt the floor vibrate with her and the perfume bottles on her dresser tinkle.

"Come here this instant!" Mama was screeching over the music. "If you know what's good for you, you'd better get in here. Now!"

Angelica heard the dreaded thump of Mama's cane against the hardwood floor. She felt a sick pitch under her ribs. Ignoring it, she slipped into her new moccasins and swung the suitcase from her bed. Picking up her purple cowgirl hat, she carefully perched it on the newel post in the hallway and walked toward Mama's room.

"So you decided to come at last, my little

angel." Mama's face was hard and cruel, belying her words. "It's about time. Come over here. By my bed. I want to show you something." Her teeth were clenched. "Come to Mama so I can teach you a good lesson."

A tightness bound Angelica's chest and the old familiar perspiration began to form behind her knees and in the crooks of her arms. She sank back against the doorjamb.

Mama's hard eyes caught the suitcase. She set her mouth in a narrow mean line. "And just where do you think you are going, missy?" she sneered, pointing the heavy cane toward Angelica's beaded moccasins. "And in those stupid shoes? A girl your size needs good sturdy shoes."

She studied Angelica with contempt. "So you're going to leave me, are you?" Small bubbles of saliva formed on the corners of her mouth. "And how far do you think you'll get? Huh?" she jeered, cocking one eye at Angelica. "Who'll have you, besides me? You can't go anywhere by yourself. If anyone looks at you cross-eyed, you bawl like a baby. You're scared of your own shadow!"

"I am not!" Angelica shouted, moving toward the bed. She felt hot tears sting her eyes. "I'm not scared of my shadow! And I'm not scared of you!"

"Keep a civil tongue in your sassy mouth, young lady!" Mama screeched and with a sharp, fast swipe brought her cane across Angelica's face.

"My face, my pretty face, my angel face!" Angelica moaned, touching the stinging welt on her cheek. Her finger came away red and sticky with blood.

"Angel face!" Mama shrilled. "Pretty face! Ha!" Mama's dark eyes seemed to pierce Angelica's forehead and her nose and her chin. "Pretty face, indeed! A face only your Papa could love. All anyone else will see is a big, fat, flabby, doughy mug! Just a fat, doughy mug!" Opening her mouth, she threw back her head and laughed.

Angelica felt her rage explode and run in hot veins throughout her body. The tears froze in her eyes. She snatched up Mama's pillow, the one with the fancy embroidered pillowcase. With a quick lunge, she covered those mean eyes, that gaping mouth with its sharp gray tongue.

Angelica pushed down on the pillow with all her strength, paying no attention to the clawlike hands grabbing at her arms, the body twisting beneath her weight, the churning legs, the humping chest. She pushed until Mama was still.

Without looking back, Angelica Bowers picked up her suitcase and her hat. Panting, she struggled down the stairs. The Airporter would be here soon. She must let the dogs in and be outside.

She stopped in front of the hall mirror, just long enough to set her beautiful new purple wool hat on her head at a jaunty angle. She was admiring herself in the mirror when she heard a strange noise. It sounded as if it were coming from the basement.

Struggling to stay calm, Angelica listened. It wasn't Mama. It wasn't the dogs. Who was it, then?

Maybe the man reading the gas meter is in the alley, or the mailman is leaving more junk mail, she thought, giving herself one more satisfied look in the mirror.

She heard a creak on the basement stairs.

Fear slid down her back like a draft. "Who is it? Who's there?" she called out bravely and went into the kitchen. The sun reflected off the stainless-steel stovetop, blinding her. "Is anyone there? Her muscles cramped with tension.

With a crash, the basement door few open and a tall, muscular man filled the space. His tattooed arms flexed, and his coarse black, curly hair formed a wild mane around his face.

Angelica's mouth went dry. "Who are you?" she croaked. He didn't answer, he just mocked her with his cruel eyes. Eyes like Mama's.

With a smirk, he moved his flat brown eyes up and down her body, up and down. Angelica's heart pounded. What did he want?

He gave her a crooked, almost-friendly smile and then moved like a cat into the light.

With a feeling of relief, she recognized him. He was that wild boy whose mother lived up the block. Elvis something. He was probably just in the wrong house. Of all times! She felt dizzy, as though suddenly a heavy weight had been removed.

"What do you want?" she asked, a new feeling of panic spreading over her. What if he asked to see Mama? She'd just explain that Mama was too ill for visitors. But then how would she explain that she was going on a trip? "What do you want?" she repeated.

"You!" he said with a leer. "I want you."

"Me!" Angelica was scarcely able to swallow. Perspiration started on her forehead and palms. He flexed the muscles in his thick arms.

The room spun around her. She watched in horror as Elvis locked the door to the basement.

"I'm getting sick of skinny old broads." He

240

turned back toward her. His eyes narrowed. "I'm ready for some fat meat."

Angelica backed toward the hallway. He lunged toward her, stunning her, sending her purple cowgirl hat rolling across the kitchen floor. "Mama!" she shouted desperately, suddenly realizing that there was no Mama.

Infuriated, he threw his body against hers, his arms nearly circling her, crushing her. Thick fingers ripped at her clothes and dug into her flesh. His hot, sweaty body pressed against hers. Angelica could not breathe.

Terrified, she twisted and tried to kick, but her legs were too heavy. She wanted to scream, but no sound came. Glancing wildly toward the back door, she stumbled toward it. She heard the ferocious barking of the dogs as they slammed their powerful bodies against it. Could she reach the door? Could she turn the handle? Let the dogs in?

She threw herself forward, fumbled for the catch, but he yanked her hair, snapping her head back. Locking his arms around her neck, he forced her to one knee.

The room was spinning now. Reaching out, she knocked the coffeepot from the stove and overturned a chair. She couldn't swallow. Couldn't breathe. The room was closing in. With one last desperate sob, Angelica slammed against the back door, but he held her tight.

"Look at all that meat." He smiled coldly at her exposed shoulder. Pressing his lips against it, he tore open her blouse.

"Do you hear all that racket?" Mary Helen asked, putting an ear still closer to the Bowers's

front door. Several thuds and wild barking re-
sounded onto the front stoop.

Both Sister Eileen and Tillie Greenwood
looked frightened. "It sounds as if someone is
being murdered," Eileen said, then went pale.
"You don't suppose?" Her eyes were wide.

"We can't just stand here, doing nothing."
Mary Helen tried the front door. Fortunately,
the latch had not quite caught. "Someone must
have gone in a hurry," she said, cautiously swinging open the door.

"No, no, no, please, don't no!" Angelica's
frightened cry rang down the short hallway. It
was coming from the kitchen.

"Let's go, O'Connor!" Inspector Dennis
Gallagher shouted, slamming the car door behind him. "It's breaking and entering, if nothing else."

The two police officers crossed the sidewalk
quickly, then took the front steps of the Bowers home, two at a time.

"Police!" Gallagher shouted from the front
door, but no one seemed to hear him above all
the racket.

Sister Mary Helen threw open the kitchen door.
A startled Elvis Greenwood looked up.
"Mommy," he said, his hands still clutching the
fabric from Angelica's blouse. "Mommy, it's not
my fault."

Sobbing, Angelica Bowers cowered in the
corner. Then, covering her burning face, she
turned toward the wall.

Sister Eileen took a step toward her. With a
thud, the back door burst open. What happened

next, Mary Helen was to say later, was like a scene right out of a horror movie.

Two enormous Royal Standard poodles, one black and one white, stood poised in the doorway. Their square bodies tensed. Their teeth were bared. The black one gave a low, guttural growl. Topknots held high, their blunt black noses sniffed the air. The white poodle fixed her proud dark eyes on Angelica.

Angelica must have sensed it. She turned from the wall. Moments ago, her small blue rabbit eyes had been filled with fright. Now they glinted with smoldering hatred.

"Go, Salt!" she shouted, pointing toward the steep staircase. "Go, Salt! Go, Pepper! Go! Eat Mama!"

Goose bumps ran up Sister Mary Helen's arms as she listened to the woman's hysterical giggle. "Go to Mama!" Angelica screeched.

Like trained commandos, the two poodles, sprang up the steps. Just as quickly, their heavy bodies thudded back down. With skidding paws, the big dogs rounded the doorway and bolted into the kitchen. Salt fixed Angelica in her sight. Like a hunter stalking her prey, the dog lowered her head. A growl came from deep in her throat. She moved stiffly toward Angelica.

Alert to the danger, Mary Helen's eyes searched the kitchen for something heavy—a frying pan, a rolling pin, something.

"It's the blood!" Angelica cried. She scrambled to get to her feet. "Salt smells the blood!" Cringing, Angelica covered the cut on her cheek with her chubby hand.

Mary Helen grabbed a cast-iron skillet from the stove, but before she or anyone else could move, both dogs plunged toward Angelica. They slammed violently against her. With driving force, they knocked her onto the kitchen floor.

"Eat, Mama," Angelica begged, twisting her face, her arms and legs scrambling like a crab, clawing, struggling to get away.

"Oh, no! No, please!" she shrieked in terror as the dogs pinned her shoulders to the linoleum. "Oh, no! Please, not my face! Not my angel face!"

The animals attacked with such ferocity that even Elvis Greenwood seemed relieved to see Inspector Gallagher enter with his gun drawn.

Sunday, November 15
Thirty-Third Sunday in Ordinary Time

Sister Mary Helen filed into her usual pew for Sunday Mass at Mount St. Francis College Chapel. The chapel was empty except for old Sister Donata who, bent nearly in two, was fast asleep in a side pew. She reached for the missalette. Today, it read, was the Thirty-third Sunday in Ordinary Time. As far as Mary Helen was concerned nothing had been very ordinary about the time since that terrifying scene at Angelica Bowers's home.

Inspector Gallagher, God love him, had taken charge. Of course, he was forced to shoot the poodles to get them off Angelica. They had torn at her neck and face. Mary Helen shut her eyes trying to blank out the horrific sounds.

But, he was too late. Although Angelica had lived long enough to answer some questions, she'd been too badly mauled to survive and had gone home to God early the next morning.

It was probably just as well, Mary Helen thought, shifting in the pew so the morning sun was not directly in her eyes. The trial for the murder of her mother would surely have ended in an insanity plea. Even poor, crazed Angelica would have been devastated to hear herself declared insane.

Elvis Greenwood had been so terrified that he had confessed on the spot. Despite the detectives' Miranda warning after he was handcuffed, Elvis had blurted out all his hatred and rage right there in the Bowers's kitchen.

Poor Tillie had whimpered pathetically while they were all forced to listen to her son blame her for not protecting him from his grandmother's cruelty and abuse.

"With each of those old broads, I was hurting you, Mommy. Just like you let me be hurt. Just like you walked away, pretended not to see, let that old bitch..." His voice faltered. "I was killing you, Mommy. You!" he bellowed at her bowed head.

"Didn't you notice, Mommy?" His mouth had twisted into a spiteful grin. "All of them were short and fat, and had that stupid brassy, dyed red hair, just like you." He sniffed. "And they smelled like that gaggy powder you dump all over yourself. Smell it?"

Elvis sniffed again. Then he pointed a thick, dirty finger, first at his mother, then at Eileen whose face drained of all color.

Tillie raised her head, her eyes glazed with shock. "Please, sweetheart!" she pleaded, but Elvis acted as though he hadn't heard her.

With a snort, he turned on Gallagher. "I bet you missed that smelly powder, didn't you, cop!

That lavender crap they all wore? And by the way, you're in lousy shape! You didn't even come close to catching me on the California Street steps."

Although Gallagher's face flushed with anger, he didn't respond.

Mary Helen wanted to come to the Inspector's defense, but under the circumstances, thought better of it. Instead, she had asked, "How did you get into the homes of your victims?"

All eyes shot toward her. For some reason, Gallagher's face was even redder than it had been. Perhaps, Mary Helen thought, she should explain her question.

"It just seems odd to me that anyone knowing a rapist is in the area wouldn't double-check their windows before going to bed."

"Why do you want to know, nun?" Elvis turned to face her. "You wanna be one of my old broads, Sister?" he taunted savagely.

Mary Helen's stomach somersaulted. For a moment, she thought Inspector Gallagher might strike the man. She, herself was careful to set the cast-iron skillet back on the stove.

"He's sick," she whispered, putting her hand on Gallagher's arm. "Sick and sad."

"I'm not so sick I couldn't find my 'Mommy,'" he gloated. "All you have to do is sit and stare at China Beach. Most of the old broads that live there take their daily walk in their 'safe' snooty neighborhood." His face twisted angrily. "So I went out there and sat on the hood of a parked car, just like it was mine. Staring out at the view like some kind of nature nut and watched and smelled"—he gave a silly laugh—"and picked.

246

"They'd seen me there. We even smiled and said hello, so when I rang their bells, they never blinked, the dumb bitches. When I said that I had car trouble, they said, sure, I could use the phone. It only took me seconds to unlatch a window. Then I could come back at night and use them!"

He chuckled at his own cleverness. He didn't seem to hear his mother's tortured wail.

The rest of the day was still a blur. Police officers, ambulances, the coroner, the forensic team, men and women with cameras and bags and tape measures, Angelica's Uncle Frank, the driver of the Airporter, and concerned neighbors swarmed through the house while she and Eileen sat on the living-room couch with Mrs. Greenwood.

Finally, when Inspector Gallagher was satisfied that no one knew another thing, he had released them all. Actually, Mary Helen was so exhausted that she wondered if she would even remember her way home. Mercifully, Inspector Gallagher sent them back to Mount St. Francis in a police car.

When Mary Helen and Eileen arrived at the convent, the other nuns were already in bed. "A stroke of pure Irish luck!" Eileen called it.

Young Sister Anne had left them a note. "You were on the evening news," she had scribbled. "At least, something was on, about nuns stumbling onto a bizarre murder scene. Details unknown. That was the teaser, anyway. You two were our first suspects. Sister Cecilia is livid. My advice is, if guilty, sleep in tomorrow morning. Let the *Chronicle* explain it!"

Now, almost two weeks later, except for an occasional snide remark, the convent community was back to normal. Thank heaven, Mary Helen thought, thumbing through her missalette to today's gospel.

She reread the familiar parable of Jesus's about the man going on a long journey. Before he left, he handed over his funds to his servants according to each one's ability. And on his return, he demanded that they had used only what he had given them.

In God's mercy, the Angelicas and Elvises of this world will not be judged by our standards, Mary Helen thought, but they will be judged with the unconditional love of a compassionate God who knows and understands the ability of each of us and what each of us was given. Difficult as it is for the human heart to accept, at this very moment, the victims and those who victimized them might be praising God together with full and forgiving hearts. So much of life and death and suffering and love remains a profound mystery!

The overhead lights in the chapel flipped on. Mary Helen heard the heavy door opening and closing. The nuns were assembling for Mass. Eileen slipped into the pew beside her.

Unobtrusively, Sister Mary Helen checked her wristwatch. Eleven twenty-five. By twelve-thirty, the liturgy would be over, unless, of course, Father Adams got carried away with his homily.

They would have plenty of time to be at Kate Murphy's home by one. Jack had been released from the hospital and according to Kate, he was doing well. So well, in fact, they were planning to have a few people in to watch the football game.

She and Eileen were invited, of course. "Everyone is looking forward to seeing you after all you've been through," Kate had said, not a little pointedly.

Mary Helen was a tad anxious about Inspector Gallagher. She never, ever remembered seeing him so upset. And she really didn't blame him. It had been an unexpected turn of events.

The bell in the sacristy rang, and Mary Helen rose with the congregation. Father Adams paused behind the altar before beginning the Sacred Liturgy.

"The Mass this morning is being offered for the repose of the soul of Gemma Burke," he announced.

Grief welled up in Mary Helen as the choir began the entrance hymn. "Though the mountains may fall, and the hills turn to dust, yet the love of the Lord shall stand...." they sang.

And Mary Helen prayed for her good friend Gemma and for her murderer Elvis, for poor pathetic Tillie Greenwood and sad Angelica Bowers and her mother. Her prayers rose for all victims of crime and abuse and hatred. For Jack Bassetti and Kate Murphy, for Loretta Bassetti and the baby, for Officer Bill Jordon, for Inspector Gallagher, for all those who had been affected by unleashed evil. She prayed that they all might truly know and enjoy the ever-faithful love of God.

"And while You're at it, Lord," she prayed, "how about those Forty-niners this afternoon?

They surely can use some Divine intervention."

"Don't you mean some Divine interception?" the Lord asked.

"Right, again!" Mary Helen said, and felt a familiar, inexplicable peace flooding back into her soul.

If you have enjoyed reading this large print book and you would like more information on how to order a Wheeler Large Print book, please write to:

 Wheeler Publishing, Inc.
P.O. Box 531
Accord, MA 02018-0531